I would like to thank Gerald Harstad and his wife Barbara for their help in Editing the book.

Detective Harriet Brown 1 The Mystery

A pampered, sensitive young lady learns her family has been murdered. Suddenly she finds her world upside down and must now struggle to survive. Assassins are trying to kill her, but she does not know why

Excerpt:

Wounded, her arms shaking, she held her colt forty-five against the wall, and moved down the hall. A dark shadow appeared, a flash, she pulled the trigger, and felt pain in her side. The assassin fell back in the room. Screaming, she sent bullets into the wall until the Assassin threw his gun out. The monitor instructed her to put her revolver down. The assassin, wounded, disappeared out the partition. Against the wall, she slid to the floor unconscious with her side and arm bleeding profusely.

Detective Harriet Brown 3 Kidnaped

Harriet's detective agency sets off to rescue a young lady kidnaped in Puerto Quetzal, Guatemala. The rescue is successful, but Harriet is left stranded with no money, phone, or passport. She has a price on her head because she was responsible for the previous drug cartel demise. The police department is tainted, where can she go?

Excerpt:

She had 300 thousand in her briefcase, the compliments of Senor Gutierrez. He could be generous after completing a four million drug deal. She had a plane. She was flying home after she dropped him off at the Rafael Nunez airport in Cartagena Columbia.

She brought the plane to a stop five-hundred-feet from his black limousine. Senor Gutierrez stepped out of the plane, walked towards the limo, stopped, turned, tip his hat, when four men stepped out of the limousine with automatic weapons. He took ten bullets before his replaced his hat.

Startled, Harriet could not move until they pointed their weapons towards her. Closing the door, she ran to the cockpit taking a bullet in the leg and arm as the windows shattered from the bullets. She pushed the left throttle turning the plane as one of the assassins ran towards the cockpit spraying it with bullets. She took one bullet across her forehead, rendering her slightly dizzy as the left propeller caught the assassin. She felt the thump as his body passed through the moving propeller leaving him scattered over the wing. Concentrating, blood flowing over her eye, she starts the remaining engine. The plane picks up speed towards the runway as the limousine continues to pepper the plane with bullets. The plane reaches the runway finally leaving the limousine behind.

Detective Harriet Brown 4 The Prince

Raul has married and has a child. She must move on. She finds herself protecting the Crown Prince of Saudi Arabian. The CIA wants him dead to accommodate the cousin of the King, Prince Fahd. He promises a decrease in oil prices along with an increase in the supply of oil when he becomes King, but first, he must have the current Crown Prince removed. Harriet's company is trying to prevent the assassination.

Excerpt:

Harriet was already out of the car when the black van bumps the smaller car hard jarring the car and Raul forward. She ran back to the black van and hit the opening front passenger door with her shoulder.

A hand with a gun in it had been coming out when the door slammed into it. The gun fell into Harriet's hands as she moved past it. The man screamed in pain.

The back-passenger door was opening. It had a leg and an arm in it when Harriet slammed into it with her back. The man screamed in pain and dropped the gun in his hand. It fell back by the rear wheel.

Detective Harriet Brown 5 Marriage

Harriet marries Raul, the Crown Prince's bodyguard, only to have it end in tragedy. She is pregnant, but she must face her old nemeses, Prince Fahd who is out to kill her and her child

Excerpt:

Harriet lifts off from the King Abdulaziz Military Air Base in the Gulfstream 630. She heads north over the Red Sea. She had an uneasy feeling and noticed a blip some distance behind her. She opens the missile bank Raul had installed on the plane. She had three missiles on each side of the fuselage. The small blip suddenly became larger, and two smaller blips appeared. They were missiles coming her direction.

She pressed the red button twice releasing her two missiles when the blips were almost on her. The explosion rocked her plane as she dove for the sea floor below. The black Panther Jet flash by as she leveled out going south twelve feet from the water. She cut the throttle back to 70 miles an hour and flipped on the automatic pilot. The flat surface of the water kept her in the air.

The Panther coming back saw only a boat on the radar screen going south on the red sea. He was satisfied he had killed her and headed home.

Detective Harriet Brown Two

The Cruise

By Christopher Charles

Contents

Prologue

Harriet Brown, a five-foot four blond haired young lady weighing a hundred and fifteen pounds, moved into her mansion after she had all the repairs completed and the blood removed. At first, she did not know if she could handle the thought of living in the same house where her father had been killed. Nadine Quiver, her former tutor offered to stay with her. She used Hypnosis to help Harriet through her anxieties by regressing her back to her childhood where she faced the neglect of her father and the loss of her mother. She progressed very well. She soon found she could enjoy the house once more. She uncovered her piano and began playing again.

She continued to attend school determined to obtain her private detective's license. This was her first love after she survived the loss of her father and the attempts on her life by Police Chief Morales who was later killed in prison. There would be no further attempts on her life from that direction.

The school offered a summer cruise to the Panama Canal where she could pick up twelve units towards her police certificate. She had the money she received for finding the 800 million dollars. She had not spent any of it yet because the Brown Detective Agency had become extremely busy from all of the publicity they had received during the trial. George Brown, Harriet's grandfather, had been by a few times, but he was retired. When he saw Harriet handling the business okay, he made fewer trips to the office. He knew Rose and Youngsu were good people. They would continue to help her.

Now business had slowed to the point no more new clients had come in for over a month. They were finishing out the last few cases that were remaining. Most of the cases were dealing with divorce issues that Mc Craw, muscular black man, handled. He received his twenty five percent, and the company used the other seventy five percent for the overhead that included the upkeep of her mansion.

Business had slowed. It was the perfect opportunity for her to take a vacation. She would be taking Nadine with her of course.

1 Planning

Cruise Ship

The ship from Norsewegian Cruise Lines pulled into the San Pedro dock in Los Angeles to unload its passengers. It had just finished a cruise to Puerto Vallarta. Captain Waverly, a tall man, was tired. The passengers were more difficult than normal to handle. He looked forward to a week off before his next cruise to the Panama Canal, he had not been there for some time. He had heard some of the port-of-calls in Columbia were having difficulty. He would need the latest reports from the office before he would decide whether he would make them a port-of-call. He disembarked from the ship and walked into the main office.

The president of the company, Harold O' Brian, a small man wearing a suit too large for his body, looked up, "Waverly, I heard you had a rough trip."

"Yes sir, a couple of the married couples got into it and nearly killed one another. Seems two of them liked trading partners. This was not the happy cruise we had advertised."

"Well, this next one will not have newlyweds aboard. It's a group of police cadets taking four courses aboard your ship. That should keep things calm."

"It will be nice to have everything calm for a change. How are the Columbian port-of-calls?"

"We are still checking. There's been four more killings since you left. We may have to skip their ports."

"Those used to be some of the best ports in the past, sir."

"Times have changed, we will not be endangering our passengers."

"No sir," Captain Waverly said. "If you don't mind, I would like to go home. It has been a long cruise."

"Yes, yes," O' Brian said. "Have you seen your First Mate Williamson?"

"He left the ship before I did. He was securing the engine room and leaving from there. That was thirty minutes ago."

"He hasn't stopped by." He flipped his phone, dialed Williamson's number, it rang until the recording came on. He flipped it closed. "Go ahead, I'll wait for him. I know you are very tired."

"Thank you, sir." Captain Waverly said. He stood, made it outside the door, when one of the cleanup crews came running towards the office. He knew it might involve him. He hurried down the steps, into the parking garage, when his phone rang. Ignoring it, he knew it was O' Brian calling him, but he was in no mood to be detained longer for something his First Mate might have done. He stepped into his car, sat on the seat releasing the trigger to the car bomb. He closed the door, started the car, then he gave in. He called O' Brian on his phone, "What is it, sir?"

"We found your First Mate," O' Brian said, "He was found in the engine room with a bullet hole through the back of his head."

"Do you want me to come back, sir?"

"I've called the police. They are going to want to question you."

"I have no idea what happened, sir."

"You are probably the last one to see him alive. Maybe you better stay."

"Yes sir, I was looking forward to relaxing in my warm bath." He flipped the phone closed and turned off the engine. When he stepped out of his car, the pressure holding the trigger in place was released allowing the car bomb to explode. It blew out the side wall of the parking garage and took out the three cars next to it. His remains became part of the cement overhead and wall. The blast carried into the cruise line headquarters causing many people to be affected.

O' Brian managed his chair. When he looked out the window, he saw fire coming from the parking garage and called 911.

The Los Angeles police were already on their way. They came blaring in with their sirens on. A few minutes later the fire department arrived to put out the flames in the garage.

When the Los Angeles Chief of Detectives Paul Ramos, late twenties, dark hair and eyes arrived, he checked out the death of the First Mate, while the fire was being handled in the garage. The First Mate was found face down below the walking steel plates in the engine room. It had all the markings of a professional hit. He did not touch anything, waited for the lab boys. He could see the cause of death, a bullet in the back of the head.

He moved on to the garage. The fire was out, but the area was still hot. There was not much to see. Parts of flesh and metal were scattered all over that corner of the garage. Shaking his head, he went back to the office building. He found O' Brian in his office. The man was not doing well. Ramos asked, "You the president of the company?"

"Yes sir, I don't know what happened."

"I'm Detective Ramos," he said extending his hand. "Who was the man in the garage? It seems he's in pieces out there."

"It could be Captain Waverly," O' Brian said retrieving his hand. "I was talking to him just before the blast."

"Was he from the cruise ship that just docked?"

"Yes sir, and so was the First Mate, Williamson. The ship just came in from Mexico."

"Anything special happened on the cruise?"

"It was a newly-weds cruise. It was supposed to be a joyful event, but two couples got into it. Captain Waverly looked exhausted when he walked in here earlier."

"What about the First Mate Williamson?"

"I didn't get to talk with him. Captain Waverly said he was going to check out something in the engine room and leave. He never left."

"Do you know if either of them had received any threats?"

"They never said."

"This looks like a professional hit," Ramos said. "Were they into drugs or human cargo?"

"No, it wasn't in their character. We hire only the best of the best here."

"I am sure you do, but we are all tempted at times." He allowed that to settle, then he said, "We will have to search the ship for any unauthorized cargo, and all current personnel and passengers on the ship will have to stay on board until I have had a chance to talk with them."

"I need to make the ship ready for the next cruise. How long do you plan on keeping everyone?"

"I'll do this as quickly as possible, but two men have been killed. The murderers could still be on the ship."

"We have fifteen hundred crew members, and sixteen hundred passengers, but about half of the passengers have already disembarked. I can give you a list of their addresses."

"That would be helpful," Ramos said. "I will start with the crew from the engine room." He started to leave when he turned back, "I will also need all of the port-of calls you made, and a list of any passengers you may have acquired."

"I don't think we picked up anyone, but I can give you a list of who left the ship and returned."

"Yes, I will need that," Ramos said as he stepped outside. Walking to the ship, he made a call to the Los Angeles Director Assistant James Clark of the FBI.

Phone:

"Detective Ramos here, sir. We seem to have two murders here that might interest the FBI."

Pause:

"Yes sir, at the San Pedro docks, we have two officers from the Norsewegian Cruise Lines dead. They just came in from a Mexico cruise."

Pause:

"Yes sir, it appears to be a professional hit. A Captain Waverly was killed in the parking garage with a car bomb, and his First Mate Williamson was killed with a shot in the back of the head. The killer probably boarded the ship, when it had docked in Mexico."

Pause:

"Yes sir, I will keep you in the loop." He closed his phone walking aboard the cruise ship. He talked to several of the crew that worked in the engine room, and those responsible for allowing people to disembark from the ship.

He learned whoever did the shooting had definitely been aboard the ship. No one had boarded the ship before they found the First Mate dead. His suspect list was close to three thousand people. He also knew the hit man had probably left the ship when the other passengers had disembarked. The best he would be getting was a description of the killer.

Mr. O'Brian remained in his office. He had a cruise ship leaving in ten days. He did not have a Captain or First Mate. He normally would have moved the First Mate Williamson into the position of Captain, but he was dead too.

He began going through his resumes. He found some likely prospects, but a phone call quickly revealed everyone was working being this was the height of the cruise season. Then he received two phone calls, one from retired Captain Henry Morgan wanting to work another season, and another one from a First Mate who he did not know. He set up an immediate interview.

Two hours later the First Mate applicant arrived. He already had his resume filled out. A handsome young man of Spanish descent entered the office.

"I am Senor Raul Gonzales," the man said shaking O' Brian's hand.

"Sit down Senor," O' Brian said. "Let me look at your resume." Taking the resume, he began looking through it. After a few minutes, he said, "It seems you only have had experience on Mexican cruise ships."

"Yes sir, I captained my last cruise when the Captain became ill. You may call for references."

"Yes, yes, I will do that. You are free at the moment?"

"Yes, I am between cruises. I have thirty days before I take up my next ship as Captain."

"Your timing could not be more perfect for us. We are shipping out in ten days for a ten-day cruise."

"You understand, I can only do this one cruise for you."

"We'll see how things are after you come back." O' Brian said. "You will also have to take on the duties of the Safety Officer. Is that okay with you?"

"That will be no problem, but I have one request, I would like my personal boat to be the captain's boat."

"I think that can be accommodated, but we will have to change the lifeboat assignments."

"Thank you, sir."

They spent the next twenty minutes working out his salary. When they were finished, they shook hands agreeing to meet on board the ship in nine days. O' Brian always liked to play it safe thinking the extra day was important. Besides, the man had an air about him, like he was from a rich family in Mexico. The fact he spoke both languages was also an important factor. He knew Captain Morgan did not.

An hour later Captain Morgan entered the office, in his late seventies, his white hair and belly were showing, but he still fitted his uniform fairly well. O'Brian knew him. He felt the tight grip as they shook hands. Both men seated themselves.

"Captain, why did you come out of retirement?" O' Brian asked. "Of course, your timing could not be more perfect."

"I wanted to do one more cruise before I called it quits," Captain Morgan said. "It is no fun sitting at home."

"We're honored to have you on this last cruise," O' Brian said. "Now, your salary will be standard. Is that okay?"

"Whatever you feel is fair."

"The cruise is leaving for Panama Canal in ten days, you should be here in nine days to give you time to familiarize yourself with the ship. Things have changed somewhat since you last took a ship out. Of course, you will have a good First Mate in Senor Raul Gonzales."

"I have never heard of him," Captain Morgan said.

"He's from the Mexican cruise lines. He's between cruises and offered to give us a hand."

"I am sure we will get along."

"Then that is it, I will see you in nine days." They shook hands, Captain Morgan left.

O' Brian was almost able to smile again. Now he just had to get his ship back from the police department.

The next day at nine sharp, O' Brian had a man in a black suit knocking on his office door. His secretary had not come in yet. He was a little apprehensive thinking of the recent murders, but he opened the door.

A short man in a black suit stood in front of him. "I am Special Agent Brooks from the FBI."

"Come in, come in, I don't know much about the murders, but are they going to release my ship?"

Agent Brooks revealed his badge entering the office. His size was small, but his demeanor was all business, "We shall see what turns up." He took out his note pad and pen. "Let's see, how long has Captain Waverly been with your cruise line?"

"Ten years plus or minus, he came up through the ranks. You could not find a better person."

"Did he have any enemies, or anyone in his private life who did not liked him for any reason?"

"No, the man was at sea most of his life. That does not lend well to a private life. He had no enemies I know of."

"What about the First Mate Williamson?"

"He was a lady's man," O' Brian said. "He kept the ladies on board happy, if you know what I mean."

"How about when he was not on board?"

"He liked to frequent the local bars when he was in port, but he was always completely sober when he was on board. He was a man's man."

"Yes, I know the ladies liked him," Brooks said. "What about jealous husbands or boyfriends?"

"He never went too far, when he was on board. He knew when to back off. He just added a little excitement for the ladies, but never anything too serious."

"Do you know of any reason why anyone would want to kill them?"

"No, we are sailing to Panama on this next cruise. There is nothing really critical or out of the ordinary. We have been there many times."

Standing, Brooks took out a card, handed it to O' Brian, "I'll be working with Detective Ramos of the Los Angeles Police Department. I would suggest you take an undercover policeman on this cruise."

"I will think about it but having a policeman on board may alarm the passengers."

Brooks nodded and left the office.

O' Brian made a call to his insurance company.

Phone:

"This is Harold O' Brian from the Norsewegian Cruise Lines."

Pause:

"Yes sir, you heard correctly, we had our Captain and First Mate murdered two days ago, I was wondering how it was going to affect our rates."

Pause:

"I don't want to take a policeman on board, how about a detective agency?"

Pause:

"You will allow us to keep our same rates."

Pause:

"Thank you, sir, I will hire a detective agency, any suggestions?"

Pause:

"The Brown Detective Agency, yes, I will look into it."

2 Preparations

Youngsu, Harriet's chauffeur, a middle aged Korean man dropped her and Mc Craw, a muscular black man, off at the Los Angeles State University. This was their last class before the summer break.

Mr. Harold Thompson, a slender man in his late forties, stood at the front of the class as everyone settled in their chairs. When everyone was seated, he cleared his throat, "The trip to the Panama Canal was an overwhelming success, but I will have to cancel it. Those of you who have placed a deposit will be receiving your money back. It seems the spaces had already been filled by another school. I am very sorry. I know you have been looking forward to this trip."

Harriet had Youngsu pick them up. She was very depressed. She looked forward to the now cancelled trip. When they arrived back at the Office, Harriet had a message waiting for her. She was to meet a Mr. O' Brian of the Norsewegian Cruise Lines in San Pedro.

Traveling towards the pier, she tried to figure out why he had called her. Was it about the refund on her ticket? She was by herself except for Youngsu driving her.

Christopher Charles

O' Brian's Office

O' Brian was in his office looking over his employee's list trying to see where he could drop a few to meet his budget. He had a band coming and a magic act, but these were accepting the cruise for payment. It was a free trip for them and free entertainment for him. His intercom beeped.

Intercom:

"A Miss Brown with the Brown Detective agency is here to see you, sir," his secretary said.

"Send her right in," O' Brian said standing.

The door opened, Harriet with a big smile on her face, entered the office.

O' Brain motioned for her to take a chair as he seated himself. He was a little surprised when Harriet arrived. She didn't look a day over sixteen wearing a suit with a short skirt. "You're from the Brown Detective Agency?"

"Yes sir, am I picking up my refund from you?"

"I don't quite understand," O' Brian said.

Confused, Harriet looked him a second, "My cruise was cancelled because another school had taken the tickets. I'm here to pick up my refund."

O' Brian smiled, "There's seems to be a misunderstanding. You are from the Brown Detective Agency?"

"Yes, but..."

"I want to hire the detective agency to go on the cruise to Panama as a safety option. Our Captain and his First Mate were killed a few days ago. The FBI suggested we take some protection with us on this trip as a precaution."

"You mean you want my company to babysit your ship?" Harriet asked.

"I didn't want to put into those terms, but yes, we don't expect any problems. It's just an added precaution."

"I will need to bring my whole crew."

"How many are there of you?"

"Five! We will need three cabins."

"I only have one upper deck cabin, the Haven." O'Brian said. "The other two will have to be below deck. Is that acceptable?"

"How many can the upper deck cabin hold?"

"Two very comfortably, it's our premium suite. We were not able to book it. That is all I have available."

"How much are you willing to pay for the length of the cruise?"

O'Brian was taken back some, "I think I indicated you would be able to take the cruise free of charge. You are in our best suite and going to the Panama Canal."

"If nothing happens, that would be a great deal, but you would not be hiring us unless you expected a problem."

"I am not going to pay you if there is not a problem. I am giving you a free ride after all."

"Say there is a problem. You would expect us to react to protect your ship and passengers placing our lives in danger, correct?" Harriet hesitated a few seconds as O' Brian nodded, continuing, she asked, "What would be our payment then?"

"That would depend on the problem. A simple dispute between the passengers would not be worth thousands of dollars."

"I agree with you," Harriet said. "Okay, small stuff is handled by the free trip, but the major action where we save your company thousands of dollars, is paid by ten percent of the savings."

"Who determines the saving?"

"You do, of course."

"Any other conditions?"

"No one is to know we are aboard to protect us, and to make us more effective. We will use aliases to hide our identities. I will also need a letter from you giving us full control of the ship if the need should arise."

"Is there anything else?"

"Yes, we need a day alone in the ship to place our spyware," Harriet said.

"I can't have you spying on our passengers," O' Brian said with emphasis.

"We will not be placing them in the passenger cabins unless there is a need later. We only need places people congregate. It may save many lives later if we are allowed to do our job."

"That is still out of the question. If our passengers found out you were spying on them, it would hurt the line beyond repair."

"You are making it very difficult for us to prevent a later problem. We gather information. That's what we do."

"It will have to be done without your spyware," O' Brian said.

"You run the risk of an event developing into something very expensive by not giving us the tools to work with."

"I'll take that chance," O' Brian said.

"How about weapons," Harriet asked. "Will you allow us to take weapons on board?"

"Absolutely not!"

Harriet smiled, "Then we will just go along for the ride and enjoy the cruise."

"That's all I want you to do," O' Brian said. "I am only hiring you to keep our insurance intact."

"There's one more thing," Harriet said.

"Yes!"

"My refund," Harriet said.

"See my secretary on your way out," O' Brian said. "You will board with the passengers to keep your identities from the employees."

"The letter?"

"Yes, again have my secretary make one up for you."

"That's not keeping my identity a secret," Harriet said.

"Okay, give me a minute." He opened his computer, quickly typed up a letter, pushed the printer button. Then retrieving it, he signed the paper, handed it to Harriet, "Will this be satisfactory?"

Harriet looked it over, "Yes, and thank you for placing your E-mail address on here. I will have my attorney e-mail you our agreement. If it is satisfactory, sign it, fax it back, and send the original back in real mail."

"Is there anything else?"

"Our boarding tickets?"

"I will need the names you want on the tickets."

"I will have my secretary E-mail them to you," Harriet said. Then she stood, smiled, "Let's make this visit about my refund to keep my identity a secret."

O' Brian nodded as he stood. He shook her limp hand thinking somehow, she was taking advantage of him, but he did not know how. "It has been a pleasure doing business with you. Remember, no weapons on board." He said this last part with some emphasis to reinstate his position.

"Yes sir, I am aware." She smiled again and left the office. She stopped at the reception desk to retrieve her refund and left. Youngsu drove her back to the office. All smiles again, she would be going on her cruise.

When she reached the office, she called everyone together in the front office. Looking around slowly, she said, "We have been hired to go on a cruise to Panama Canal for ten days. We have three cabins, two of them will be below deck, and one is above deck. Youngsu and Mc Craw will occupy one of the below deck cabins, and Rose with the equipment will occupy the second below deck cabin. Nadine and I will occupy the upper deck cabin.

We will need aliases. I need to be from a wealthy family on a cruise with my friend, Nadine. Youngsu and Mc Craw barely managed to purchase their tickets, and Rose is a loner to allow her to use the equipment. Rose's below deck room will be our office since she will have the extra space. Are there any questions?"

"Weapons?" Mc Craw asked.

"I was told there would be no weapons, and we cannot use our spyware, but we are taking our spyware along in case there is a need later. We will have to get it aboard. Youngsu, that will be your job."

"Any other questions?"

"Yeah, how much are we getting paid?"

"We are only getting the cruise unless something goes wrong, then we are getting ten percent of what we save them."

"That doesn't sound like we are going to make anything," Mc Craw said.

"I don't know," Harriet said. "The Captain and First Mate of the ship were murdered two days ago. They want us aboard for insurance purposes, but he has effectively tied our hands. I expect a problem. That's why I went for the deal. We will not be able to prevent a problem. We can only keep it from getting out of hand. Now, any other questions?"

No one said a word

"Good, then I am off to see the FBI to get an update on the murders," Harriet said. "Rose, you should find a good contract lawyer, and get that contract off as soon as possible. I want our ten percent in very solid. That's the Norsewegian Cruise Lines. Otherwise we will enjoy the free vacation. We also need aliases. We are going to be just passengers unless something goes wrong. Maybe we should keep our first names."

"Total aliases?" Rose Blanchard asked. Her mother was of Mexican descent, and her father was Arabic. She spoke Spanish and Arabic very well.

"Yes, back it up with IDs and such."

"Got it. Nadine also?"

"Yes," Harriet said as she opened her phone. She pressed her speed dial.

Phone:

"Director Assistant James Clark, guess who this is?

Pause:

"Yes, I am glad you did not forget. I need to meet with you immediately. It is very important."

Pause:

"Twenty minutes is fine, I will meet you at your office," Harriet said, and flipped her phone closed. "Youngsu, we need to be going." She followed Youngsu out to the limousine.

Rose, a lady in her late sixties, trimmed, called Mr. Godfrey. She had used his attorney services in the past. She quickly related what they wanted in the contract and faxed over the present contract. He was going to work out the details with Mr. O' Brian. They would have the contract back before they set sail.

Later, entering the Director Assistant's office, Harriet smiled as she approached James Clark, a tall man with wavy brown hair and wide shoulders.

He immediately began backing up, "You're not going to plant a bug on me, are you?"

Harriet lifted her hands showing nothing in them, "No, not today," she said. "I am here on outside business."

He stopped backing up, feeling a little foolish, he offered her a chair, "Then please be seated and tell me all about it."

Taking the chair, she said, "I was hired by the Norsewegian Cruise Lines to take their ten-day Panama Canal Cruise because of the deaths of one Captain Waverly and his First Mate Williamson. What do you know about the case?"

"There is not much to tell at this point," Clark said. "It had the markings of a professional hit, but we know little else. Captain Waverly was blown up in his car, and Williamson was shot in the engine room. We have Special Agent Ted Brooks in charge of the case. Maybe we should bring him in on this if you are going to become involved."

"I don't know him," Harriet said. "I really prefer to work with you."

"You will work with both of us, but he will be my leg man," Clark said, "Is that satisfactory?"

"As long as I have a direct line to you," Harriet said.

"That is workable," Clark said. He pressed the speed dial on his phone, "Brook, I have a development on the cruise line murders."

Pause:

"Good, I'll see you in a few minutes." He turned to Harriet, "You will like him, he is very agreeable."

A moment later Special Agent Ted Brook entered the office. Harriet did not stand as he came around to the desk.

"Brook, meet Miss Harriet Brown," Clark said.

"Yes, I know the Brown Detective Agency that was in the news." He extended his hand. She shook it slowly.

"She is here concerning the cruise line murders," Clark said. Then looking at Harriet, he said, "Please go on."

"The Norsewegian Cruise Lines has hired my company to take the cruise to the Panama Canal."

"No offense, Miss Brown, but it would have been better to send our people undercover."

"I think they wanted to downplay the murders, sir. Who would want to take a trip with possible murderers aboard? The fact the FBI was aboard would give that impression."

"What do they expect from you?" Brook asked.

"Not very much," Harriet said. "We cannot use any of our equipment on board or take any weapons. I think they needed to satisfy their insurance. Otherwise, I cannot see where we will be very effective."

"So, you are a token for the Insurance Company?" Brook asked.

"Probably something like that."

"Then what do you want from us?" Brook asked.

"Cooperation, if we find something," Harriet said. "We may need information, or we may need your help. We are going to be locked on a ship without our tools to work with making us very vulnerable."

"Do you think the killer will be on the ship?"

"No, but don't you think it is unusual for the Captain, and his First Mate to be suddenly killed?" Harriet asked. "Then you have to think what this has forced the Norsewegian Cruise Lines to do?"

"Why they would have to hire another Captain and First Mate," Brook said.

"Exactly, then you have to ask, what is the advantage of this to the killer, or the one that ordered the murders?"

"He would have control of the ship."

"Now you see my problem," Harriet said. "Adding to this, they do not allow any law enforcement people aboard, only us, a token, because the insurance company needs to be satisfied. Continuing in this thought, once he has control of the ship, what would be his advantage?"

"He could change its course, and take it to another destination," Brook said.

"Then you have to ask where he would take the ship, and to what advantage?"

"Maybe he is going to pick up someone at sea, or take on a cargo," Brook said.

"It has to be something worth killing the Captain and the First Mate for," Harriet said.

"What would you want us to do, Harriet?" Clark asked.

"Maybe place a military ship near the Panama Canal, one that can disperse Helicopters and a military commando team."

"I don't know if I have that much clout with no real evidence," Clark said, "But I will see what I can do."

"Then I must be leaving," Harriet said. "I am hoping I am wrong in these scenarios', and I can have a pleasant vacation."

Director Assistant Clark stood, "Let's just believe you will have a well-deserved vacation, and the killings were for a local problem. I will keep you updated as promised on the case."

"Thank you for your time, sir," Harriet said standing. They were not taking her serious. She smiled, excused herself, and started to leave. Stopping at the door, she turned back to the Director Assistant, "I will be sending a decoder by with Mr. Youngsu for communication purposes."

Clark smiled and nodded.

After she left, Brook turned to the Director Assistant, "You think she was being a bit paranoid?"

"Normally I would say so, but I have learned to trust her instincts, but I don't know how I am going to convince the military with no direct evidence. They don't spend millions to move ships and people on instincts."

Harriet climbed into the limousine. She had finally told someone of her apprehension in taking this trip. She would still be going, but at least if something does happen, Clark will have a better understanding, and react quicker.

There was still a lot of preparations that had to be done before they walked aboard the ship. Rose had developed a communication system for them evolving wearing an earpiece. It fitted the ear quite well and was invisible with her hair down covering her ear.

Rose had found a schematic of the inside of the ship. She found the location of the two staterooms for herself and the boys. It was not even in the ship's personnel section. It did not have a port hole, and it sat very close to the engine room, meaning it would be very noisy. In fact, the next cabin was on the deck above them. Both rooms had two bunks. It would be her room they needed to camouflage hiding the spare bed. They would be placing the equipment in that space.

Once she had the dimensions, she gave them to Youngsu who set about constructing a wall that mimicked the bulkhead on the ship. They would be sending the construction over via the mail, where they would pick it up on the ship. They would also send over Harriet's Colt 45, and some of their spyware that way as well.

Next, she had to develop a way to communicate from the ship that would not be detected. That would involve sending and receiving encrypted messages. It would sound like ordinary noise until the encrypted machine turned it into English. This would prevent the ship's personnel from picking up their transmissions.

They would be able to send encrypted messages from the ship to the FBI by using the satellites, but they would need a strong transmitter to send messages, and to receive a message.

Youngsu constructed the antennae he would need and packed it into one of the boxes they were mailing. They were sending it priority to arrive on board the ship a day before they boarded. Youngsu dropped off an encrypting machine to FBI Office. He made sure the Director Assistant was made aware of it and placed it in the computer room.

Harriet made an appointment with Chief of Detectives Ramos at the same restaurant she had been shot at previously, but this time she would meet him inside. He handled the murder cases for the Los Angeles Police Department. They became friends during the investigation on the Morales' case earlier.

Youngsu drove her up to the restaurant and opened the door for her. She stepped out and entered the restaurant. She found Detective Ramos sitting by himself in a corner booth away from the windows. Remembering the previous drive-by shooting, he was not taking any chances. Maybe she would finally forgive him this time.

He stood when he saw her approach, offered his hand. "I am glad you could make it before you left on your cruise."

"Thank you, Paul," she looked around, "Not even a window, I should be safe this time." She smiled and took a seat across from him.

He found his seat. The waitress came over, took their order, and gave them a cup of coffee. Settled, he looked at her, "I am no longer the Chief of Police. They brought in a man from the outside because of the internal problems."

"It was more than that," Harriet said. "Mr. Johnson had made some very damaging statements regarding you. These still linger in people's minds even though they were proven false. I am surprised they allowed you to keep your Chief of Detectives position."

Ramos swallowed hard, "I didn't think about it from that perspective. Let's move on to your upcoming cruise. Is there any way I can help you?"

"Then you believe the Captain and his First Mate being killed has something to do with this cruise?"

"Yes, and I am not sure how deep it all goes," Ramos said.

"The new Captain, and the First Mate have to be suspected."

"Yes, that gives the person ordering the killings the control of the ship. What advantage would that be?"

"They can take the ship anywhere they may choose or allow anyone to board like a pirate raid." Harriet said.

"They would probably take the valuables from the passengers, but that would not warrant the murders. It has to be something more."

"We are going to set up a decoding machine for the FBI. That way we can transmit privately. We will still have our satellite phones for more direct communication."

"Would it help if I took a position in a hotel in Panama?"

"Can you do that?"

"I can if I take my vacation now."

"If you could bring along a few of your friends, that would make more sense," Harriet said. "If something is going to happen, it will be in that location."

"I will see what I can do," Ramos said.

"I talked with Clark. He didn't take this all that seriously. I suggested a naval ship with helicopters and commandos, but he didn't think that was possible."

"I'll be down there, and maybe I will have at least one helicopter lined up when you arrive."

Harriet smiled, "It may not be the navy, but at least you will be doing something we might need to use."

The waitress brought their food, and the conversation changed to lighter subjects. Harriet could see he liked her and encouraged it a bit. She wanted a backup. He was willing to risk his life and sacrifice his vacation for her. That meant a lot.

Aboard the Ship

On the ninth day Captain Morgan arrived, and went aboard the ship to become acquainted with it. It had some new features, but the basics were still the same. He would not have any trouble handling it.

First Mate Senor Raul Gonzales stopped by the main office before boarding the ship. He entered Mr. Harold O' Brian's office.

O'Brian stood, they shook hands as he said, "I am glad you stopped by before you went aboard." He motioned for Gonzales to sit down.

"You wanted to talk to me?" Gonzales asked. He had received an e-mail from O'Brian to come to his office for a briefing.

"I wanted to apprise you of what you can expect aboard the ship."

"Yes sir."

"Captain Morgan has been out of the business for a few years. He will be relying on you to pull him through some of the tough spots on the cruise. I would like you to double check his decisions."

"Yes sir, anything else?"

"Yes, I have hired a detective agency to come aboard. Since we had the sudden deaths of our former captain and first mate, my insurance company requested I hire them or take on undercover agents. I preferred the detective agency."

"As long as they don't interfere with the function of the ship, I can handle it."

"They will have no weapons, or the use of their spyware," O'Brian said.

"Then it seems you have already taken care of the problem," Gonzales said. "Does the detective agency have a name?"

Christopher Charles

"Yes, the Brown Detective Agency, it is run by a Miss Harriet Brown. She will be using an alias. She will be in the Haven Suite on the upper deck. You should give her a free hand as much as possible to satisfy my insurance company. We don't want it to seem we are preventing her from doing her job. She also has a letter stating she has control of the ship if there should be an emergency requiring it."

"I am to honor this letter," Gonzales asked.

"Only if there is a real emergency like a raiding party," O' Brian said, "But otherwise no."

"As long as she does not interfere with the running of ship, I think we can get along."

"Good, I hoped we could make this work."

Gonzales nodded, stood, "If that is all, sir, I need to board, and get settled in."

"Yes, yes, thank you for coming by."

Gonzales turned, and left the office. Walking towards the docked ship, he was thinking how he would handle Miss Brown. He did not have her alias yet, but that should not be too difficult to figure out.

He met Captain Morgan on the Bridge looking over the equipment. "Good Morning, sir I am your First Mate, Raul Gonzales"

Captain Morgan reached out, took his hand, "Nice to meet you, I hope you have had experience working a ship of this size?"

Gonzales looked slowly around the Bridge, "I see no difficulty here, sir. All the equipment is standardized."

Captain Morgan looked at him hard, "I know who sent you, and I know what I have to do."

"Then you better know there will be a detective aboard bringing God knows what with her. We will not speak of this again until the time of the event. Do we understand one another?"

"Yes, I understand my position."

"Good, now I need to see to our evacuation and lifeboat capability. I heard this has been seriously lacking aboard this ship."

"Yes, go ahead," Captain Morgan said in a defeated voice.

Gonzales nodded, picked up the mike to the ship's speakers, "This is First Mate Gonzales speaking. All personnel proceed to the theater immediately. That means everyone be there in five minutes." He turned back to Captain Morgan, "You coming?"

"No, you go ahead, and handle it. Do you know who the detective is?"

"No, she has assumed an alias, but she will probably be in one of the top deck suites." He did not want to give the captain too much information at the moment. Going to the ship's computer, he brought up the ship's personnel, and printed it. Then he brought up the crew's lifeboat assignments. Looking them over, he said, "Part of the crew will have to be in rafts."

"Yes, the passengers have the lifeboats except for the crews going with them."

He hit the print button, and the list came out of the computer. Picking up the paper, he started for the door, stopped, looked back, and asked, "You can handle this?"

"I can do my part," Captain Morgan said.

"Good!" Gonzales said, and proceeded down the stairs. He headed towards the theater. How many lives can he saved will depend on how well he does his job. Walking into the theater, he stepped up on the stage, and picked up the mike. He looked at his watch. It had been ten minutes, people were still coming in. "Take your seats immediately, stop your talking." He waited another two minutes. Finally, everyone had seated themselves. They remained very quiet waiting for him.

Then he spoke, "When I say five minutes, it means five minutes, not twelve minutes. If this was a lifeboat drill, we could all have drowned by now. We are going to spend the next few hours working on our lifeboat drills. There will be no talking except where it is absolutely necessary. All personal items are left behind, that includes cell phones. The only thing you will be taking to the boats will be your lifejacket. You will be putting them on at your station, not in your room, or moving through the hallways, but at your station. Is that clear?"

Everyone said, "Yes," loudly.

"We need to take roll at each station immediately. We cannot do that while you are in your cabin looking for something or putting your lifejacket on. In a time of emergency, the ships electrical system will be out, so your cell phones will not work. It will be dark in your cabin so have the location of your lifejacket in mind. To look for personal items will take precious minutes away from getting your lifeboat into the water. One of those minutes may cost you your life. Yes, we will be using the lifeboats on this cruise for the drills.

He allowed this to settle a moment, then he continued. "All of you have been assigned your stations. Those of you assigned to the lifeboats will be in charge of that lifeboat. You will take roll call to insure everyone is there. If it was a real emergency, you would start loading immediately as you checked their name off. Those activating the davits will lower the boats and stay with their boat. I want those people to remain here after this meeting is closed.

Those assigned to the rafts will first load them, then go aboard. You shove off immediately, then wait for your tow line from one of the lifeboats. Remember you in the lifeboats are to come back for the rafts and pull them away from the hatch. If the sea is too rough for the lower hatch, then the rafts are thrown overboard. The crew assigned to them will take the second option, and board the lifeboat assigned. Once in the water the rafts are retrieved, opened, and boarded. The line remains attached to the boats. Any questions so far?"

No one said a word.

"Good, supplies for the passengers and crew will go with the rafts. That means I want survival equipment for a land drop that includes tents, food, and water. These are to be packaged, ready for a quick transport aboard the rafts. The crew going with the rafts will be responsible for a quick loading, and moving away from the ship for the pickup by one of the lifeboats, any questions?"

A hand goes up.

"Yes!"

"Why do we need land supplies?"

"We are travelling along a jungle coastline. I believe you would complain if you had nothing to eat but monkeys. Put together a package that will require six people to carry. Two of the crew will secure the raft to the hatch as they inflate it. Once it is inflated, they will board the raft to receive the package, one package per raft.

Those carrying the packages will board with it and cast off. This needs to be done in less than two minutes. That means from when the raft hits the water. There are forty rafts, and four hatches, that is twenty minutes total. This has to be done very smoothly. I want the chiefs to remain here for further instructors. The rest of you move to your stations. Let's move it!"

Christopher Charles

The people in the auditorium began moving out quickly. The men who work the davits, and the Chiefs moved closer to the front. The Chiefs were the head of each department.

When they were all seated again, he said, "I want this boat drill to go smoothly. That means everyone has to know his job well. I expect you to train your people. Those working the davits see to the proper maintenance. I want those lifeboats moving up-and-down twice today before we start our first drill. The drill will include taking the boats down as far as possible. Okay let's get to it!"

Gonzales walked out on deck. He watched them lower all the lifeboats on the starboard side facing the dock. All of the boats could move down until they were almost to the dock. They seemed to be working fine. He checked the port side. One of the lifeboats had not moved, two others went halfway and stopped. It seems the davits had not been used for some time.

He went below deck to watch the crew put together cargo for the rafts. One of the chiefs came up to him, "We don't have any tents or mosquito netting here, sir."

"Then you better find some. I am going to have a lifeboat drill in two hours."

"Yes sir." The Chief said with worried look his face. He yelled in his phone as he walked away. "You heard me! Just get something now! Use the internet!"

Gonzales smiled, and thought, "Maybe he would have a crew yet."

Two Hours Later

The Chief had somehow found the tents and mosquito netting. The packages with the survival gear were finally completed. It seems most of the supplies were already on board. The lifeboats could now go up-and-down smoothly.

Detective Harriet Brown

The lifeboat drill horn sounded!

This was not the first lifeboat drill for the crew. They knew what they had to do, but this was for speed and perfection. In the past it was not all this serious. They were lucky to have everyone in the correct position within an hour. Now the man wants five minutes and in the boats.

The crew scrambled to their station donning their life vests. One of the crew members began calling out names as they boarded the lifeboats. When all of the names were called, the lifeboats lowered almost to the dock with the crew in them, the davits working perfectly.

Those at the lower hatches moved the rafts to the side of the ship, and the supply bundle came up behind them. They moved back quickly taking the life raft and supply bundle with them, as another life raft came in. This continued until all of the raft's bundles had been to the door with the Chief in charge yelling out orders.

Each Chief reported when he finished. After the final call Gonzales looked at his watch, picked up the mike, "You took five minutes to arrive at your station, another ten minutes loading the lifeboats, and lowering them to the water. Those of you with the life rafts took five minutes to reach your stations, and thirty minutes to unload the rifts. Replace the coverings on the boats, return to your duties. We will have another drill until you can do this perfectly. You will have passengers to teach tomorrow, Chief Myers to the Bridge!"

Ten minutes later Chief Myers stepped up on the Bridge, approached Gonzales, "Chief Myers reporting, sir."

"Yes Chief, how can we make the lifeboat boarding faster?"

"It's the calling out of the names that slows the process down, and when the passengers arrive, it will be even worse. Some will not hear their name at first or be too nervous to answer."

"How about having the passenger and crew members call out their names as they board the lifeboats. You need to be in the water quickly to retrieve the life rafts."

"That might work, sir, if we split the list up with the crew coming aboard to make it easier to spot the name on the list."

"Use large print, and make sure the crews all have flashlights attached to their life vest."

"Yes sir, I will see what I can do." He saluted, turned, and walked fast down the steps. He had no idea where he would get the flashlights. Maybe the gift shop had a source.

Two hours later he called another drill. The crew moved to their stations faster, but they did not have passengers yet.

Gonzales called Chief Myers to the Bridge again. He had a concern on his face. Arriving to the Bridge, Myers saluted, "The crew asked me how they were going to be ready for the passengers by tomorrow morning if they must attend the drills all day?"

"They may have to work all night, but we will have the lifeboat drills until we can perform our duties," Gonzales said. "Now, we need a way to be sure no one is left on the ship. They will mean having four people on each deck, two at each end, moving towards the center checking each cabin or spaces to be sure everyone is on deck. We may have someone unable to move for some reason, or someone hurts themselves in the excitement. These will have to be the maids because they will already have the keys to the cabins.

Rearrange the stations to make this possible. They will go out with the last raft or lifeboat. I also want you to lower my boat when the lifeboats are lowered. You can supervise and support the lifeboats once they are in the water. When all of the boats and rafts are in the water, you are to come back for the Captain and myself. Is that clear?"

"I understand, sir, I am to be in your boat when we actually lower the boats into the water."

Gonzales nodded, "Good, we will have another drill in two hours to work out the kinks. We cannot instruct our passengers if we do not know how to perform our duties."

"Yes sir, one more drill."

"It may be the last one if we have a smooth run this time," Gonzales said.

"Yes sir, I will tell the crew," Chief Myers said as he turned, and left.

Gonzales smiled to himself as he watched the man leave. The crew preformed the next drill perfectly. They did not want to work all night long.

3 The Cruise

The day arrived. Harriet and company carried their bags to the dock and went through the security line. They were every bit as thorough as airport security to the point of checking all the shoes coming aboard.

Harriet had a large trunk brought aboard carrying all of her clothes and personal items. She and Nadine, her former tutor, dark hair, early forties, boarded separately from the others to make their identities work better. They had all changed their last names.

A porter trudged her heavy trunk, and Nadine's suitcase to their suite on the top deck. It had a balcony facing the ocean, large closets, queen-size beds in each bedroom, and a shower in each bathroom. There was a dining table, three chairs, sofa, balcony, and a sun deck off the living room. It also had a grand piano, and a large Jacuzzi in the middle of the room.

Rose carried her own suitcases and trudged down several decks until she reached the bottom one. Moving along the corridor with only the one bulb overhead to light the way, she made it to her stateroom. Inside were two small racks they called beds with three feet between them. There was no porthole. If the lights should go out, it would be pitch dark. Fortunately, she had brought along a flashlight for that event.

Mc Craw and Youngsu stopped by the post office and picked up their packages that contained the camouflage boards and Harriet's gun. No one questioned them. It was in their names, and they had the correct IDs. They also looked like part of the ship's crew. They just figured it was something the ship needed.

Moving down the lower deck hallway, they finally found their cabin next to Rose. They dropped their bags off, took the camouflage and the pistol to Rose. She allowed them in, and Youngsu sat about constructing the camouflage. In minutes, he had it in place. It had a loose panel that would allow them to crawl inside and to store their spyware.

Passengers coming aboard, brought with them a great deal of confusion. It was a perfect time to place their antenna and spyware. Carrying his toolbox, wearing a crew below deck uniform, he worked his way to the upper decks, and onto the top of the ship. He placed his antenna up next to the other ones and proceeded to the wheelhouse. At the moment no one was there. He quickly placed his golf ball size bug up under the forward counter. It would pick up all the conversation in the Bridge.

He worked his way quickly to the officer's quarters and placed a bug in captain's and first mate's cabin. They were both out on deck greeting passengers. He also slipped one in the mess halls of both the crew and the officers. Though, most of the officers would be eating with the passengers in the dining rooms. Thirty minutes later he was done.

Walking back towards the lower deck, the First Mate stopped him, and told him to go to the crews' quarters, and fix a water leak.

Saluting, he said, "Yes sir. He moved off with his toolbox. He knew the layout of the ship from the semantics he had studied earlier. The First Mate, being unfamiliar with the crew, sent Youngsu thinking he was one of them.

Going into the crews' quarter, he found a water pipe leaking badly in one of the showers. All it needed was a tightening with a wrench. He quickly fixed it and dropped a few bugs in the area. Now, he headed back to Rose's cabin, that was on a lower deck, to see if the bugs were working.

Rose nodded everything was fine.

He picked up Harriet's gun and earpiece, placed them in his toolbox, and headed topside. He knew the location of Harriet's cabin, and knocked on the door quietly. He quickly entered, handed Harriet her Colt 45, two clips, her earpiece, and four bugs. He didn't say a word and left the cabin quickly. He had completed everything that needed to be done and descended to his cabin below.

Harriet hid the gun in the ventilator and shoved the cover back in place. She worked the earpiece on. Even without her hair covering it, the bug would be difficult to spot. She pushed it in a little tighter.

Time to move, she knew the weigh-anchor Champagne party was in the large lounge on the main deck in thirty minutes. Harriet wanted to be there. She knew the Captain and his First Mate would make an appearance. She put on her sexiest dress, walked quickly down to the main deck and lounge with Nadine beside her. In her bag were five bugs she wanted to place on the Captain and the First Mate.

Coming into the hall, it was half full. People were still coming aboard and unpacking their clothes. Harriet spotted the Captain and started that direction with a bug between her fingertips, when she ran straight into the First Mate. She stumbled, as he caught her. She knew immediately who he was, pushed the bug into his inside coat pocket, and pressed it home.

He caused the incident to prevent her from reaching the Captain, "Excuse me madam, I did not see you."

Harriet, recovering from her footing, looked up at him, "Thank you for keeping me from falling. You are…"

"Senor Raul Gonzales, First Mate at your service, my job is to make your stay aboard our ship one to remember."

"Your accent says you are from South America," Harriet said slowly. Then cocking her head slightly, she said, "I would say you are from Columbia."

"You are very clever, Miss…."

"Harriet Cummings," Harriet said.

"I see you are with a friend?"

"It's just Nadine and me. This is our first cruise. We usually fly when we travel."

"Then maybe we can see more of each other," Gonzales said. He bowed, kissed her hand, and said something in Spanish.

"That would be my pleasure," Harriet said.

He looked at his watch, "Duty calls." He turned and left the lounge.

Harriet heard Rose's voice in her earpiece, "He just told you in Spanish he would see you in bed."

"Not a nice man," Harriet said. She picked up a glass of champagne, and walked over to Captain Morgan, who was surrounded with four elderly couples trying to impress him.

She worked her way between them and the Captain, coming in tight enough to have one of the elderly men push her, when he turned slightly. This sent her into the Captain, where she pressed the bug into the inside of his coat pocket, while she stabilized her glass of champagne in his face.

She looked up at the Captain innocently, "Sorry, I didn't think he was going to turn that way."

The Captain backed up to avoid the glass of champagne, "No harm done. I need to be going. We are leaving within the hour. There are many things I need to do before then. I will see you all on the cruise." He quickly turned and left the lounge.

Harriet could see he was under a lot of stress. His voice said it and his mannerisms said it. The First Mate Gonzales was comfortable and in control. It was obvious who was in charge.

She walked over to the piano, sat down, and lifted the cover. She ran her fingers over the keyboard. She played a light tune to get the feel of the keys, then she pounded out a piece she would play for a symphony. When she was finished, everyone clapped. She stood and bowed to the crowd.

A few pieces of the band came in to play a light melody to put everyone into a good mood. When she stood to leave, the band leader pulled her back. They played a half hour of songs together.

The speaker sounded and announced the ship would be weighing anchor.

"Those that were not on the cruise needed to leave, and those that wanted to say good-bye up on deck, needed to go there."

Harriet and Nadine made their way back to their cabin while Rose was listening to the new bugs.

On the Bridge, Captain Morgan was alone with his First mate. "I don't think I can do this."

"You better get a grip on yourself," Gonzales said. "I am not going to carry you on this cruise."

An officer in a white uniform walked onto the Bridge, "We are ready to weigh-anchor, sir."

Gonzales looked at Captain Morgan, "Are you ready?"

Captain Morgan nodded, "Let's weigh-anchor." He reached up, pulled the cord, the whistle blew twice.

People began moving off the ship. Others were coming to the main deck to wave to people from the rail. Ten minutes later the gangplank withdrew. The ship's horn blew twice more, the ship pulled away from the dock. Harriet and Nadine were watching the whole episode from the stateroom balcony. It would be the last land they would see for a couple of days.

Rose had checked the spyware. It all worked perfectly. She had picked up the conversation on the Bridge. She had isolated each location on her machine. Being voice activated, it only came on when someone talked. It did not require her to be wearing the earphones all the time. She could always go back and hear the conversations a few minutes later. This allowed her to move about the ship. After an hour or so, she went back to her cabin, and listened to what it had recorded reviewing each location.

Youngsu continued to move through the ship carrying his toolbox checking light bulbs and the electrical systems. He placed more bugs until he was down to two. The equipment could not accept anymore.

Mc Craw took advantage of the open-air deck chairs to take in the sun. He kept his face covered with a bath towel. He did stop by the open food bars, café style, to take some food back to his cabin.

Harriet and Nadine were walking by one of the education halls. On the stand outside the hall she noticed a sign reading:

Police Education'

She peeked inside, and saw the room was filled with twenty men. They all appeared to be of Spanish descent. She turned to Nadine, "This is who replaced my class."

"They look very military," Nadine said.

"Surely the cruise line knew of the switch. I asked for my refund after all. So, three events have happened, two deaths, and the replacement of her class. Either something is being set up to happen, or something is being set up to prevent something from happening. Rose, have you been listening?"

"What do you have?" Rose asked over the earpiece.

"A class of twenty plus men are in the education hall. They looked military or police of Spanish descent. I think we should bug one of them. See what Youngsu can do."

"It could be an innocent class of policemen taking the cruise and being educated from another country," Rose said.

"Yes, it could be." Harriet said. "We need to know where they are from. That could give us a clue."

"I will see what I can pick up."

"Thank you, Rose," Harriet said watching two of the men leave the education hall. Following, she saw them enter a large dining room on the main deck. It was a little early for her to eat, but she watched them take a table near the window. She led Nadine to the table next to them and sat down.

The waiter came by, asked them what they wanted. Harriet ordered sherbet ice cream. Nadine ordered a cup of coffee. The waiter nodded and moved to the next table. Each of the men at the table ordered a club sandwich in English and a cup of coffee. When the waiter left, they began talking in Spanish to each other.

"Most of the conversation concerned the girls they were going to pursue later, but their accent was definitely South American maybe Columbian," Rose said into her ear plug translating the Spanish.

The conversation did not give them any more information. When they left, Harriet quickly finished her ice cream, "We need a bug in one of their cabins."

"We don't have that many anymore," Rose said in the earpiece.

"We just need one or two."

The next day, when the class was in progress, Youngsu managed to place a bug in one of the South American's policeman's state room. He only had one bug left.

The ship moved through the calm water off of Mexico. At twelve noon, Gonzales sounded the abandon ship. He announced over the loudspeaker, "All passengers will go to their assigned lifeboats, and bring with you your life vest. Leave all personal items and phones behind because there is not room for anything extra on the lifeboats. Your phones will no longer work when the ships electricity is off.

There will be no talking except when necessary for instructions, so you may hear those instructing you where to go. You will find your boat number by looking on your cabin door or on the information kit you received coming aboard. It is important to move quickly because the ship may only stay afloat ten minutes in a real emergency."

The passengers began moving in all directions. The crew began guiding them. The four crew members on each deck were moving people out towards the boats. It took one full hour before everyone was in the correct place.

Harriet and Nadine were assigned the same boat near their cabin, but Rose and the others were assigned to another boat. Rose left all of their gear behind in the cabin. The recording devices were behind the partition.

Youngsu's bag under his bed had its own small partition. He slipped his phone into his sock, lowered his pant leg to cover the bulge.

Knowing the ship layout allowed Harriet's team to find their lifeboat quickly. Many of the other passengers were confused. Some found themselves at the wrong boat and had to hurry to find the correct one. Roll call was taken by having the passengers call out their names when they entered their boat. It was slow until the passengers understood what they were supposed to do. Stragglers came in later. Eventually they filled the boats.

Gonzales looked at his watch. He knew he would have to speed up the time. He blew the horn, announced over the speaker, "We will have move faster next time. There was too much noise making it hard for the others to hear instructions. Please only talk when necessary.

We need to cut this hour down to ten minutes. That means putting your life vest on at the lifeboat where help can be found if you have a problem with it. Remember, every second counts when the ship is sinking. Thank you for participating in the drill. We will have more of them until we can cut the time down."

He handed the mike to the mate on the Bridge, looked at Captain Morgan, "We will have to have another one today to step up the time."

"Let's not make the passengers hate us."

"I think saving their lives will be more appreciated," Gonzales said, as he watched the passengers step out of the boats. Then thinking to himself, "I bet some of them thought it was exciting." He noticed Harriet climbing out of the boat. "Let's invite Miss Harriet Cummings to dinner tonight, sir. I am sure she will enjoy it."

"Miss Cumming, is that the one who played the piano earlier?"

"Yes, I also think it is wise we get to know her."

"I'll have an invitation sent," Captain Morgan said as he smiled. His First Mate has found his first victim."

4 The Captain's Dance

Harriet read the schedule. They were still a day out before they reached their first port of call. The Captain's dance was scheduled tonight. She wanted to attend. The band had already asked her to play the piano for them.

She had other things on her mind. She had an invitation to sit at the Captain's table. It came to her stateroom earlier in the day. It was a privilege given to those on the upper deck. It would allow her to get closer to the First Mate. She wanted a better read on him. She felt something else, but she ignored those feelings. She would keep this all business.

Nadine walked beside her as they entered the large dance hall on the main deck. She wore a sleeveless long flowing yellow dress that extended to the floor. The band was already playing dance tunes. She saw the Captain sitting at the table next to the window. A few people were dancing on the floor.

The First Mate Gonzales was dancing with one of the older ladies from the table. The large table accommodated twelve people. Other tables were close-by leaving the dance floor area open towards the middle of the room.

Approaching the table, Captain Morgan stood, "Welcome to our table Miss Cummings and your friend is?"

"Nadine Martin, she has been my companion for many years."

"Please be seated ladies, we are opening the champagne."

The First Mate Gonzales had returned from the dance floor and seated the older lady. When he saw Harriet about to take a seat at the other end of the table, he said, "Miss Cummings you need not sit so far away." He pulled out a chair next to his seat, and continued, "I have been saving these seats for you and your companion."

Harriet took the chair offered. "Thank you, Mr. Gonzales, but why do we rate such a privilege?"

"It is to make up for my bad behavior earlier when I had to leave so abruptly."

"And mine too," Captain Morgan said. "We had our duties to perform and cut you off rather harshly."

Harriet took the seat offered as Nadine found the chair next to her. Gonzales took the seat next to Harriet.

The Captain remained at the head of the table next to the First Mate. He opened the champagne bottle, "Now that we are all here, we need to make a toast." He began pouring the champagne and passing the glasses around the table. When everyone had a glass, he said, "Here's to a very enjoyable trip you will always remember." He took a sip of the champagne and smiled the best he could. He knew what was going to happen to these people.

Gonzales saw the look in the Captain's eyes. He quickly said, "Let's make this night one of fun and enjoyment." He took another sip with a big smile.

Harriet barely had time to lay her glass down when Gonzales took her hand, "Come, they are playing a Waltz."

"Yes, it is very lovely, but I don't think…."

Before she could finish her sentence, he had her on her feet following him to the dance floor. Putting his arm out, he said, "It's a six-count beat starting with your right, just follow my lead."

He didn't have to tell her. She knew what a Waltz was. She had played the Waltz on the piano thousands of times, but she had never danced to the music. She felt his strong arms take control as he moved her around the dance floor. She allowed her legs to move the direction he moved her as she felt the music take her. Going with the music, she felt herself floating across the floor. He took long steps causing her dress to flow around her. His left hand went up as he pushed her into a spin. She came back out of the spin to find herself in correct alignment with him.

Suddenly he spun around her, then she found herself spinning around him ending in a cross-step. It made her feel suddenly free. Going with the music, they floated across the floor. When it was over, he suddenly dropped her to his left, and then caught her before she hit the floor. Standing, the audience clapped their hands thinking the dance was for them.

Harriet blushed. She worked her way back to her seat. She never knew she could dance so well. It had to be all of her music training she had growing up.

First Mate Gonzales, all smiles, brought her back to her seat. "You dance extremely well Miss Cummings."

"Thank you," Harriet said. She felt her muscles going weak. She needed to get control of herself. She tried to shrug it off by taking a drink of her champagne.

Christopher Charles

The music turned to a slow foxtrot. Gonzales allowed her to take her drink, then he had her up again.

She started to protest, but she could not get the words out of her mouth. She survived the first dance of her life, could she do it again. This was different music. She knew the beat. She expected a slow movement across the floor. Instead, he took long steps moving her across the dance floor. He held her close and moved his right leg between her two legs. He had complete control as he moved her backward, her steps following his. They were moving as one.

He didn't speak to her allowing his dancing to speak for him. She had never been this close to a man before, her soul blending with his as they flowed across the floor. His hand in her back seemed to be on fire as she felt the radiating heat. She felt every movement of his body as she blended with him.

When the dance was over, she almost collapsed on the floor. Only his hand still on her back held her up. Slowly her emotions settled, the spinning stopped, allowing her to be led slowly back to her seat. She had enough dancing. The audience did not applaud this time. They were in awe of the display of emotion.

Harriet suddenly realized everyone had been watching them. She felt embarrassed as she took her chair. Neither of them said a word during the dance, or as he led her back to her seat. He did not have to. Their emotions ran too deep.

He took the seat next to her. Immediately he turned his attention to the other ladies at the table.

Harriet did not say a word. She sipped her champagne. She was thankful when the food began to be served. Eating in silence, she noticed Gonzales had come out of the trance rather quickly. Was she just played, or did he really have feelings for her? She went through her meal quickly and continued to look at the others talking.

Nadine, beside her, knew something had happened out on the dance floor, but she did not want to talk about it there.

Finally, Captain Morgan decided he had to rescue Harriet. He knew she had played the piano earlier, "Miss Cumming, I understand you play the piano beautifully. I wonder if we could encourage you to play for us."

Harriet looked around at the expecting faces. Many of them had heard her play earlier.

Finally, closing off her emotions, she said, "The band is playing so well, I would hate to interfere with their music."

"I am sure they would not mind," Captain Morgan said, as he looked up at the band leader and nodded.

The band stopped playing. The band leader bowed slightly, "It would be our honor sir, to hear her play."

"There you are, Miss Cumming, the floor is all yours."

Gonzales quickly stood, eased Harriet's chair out of the way as she stood. Smiling, he said, "I have not heard you play, but everyone says you play beautifully."

She could not reply. She swallowed hard, made her way to the piano, and sat in front of it. She stared at it a moment. She knew they expected her to play, but she still felt the earlier emotions. She did not notice Gonzales had walked up behind her. She felt the waves of emotions flow over her as she placed her hands on the keys.

Moving them fast, she took her emotions out on the piano as her fingers flowed over the keys producing a quality of music, she did not know she possessed. Everyone stopped eating becoming captivated by the music. They were feeling her emotions with her as they had been watching her dancing previously with Gonzales.

She had half of the audience in tears as she came to a completion. When she had finished, she could not move for a moment. Then Gonzales took her arm as she stood and led her back to her seat. The audience did not clap until she was seated. Then they began to stand and clap until everyone was standing and clapping.

Harriet could not take it anymore. She stood quickly and ran from the dining room. She ended up on the fantail of the ship looking out over the ocean. It was calm. The moon filled the clear sky. She had tears streaming down her face. She felt so foolish. She even ran out of there. Everyone knew how she felt. She still did not understand what had happened.

She watched the churning water below allowing her emotions to settle. She heard soft footsteps behind her. She recognized them immediately. She felt the reassuring arms of Nadine go around her.

"It's okay hon," Nadine said. "It was simply beautiful. I don't think many made the connection, it was your emotions they were hearing."

Harriet turned into Nadine arms, "What did he do to me? I felt so naked."

"Some call it love, others would say your hormones were suddenly aroused and took control of you."

"I can't ever be around him," Harriet said, "It may happen again."

"You will be more prepared the next time. Don't allow him to get that close and enjoy his company."

"He's our mark, how am I going to control that and do my job?"

"That's the point, he was affected too. You already have him. You just need to control your own emotions."

"I am to use my love emotion as a weapon?"

"Women have been using it for eons very effectively," Nadine said. "Now let's get you back to our cabin and cleaned up a bit. Then maybe you can finish your dinner. It certainly cost enough."

Harriet stumbled back to their cabin, cleaned up her tears, and reapplied her makeup. Then putting on a smile, she followed Nadine back to the ballroom. Gonzales pulled her chair out for her allowing her to sit next to him. She could feel her emotions wanting to come, but she held them in check, and took her seat.

"Thank you for coming back," Captain Morgan said. "I feel we have abused you quite severely, please forgive us. I should not have asked you to play the piano when you were already under a great deal of emotional stress. Though, it was the most beautiful piece of music I have ever heard."

"Thank you, sir," Harriet managed to say. "I am quite alright now."

"I apologize for dancing so emotionally with you, but I could not help myself, you dance so well." Gonzales said.

Harriet looked up at him, "That was my first dance."

"Then you must have taken lessons," Gonzales said. "You flowed with the music so perfect."

"That was her first lesson, Mr. Gonzales," Nadine said. "You must be a very good teacher."

The First Mate became embarrassed. "It must have been an emotional thing," He said standing, "I think I had better check the watch, sir."

"Yes, that might be good," Captain Morgan said seeing he was upsetting Harriet again.

When he left, Harriet felt a sense of loss, and relief at the same time. She forced a smile taking a drink of her champagne. She finished her dinner as the conversation moved around the table. She felt better.

Captain Morgan noticed it, "If you feel up to it, we would all like to hear you play the piano again."

"Okay, but I am going to play something less emotional."

Captain Morgan motioned to the leader of the band.

He nodded, brought the band music to a stop. Then announcing over the mike, "Miss Cummings has granted us more music on the piano."

The audience clapped as Harriet walked to the piano. She would play something light allowing her fingers to flow over the keys. She felt like a butterfly erupting from her cocoon allowing the emotion to fill her body expressing themselves on the piano keys. She did not play any particular song creating the music as she felt the emotion. It was simply beautiful.

When she finished, the emotion spent, she slowly stood, bowed as the audience gave her another standing ovation. She walked back to the captain's table smiling.

Out in the hall, First Mate Gonzales listened to the music. When she finished, he wiped the tears from his eyes. What did that girl do to him? She had some kind of emotional power over him, that he had never felt before.

5 Cabo San Lucas

The next morning Harriet woke up early. She knew the ship would be anchoring at Cabo San Lucas this morning. She wanted to watch and stood by the rail beside the pool. Nadine was still asleep in the stateroom.

The ship came into the harbor slowly. Lining up with the incoming swells, it dropped the bow anchor, and continued to lay out more chain as the ship moved very slowly towards the docks. Then it dropped the fantail anchor taking back in the chain from the bow anchor as the ship moved slowly forward as it let out the fantail chain. Finally, the ship stopped, the chains remained still. She was very impressed.

She watched them lower the tenders, the boats that transport the passengers back and forth from the ship to the dock. She heard a noise and looked down. They had opened up part of the ship on the lower deck level. It was a hatch. They pushed out a thick two-foot bumper. The tender came up next to it. A line was thrown, someone pulled it up tight, wrapping it around a cleat inside the hatch. She learned all of these terms later.

She was watching the activity below and did not notice First Mate Gonzales approach her from behind.

He came up beside her, "They have a great snorkel reef here you should see."

She turned and looked up at him. She could feel the night before emotions coming back. She quickly controlled them. She needed information from this man. He was the key to the two murders. Rose had not been able to pick up anything from the spyware. If she remained close to him maybe he might allow something to slip. "How does one get there?" She asked.

"If you allow me to be your guide, I will take you there."

"Can I trust you?"

"I will be the perfect gentleman."

"I can count on that?"

"Certainly, you can even call me Raul."

"Only if you call me Harriet, and you remain the perfect gentleman."

"Harriet, that is a very nice name, yes, I can still remain a perfect gentleman."

"Then what should I bring along?"

"Wear a swimming suit. You will be getting wet and bring something along to keep warm. I will have everything else we will need in the boat."

"This will be a private tour?"

"I said I would be a gentleman," Gonzales said.

"I believe I can accept the word of the First Mate whose name is Raul," Harriet said. "Where should I meet you in thirty minutes?"

"I will have our boat ready by the lower deck hatch where the other boats will be picking up passengers."

"What about Nadine, my companion?"

"You can bring her along if you choose."

"Okay, I will see you in thirty minutes." Harriet said walking fast towards her stateroom.

Gonzales watched her walk away. He did not know if she would be alone. He needed to keep her off balance. This operation had to be done just right.

Harriet entered her stateroom. Nadine was still asleep. She sat on the bed and woke her by pushing on her, "The First Mate is taking me snorkeling. Do you want to go along?"

Nadine opened one eye, "What time is it?"

"It's almost nine, you are sleeping the day away."

"Just leave me be for a while."

"I'm going snorkeling with the Raul, the First Mate."

"Since when has it become Raul?" Nadine asked trying to wake up.

"Since a few minutes ago," Harriet said, "I'm going snorkeling with him."

"Do you even know what snorkeling is?"

"It's when you put on a wet suit and go underwater. It sounds scary and fun."

"There's no wet suit," Nadine said. "You put on a face mask and snorkel. You swim around on the surface of the water looking at the fish below."

"It doesn't sound too hard," Harriet said.

"When did you learn to swim?"

"Okay, I will hold on the side of the boat and look under the water."

Christopher Charles

"Be sure that is all you do," Nadine said.

"He said you can come along."

"And do what? Watch you put your face in the water?"

"Maybe be my chaperone."

"The reason you want to go is to get information out of him. Me being there will not allow that unless you think he will take advantage of you."

"He's the First Mate. He promised he would be a gentleman."

"Then you will be getting your bathing suit wet after all," Nadine said.

"You're not coming?"

"I think you will be okay," Nadine said as she rolled over on her bed.

Harriet stood, walked to the closet, and pulled out her bathing suit she had purchased before the trip. She had not worn it yet. In fact, she has never worn a bathing suit. She worked herself into it. Then looking in the mirror she felt embarrassed. She looked good, but her top hung out a bit. She tried pulling more of the bathing suit higher, but it only improved the situation slightly. She still showed too much. She pulled a sweater over her swimsuit and found her thongs.

"You better be taking some sunscreen, hat, and sunglasses," Nadine yelled from under the covers. "The sun's much hotter down here."

"Thank you, see, maybe you should be coming along"

Nadine did not answer.

She had her thongs, sunglasses, sunscreen in her sweater pocket, and her hat. She was ready. "Your last chance," Harriet yelled.

"Go have fun but hang on to the boat."

Harriet smiled as she left the suite. She worked her way down to the lower deck hatch where the boats were picking up people and taking them ashore. She saw the First Mate waiting for her by the hatch.

When he saw her coming, he motioned for his boat to be brought up, a special red speed boat able to accommodate four people. One of the mates brought the boat in next to the ship with the bumper guards on the side. He placed it on idle as he quickly jumped to the hatch and tied it down.

"Just in time," Raul yelled as he stepped aboard. The back seat was filled with flippers for the feet, face masks and snorkels for the face. There was also a blanket and a basket full of food.

She smiled, took his hand, as he helped her aboard.

"Is your companion, Nadine, coming with us?"

"She wanted to sleep in this morning."

"She's going to miss a great outing," Raul said.

"I will tell her all about it when we come back." Harriet said as she started to work her way over the first seat.

"No, no, you are going to be driving the boat," Raul said as he stepped back across the seat. He sat down on the passenger side.

The security officer by the hatch was confused. He had the line in his hand, but he did not know who to throw it to.

"Give it to her," Raul yelled, "She is piloting the boat."

Harriet still standing, looked up as he tossed the line to her. She barely caught it as she balanced herself against the rolling boat. She quickly grasped the windscreen as she fell back into her seat with the line. She tucked the line beside her seat as the boat drifted from the ship.

"Maybe you ought to push the throttle forward some to take us away from the ship." Raul said.

Harriet looked at the lever beside her, "Do I push this lever?"

"Yes, push it forward, and steer the boat out away from the ship."

Harriet pushed the lever all the way forward and turned the wheel sharply. The boat spun out sideways and took off towards the shore.

"Ease up on the throttle and steering," Raul yelled hanging onto the side of the boat.

Harriet immediately brought the lever back to slightly above idling, straightening out the wheel, she yelled, "Whoa, I didn't know it had this much power."

Raul swallowed hard. Slowly he said, "Now that you have control of the steering, maybe you can turn us out more. We are heading down the beach."

Harriet adjusted the steering. She had them going the right direction, before she asked, "Can I increase the speed?"

"Yes, move the throttle forward slowly allowing the speed to pick up."

Harriet shoved the throttle forward, the front of the boat lifted as water flew over the windshield. The boat broke through the swells spraying them both with water.

"I told you to wear your bathing suit." Raul yelled over the noise.

Harriet smiled as she allowed the water to splash her face and arms.

"See that rock formation," Raul yelled. "Head that direction. You will find a sea lion colony there." The boat skipped over the top of two swells in a row sending water over both of them.

Harriet began to get the feel of the boat. "Can I turn it some," she yelled.

"As long as you head for that rock formation," Raul yelled back.

Harriet began moving the boat back and forth bringing her side of the boat very close to the water as she made a tight turn. When she took the turn hard to the left, Raul's side, he became very nervous. The water came up to the top of the gunwale. She smiled straightening the heading.

She stood, allowed the water to strike her in the face as she made some more sharp turns. Screaming, she sat down, and straightened out the boat again.

Raul did not realize what he set loose. He anticipated she would be very apprehensive and helpless. Instead, she was a tiger on the loose.

Harriet slowed the boat some when they approached the sea lion colony. She did not want to scare them. They were sunbathing on the rocks as the boat moved quietly by them. One of them lifted his head to see slightly, but that was all the reaction they received going past them.

They were approaching Santa Maria Cove. She kept the speed down as they approached.

"We are going to anchor out two hundred yards from shore. There is a reef here that is loaded with fish and plant life."

She moved the boat into the cove. Slowly she brought the boat to an idle. No one else was here.

Raul stood, moved to the back seat, picked up the anchor, and threw it overboard. It dropped thirty feet and stuck. He quickly tied the line off on the boat cleat using a figure eight.

Christopher Charles

Then looking at Harriet, he said, "We're here. Your flippers are in the back seat along with your mask and snorkel. You may have to adjust the face mask."

Harriet took off her wet sweater and climbed over the seat. She sat on the gunwale with her feet on the back seat. The small swells lifted the boat up and down. She watched him slip into his fins. She was not sure what they were for. She watched him adjust them. She put on her smaller fins, adjusted them like he did. They felt snug and awkward. She could see it would be difficult to walk with them on.

He handed her the face mask and snorkel. She watched him a moment to see how he put it on. He took it off and adjusted it slightly. She tried hers on. Loose, she tried to adjust it, but she only managed to make it worse.

"Here, let me have it," Raul said. "Sometimes these things can be tricky." He quickly adjusted it to her head as she held it in place. He placed her snorkel into her mouth, smiled, "I think you are ready." He gave her a hard shove. He watched her flip over into the water.

It may have been the rough ride he took coming here and this was pay back. Anyway, he felt good as she disappeared below the water.

Harriet grabbed her face mask out of reflex as the water enveloped her. This was the first time she has ever been in water other taking a bath at home. She looked around quickly. The boat was above her; she took a quick breath through the snorkel. It filled her lungs with water as she flailed her arms bringing her to the surface.

She could not breathe. Ripping the facemask off, she continued to thrash her arms trying to stay afloat and breathe. The water in her lungs tried to come up as new air tried to go down. Finally, the lack of oxygen took its toll leaving her face down in the water.

Raul had ripped his facemask off. He was already over the side when she came up splashing. She had drifted twenty yards from the boat. He swam quickly to her turning her face out of the water.

She began gasping for air again as he placed her into a cross chest carry swimming back to the boat using a scissor kick. When he reached the boat, she leaned forward, and continued to cough up water.

Gradually regaining control, she was able to stop the coughing. She noticed Raul held her with his arm going across her chest and under her arm. Taking in a few more breathes, she said, "This is not behaving like a gentleman as I was promised."

Seeing she had composed herself, Raul released her and held her hand to the boat. "Sorry for behaving badly. I should not have pushed you in when you were not ready."

She did not say anything for a moment. Then quietly she said, "I have never been swimming before. This is my first time in water over my head."

Raul, taken back, "You did know snorkeling requires swimming?"

"I thought I would be looking over the side of the boat."

Raul smiled, "Let me make it up to you. I will teach you to swim."

"Okay, if you don't let me drown."

"I will not let you drown, that will be the first thing we will work on. Let me have your hand."

Harriet looked at him. She felt she could trust him. He was trying to make up for almost drowning her. She allowed him to take her hand.

Taking it, he said, "Now slowly release your other hand from the boat while I hold this one."

She slowly released her tight grip, but she depended on her right hand he held to keep her afloat. She did not take her eyes off of him looking for any hint he would try to intimidate her again.

"I will not let go of you, just relax, and lean back into the water letting your head float." He watched her leaning back. "Now, extend your other arm out. Relax it on the water allowing it to float too." Her left hand and arm floated.

He could still feel the tight grip she had on his left hand. "Now relax your grip on my hand allowing it to float. I will still touch your hand." He felt her grip become less ridged until he only touched her fingers.

Her head remained above the water. A small swell came in sending the boat higher, then down taking her head below the water slightly. She started to raise her head when he took hold of her hand again.

"Easy, that was only a small wave going over your face. It was not drowning you. Let's do this again." He slowly released her hand until she floated free of him with the water line coming to her chin when she did not move.

"There, that is your float level with the heavy fins. Take them off and your float level will probably be below your chin. Now you can see, if you do nothing, you can float, and breathe as much as you want."

"I'm being taken somewhere?" Harriet yelled looking side to side as she drifted from the boat and Raul.

"Move your legs up and down. Let your fins work. They'll move you back here."

Harriet kept her arms out in her float position. She kicked her legs moving the heavy fins. Suddenly she found herself up beside the boat and Raul. Amazed, she turned her head around and tried it again on her back going further from the boat. Twenty yards out, she yelled, "What do I do with my arms?"

"You can move them back and forth at your side, or for more speed put your hands over your head and touch them." Raul watched her put her hands together over her head, and yelled, "Not together, only touch them. Now cup them slightly and pull the right arm down hard as you continue to kick your legs. Then take the right arm back to position and move the other arm hard down to your side."

Harriet did it, and found herself moving very fast from the boat, and yelled, "How do I come back?"

"Lean forward, put your face in the water in the same position. Then you pull with each arm touching each time."

Harriet stopped kicking allowing her body to stop moving, then gathering up her legs, she placed her head into the water, and pushed her leg out behind her. Now face down in the water, she felt an immediate twinge of fear when she could not breathe.

Remembering what Raul had said, she placed her hands together, and moved the right arm down pulling her forward. She kept kicking her feet as she moved the other arm down. Her fins working, she really moved through the water, but she needed to breathe. She decided to take one more combination of strokes before she lifted her head up to breathe.

Completing the combination, she raised her head, and found herself at the boat in front of Raul.

Smiling, he said, "Now all you have to do is learn how to breathe. Place both hands on my left arm."

Harriet felt herself sinking. She immediately grabbed his left arm.

"Now hanging onto my arm with both hands, allow your body to remain floating behind you, and place your head in the water.

Christopher Charles

When she was in position, he said, "Okay, keeping one hand on my arm at all times, you will rotate them. When the right arm goes down, your head is in the water blowing bubbles, but don't blow all of your air out. When you left hand goes down, you turn your head to take a bite of air. If you feel water over your mouth, don't take in the water, wait for the next series of strokes. This is only a bite of air. We do not want to fill your lungs with water again."

Harriet began practicing until she could do it automatically. She stopped, "Okay, let me try it."

Raul nodded, he pushed her out from him.

She leaned back and did her back stroke away from him. When she was a hundred feet from him, she leaned forward, and went into her crawl stroke back towards him. She found her rhythm when she reached him.

He stopped her from crashing into the boat, "I think you can swim."

She pushed off from him again and did her back stroke. This time she went two hundred feet. She struck something with her head. Stopping, she kicked her feet to stay afloat. She turned around, found her face mask and snorkel floating in the water. Picking it up, she placed mask over her head.

Working the snorkel into place, she looked down in the water, and moved into her forward strokes. She was fascinated by the reef below her. She remembered to blow out the water this time before she took a breath. She looked up at Raul a few feet in front of her.

He smiled, "It looks great, huh?"

She smiled moving out away from him. She wanted to dive deeper under water, but she did not want to stop breathing through the snorkel tube. Scared, she finally said, "Okay, time to do it." Taking in a breath of air, she ducked her head, and felt her feet go above her. She found herself going deep.

She looked around quickly at the coral reef for a few seconds. Now she wanted to go back to the surface. Okay, he said she is supposed to float. She stopped moving. She felt herself going upward. Then once she saw the sunlight, she kicked her legs taking her up quickly.

Coming to the surface, she remembered to blow out the water from the snorkel before she took a breath. She blew hard sending the water in the tube blasting out the end of it, then she took a slow breath back in.

Suddenly feeling better, she dove again and swam though the reef. She took several more dives until she felt more confident. Finally, tired, she came to the surface. She saw the boat a hundred yards from her. Raul stood on the boat looking for her. She put her head down and began a power stroke towards the boat. She could feel the swell go over her snorkel, but she always blew the air out before she took a breath.

When she reached the boat, she felt Raul's hand over hers.

He looked down at her, "Are you ready to call it a day?"

"Can you teach me to dive?" She asked handing him her snorkel and mask.

"Maybe, do you want a lift aboard?"

"Yes, please," Harriet said. She felt him take a hold of her hand lifting her up. When she had her feet on the side of the boat, he pushed her back into the water. She felt herself go under the water. Once the momentum downward had stopped, she did a couple of kicks with her fins. She found herself back on surface. Looking up at him, she yelled, "That's the third time you have not acted like a gentleman."

"Look at all that you have learned. It didn't even bother you this time. You should think of it as your first lesson in diving. It's called a belly flop except you were on your back." He was smiling.

"Are you going to be pulling me up?" She asked, pretending to be angry.

"Hand me your fins first."

Harriet worked her right fin off and handed it to him. Then she took off the left fin, handed that to him, looking up, "Is it my turn now?"

Standing on the side of the boat, he reached down took hold of her arms. He started to pull her up when she raised her feet up to the side of the boat. Pushing hard, she had him flying off the boat. Not expecting it, he released her hands. He fell face first into the water.

She quickly came to the surface, took two quick strokes, and pulled herself up over the edge of the boat. She started to swing her left leg in, when she felt a hand take hold of it. She looked down to see Raul coming to the surface.

"Let go!" She yelled, "Or get a foot in the face." She was ready with her right foot, when he let go, allowing her to swing her left leg on into the boat.

As he came in over the back of the boat, she said, "We call that a real belly flop."

"Okay, I may have deserved that," Ramos said. "Are you for heading back?"

"If I can drive the boat," Harriet said.

He began pulling the anchor in, "The boat is all yours after I get this in."

The anchor would not move. He pulled and pulled, but it was stuck on something.

Placing her arms over her head, she fell forward into the water, using the only dive she knew. Kicking her feet, she went down thirty feet. She saw the anchor. The water was very clear, but not as clear without the head gear. She saw the anchor, caught between two pieces of coral. The line seemed loose, she eased it out from behind the coral. She felt it going upward. She hung on going with the ride. When she reached the surface, she took hold of the side of the boat and climbed in.

Raul noticed how fast she climbed into the boat, "Were you afraid I would leave you?"

"The thought did cross my mind," Harriet said, "But I got your anchor loose."

"Yes, most impressive," Raul said. "You earned the privilege to drive the boat."

She moved to the front seat as Raul secured the anchor. She had the boat started when he reached his seat. Pushing the throttle to full forward, the boat took off throwing Raul back into his seat.

When they were out of the cove, she stood, and moved the boat into the swells striking them head on sending the boat high into the air. She felt more confident now that she could swim. The water coming off the windscreen struck her in the face with each swell. She shook it off and looked for another large swell.

Raul watched her. He became a little uncomfortable, when she took the next swell. It threw the boat sideways. "Can we slow the ride down for the passengers please?"

"Yes sir," She said slowing the boat. She saw the sea lions still on their rock as she passed the rock formations. When she could see the ship in the distance, she punched the engine to full throttle again striking the swells more on an angle creating less splash. She headed straight for it. Twenty minutes later they were coming up to the ship.

"Put the bumpers out," Raul yelled from his side.

Harriet brought the boat to idle. She flipped the two bumpers over the side to protect the ship. Easing the throttle back and forth, she learned how to move it slowly towards the ship. Raul did not say a word watching her learn. "Yes, she picks up things very fast," he thought. "He will have to be careful what he teaches her."

After five minutes of experimenting she had it down and eased the boat up to the ship with the security officer becoming very impatient. There were two other boats waiting to come in next. Finally, the boat was against the ship. The lines were thrown.

Harriet quickly slipped on her clothes over her swimsuit, picked up her hat and sunglasses. She allowed the security officer to help her up. She turned back to Gonzales climbing out of the boat, "Thank you for a very pleasant boat ride and the swimming lessons." She turned quickly, went through the security machine, making her way towards the stairs.

Gonzales watched her go. He liked her energy and spirit. He wanted to go after her, but the security officer handed him a message from the Captain. He looked at it, nodded. He was late getting back to the ship. The ship needed to set sail in twenty minutes.

A junior officer jumped into his boat. He took it to the davit at the bow of the boat. He wiped the boat clean of saltwater and took it back up to its original position. The swimming gear was removed, cleaned and stowed.

Gonzales went to his cabin, showered and changed. He put on his uniform and headed for the Bridge.

When he entered Captain Morgan turned, "It was nice you could make it. How was our Miss Cummings?"

"Very charming, sir." Gonzales said. "She learns very quickly." Then changing the subject, he said, "Shall we weigh-anchor?"

"Yes, of course," Captain Morgan said. He pulled the horn telling the crew to weigh-anchor.

The anchor came in. The ship moved out of the harbor. When they were ten miles out, the ship slowed until there was only enough forward motion to hold headway. First Mate Gonzales blew the emergency horn, and said over the loudspeakers, "Report to your lifeboats immediately." He waited a minute, "Report to your lifeboats immediately!"

Harriet was in her stateroom enjoying her bath allowing the jets of hot water from her Jacuzzi to sooth her body. She heard the lifeboat call. Scrambling, she found a towel, and tried to dry herself quickly. She managed to dry a few places, before she attempted to put her clothes on. They stuck to her wet body. She jerked and pulled until she had most of her body covered. She did not bother putting her shoes on, taking them with her. She grabbed her life vest and headed down towards her assigned lifeboat.

It had already been twenty minutes when she arrived at her station. Everyone was in the boat waiting for her. She climbed into the boat with a towel around her shoulders carrying her shoes and life vest. She found her seat as they lowered the boat to the water. She looked up to see Gonzales looking down at her smiling. She would get even.

Over the speaker, Gonzales said, "That was much better, but we need to shave ten more minutes off that time. This ship can be underwater in ten minutes. We need to come in under ten minutes."

Easier now that the crew could recognize the passengers. Strange names were no longer hard to find. They had most of the passengers marked off before they entered the boat. Harriet's lifeboat was the one taking twenty minutes. That was because of her.

Gonzales turned back to the Captain on the bridge, "We are improving. I'll have them down to ten minutes next time."

"You may have to talk to our Miss Cumming before that happens."

"It looked like she was taking a bath," Gonzales said with a smile. "Maybe I should try and make it up to her with a tour of the ship."

"I would wait a few minutes before you ask her. She might want to put some clothes on."

"You might be right."

Ten minutes later a messenger knocked on Harriet's door. Nadine opened it, took the note, and said, "One moment." After closing the door, she looked at the note, "It seems our First Mate wants to take you on a tour of the ship."

"Probably to make up," Harriet said as she worked her hair. She thought a moment, "It will be a good opportunity to learn about the ship. Tell him I will go."

Nadine opened the door, looked up at the messenger, "She will go."

"She is to meet him on the Bridge when she is ready," The messenger said. He was instructed not to push her.

"Thank you," Nadine said, "She will meet him on the Bridge."

The messenger nodded and left.

Nadine closed the door, "He is probably going to instruct you on how to be faster for the lifeboat drills."

"You are probably right. I did cut into his twenty minutes quite severely. Now, what should I wear?"

"If he takes you down into the bowels of the ship, you will want pants, a long sleeve shirt, and low heel shoes, maybe your tennis shoes."

Thirty minutes later Harriet walked onto the Bridge. She saw Gonzales in his uniform standing by the side window looking out. He did not look her direction.

She wandered about the Bridge looking at the various screens. The personnel were a little nervous, but they allowed her to move about. The Captain was in his cabin below getting ready for his evening meal and theater.

She noticed a screen in front of the man steering the ship. He stood behind the wheel keeping his eyes on the screen. "Is that telling us where we are going?" Harriet asked.

"It tells us where we came from and where we are heading now. The ship follows these headings until they are changed. You can see where we left Cabo San Lucas. We are following this line. You can see here where the ship is on this line."

"What about these two levers?" Harriet asked.

"Those are the thrusters that move the ship," The Second Officer said. "They are not all the way forward, but if they were, we would be going thirty knots. Being only halfway forward, we are going about eighteen knots. It gives us a smoother ride, especially this time of day when people are eating."

"Why do you have two thrusters?" Harriet asked.

"We have two engines. They are electric diesel meaning what actually drives the ship are two large electric motors each attached to a shaft that has a screw, that in turn drives the ship. The electricity to drive the motors come from the diesel engines. We also have other engines that produce electricity to light parts of the ship."

"But why two electric motors?" Harriet asked.

"It gives us more speed and flexibility. Say we want to turn the ship quickly. We can reverse the one motor and push the other motor forward with these levers. That will force the ship to turn quickly or maneuver around tight corners when we dock. You can almost steer the ship with the levers if the rudder should go out."

Gonzales noticed he was being ignored standing by the window. He walked over to them talking, "I am sure Miss Cumming is not interested in all of this information."

"I find it extremely interesting," Harriet said.

Gonzales remembered she had a piece of paper stating she could take over the ship in an emergency. "I really wanted you to come up here and enjoy the view." He waved his arm across the panoramic view of the ocean in front of them.

The sun had set, the moon was shining on the smooth ocean surface. Half of the ocean was still in sunlight as the sun set on one side. The other half in moonlight was rapidly taking over. The curvature of the Earth took both lights to one hundred eighty degrees. Within a few minutes the sun was gone taking its ribbons of fire with it.

Harriet did not say a word until the sun was completely gone. Finally, she said, "That was very spectacular, sir. I am glad I did not miss it."

"Then we are off to a good start," Gonzales said, "Let me show you the rest of our wonders."

Before she took Gonzales' arm, she turned back to the second officer at the wheel, "Thank you for showing me how to run the ship."

"It was my pleasure, Miss Cumming," the Second Officer said.

Taking her arm, Gonzales led her off the Bridge. He took her through the decks and into the casino. It was filled with blackjack card tables, slot machines, roulette tables, and a couple of tables where a game of poker was being played. He stopped at one of the empty poker tables, "Do you know how to play poker?"

"I have never played," Harriet said. "Does it require money to play?"

"Yes, that's what makes it exciting," Gonzales said, "It's the possibility you could lose everything."

"Why would someone want to chance losing everything?"

"Because there is a chance you could win everything."

"Is that called gambling addiction?"

"I believe that is the term," Gonzales said.

She was not quite dressed for this room. She felt out of place. This was not what she expected, "I thought we were taking a tour of the ship."

"We are, but a few hands of poker will not take very long," Gonzales said.

"I did not bring any money along for the game," Harriet said.

"We don't use money. The ship will give you credit for any amount of chips you want."

"If I lose, I will have to pay the ship back, correct?"

"That is how it is arranged," Gonzales said. "I think you will enjoy the game." He motioned for one of the stewards.

The young man came over immediately, "Yes sir?"

"Give Miss Cummings two thousand dollars-worth of chips."

"Yes sir," the young man said. He turned disappearing around the poker table. Two minutes later he arrived with a tray of poker chips.

Gonzales took the tray of chips, handed them to Harriet, "Now you can try your luck."

"I told you I have never played before."

"The game is simple enough. It is the betting that becomes exciting."

Christopher Charles

"Are you going to play?"

"Of course, I would not leave you alone on this venture," he said as he pulled out a chair for her. He took the chair beside her, snapped his fingers. One of the stewards placed a tray filled with two thousand dollars' worth of chips in front of him.

The table quickly filled with other men. Especially when they heard she had never played before. A pack of hyenas were coming to take down a young female antelope.

When they were seated, Gonzales asked for a pen and paper. The young steward quickly retrieved them. Then looking around the table, he said, "You will have to be patient with the young lady as she learns the game."

He began writing down the different types of winning hands going from a pair to a straight flush. Then he said, "These are the various types of winning hands with the bottom one being the most valuable. If you get a flush or a straight the highest card wins."

Then he looked around the table, "All of the hands will be won on card value, and not on the amount you can bet, meaning you cannot buy a pot by betting more money than the others at the table.

No one will go light, meaning if your bet is not on the table, you step out of the game, and allow the game to continue unless there are two remaining, then you cannot bet more than the amount the last one has remaining. We are not here to place anyone into a debt position."

"Which of cards have the most value," Harriet asked.

"Let me lay it out for you," Gonzales said, and placed face-up the ace through one. "The ace is the highest card and the one is the lowest. If there are two flushes, the highest three cards win. Do you have any more questions?" He asked softly hoping there would not be.

"No, I think I have enough to get started," Harriet said.

"Good, I will deal the first hand to keep it slow for Miss Cummings," Gonzales said. "This will be 'Seven-Card-Stud'. I will deal the first two cards down and one up. Only you should look at your down cards. You will be dealt seven cards, then pick the best cards out of the seven to make up a five-card hand.

You bet after these cards are dealt or you fold your cards giving up your hand. The highest card starts the betting." He quickly shuffled the cards, handed them to the man next to him, "Would you like to cut the cards?"

The man took off half of the cards, placed them on the table. He took the remaining half, placed it on top, "Cards are cut."

Gonzales quickly took the cards, "Twenty dollars to buy in," He threw in a chip. "Miss Cummings you will need to place a chip in to play."

Harriet looked at him, smiled, and placed a chip into the growing pile in the middle of the table.

"Pot's right," Gonzales began dealing the cards. He dealt two cards facing down and one card facing up.

Harriet had an Ace showing. She did not look at her two down cards. After the cards were dealt, Harriet's ace remained high. She looked at her ace, "It looks like I beat everyone, what do I do now?"

"You place a bet on the table, and the others must follow or fold from this hand."

"Okay, I think I will bet five of these chips," Harriet said. She placed them out on the table. "Did I do that right?"

"That's a hundred dollars."

"Was that too much?"

"No, I just wanted you to know how much you bet." Gonzales said. Then looking around the table, he said, "Is anyone staying?"

Three of the six men who had come to the table placed their hundred dollars on the table.

Gonzales placed his hundred dollars in the pot, "Pot's right." He quickly dealt another card up around the table. Gonzales had two kings, another man at the table had a straight going, and one had a possible flush (all of his cards were in one suit.)

Harriet went down her list looking at each hand on the table. She received another ace giving her two.

"It seems you are still high, Miss Cummings," Gonzales said. "You may place the first bet."

"Then I am going to place ten of these chips," Harriet said. "I can do this, right?"

"Yes, you may bet as much as you want until you run out of money," Gonzales said as he watched her place the chips into the pile in the middle of the table.

Seeing she only had the aces, all of the remaining men, and Gonzales placed a like amount.

"Pots right," Gonzales said. He proceeded to deal another card.

The man with the possible flush received another card to help his cause. The man with the straight felt he was in over his head and closed his cards. Gonzales received another King giving him three Kings showing. Harriet received a queen.

Gonzales looked the table over, "I think I am high with my three kings this time Miss Cummings. I will bet three hundred dollars." Placing a stack of chips in the pot, he looked at Harriet, "You might want to look at the down cards before you bet, Miss Cummings."

"Then I will not bet properly," Harriet said. "Do I bet the same as you this time?"

"You can bet higher, but I cannot tell you how much you should bet."

Harriet looked at the hands on the table and then at her list. She could see the full house developing. More, she also knew the best hand Gonzales could have would be an ace high full-house, or four Kings. She also knew she had one more card up, and another card down to bet on. Finally, she said, "I will bet four hundred dollars." She took the chips from the dwindling stack and placed them in the pot."

The man with the flush looked at Gonzales' hand. Did he have another pair hidden in the down cards? Not wanting to give up on his flush, he placed four hundred into the pot.

Gonzales looked around, "This will be another card up." He dealt the cards giving the man with the flush a King in his suit. Gonzales dealt himself a Queen giving him a possible full house. Harriet received another Queen.

"It appears I am still high," Gonzales said, "I will bet four hundred on my King high full house." He placed the chips on the pile.

Harriet knew Gonzales did not have four Kings, but he could have another queen in the face down card. Not wanting to change the rhythm, she said, "I bet another hundred." She placed five hundred dollars into the pile.

"The pots right, this will be down and dirty." He dealt another down card around. He looked at his down cards and saw the other queen. He had his full house. Harriet did not have hers. The only thing that could beat him was an Ace high full house or four aces. That meant she would have to have two aces in the hole. He noticed Harriet had looked at her down cards. She did not show any unusual emotion. Guessing she did not have it, he said, "I will bet five hundred dollars."

Harriet thought about raising him, but she was low on chips. Then deciding to go all out, she said, "I bet the rest of my chips, eight hundred dollars."

The man with the flush dropped out immediately. Way too rich for him with only a flush.

Gonzales looked at Harriet closely. He could not bet more according to his own rule. He felt sure she did not have anything. He had her Queen, maybe she has another Ace hidden. Then again, she would not know anything about bluffing, but she learns quickly. Finally, he said, "I will call Miss Cummings." He placed five hundred dollars' worth of chips into the pile.

"Is that it?" Harriet asked.

"You have to show us your cards to prove who won the hand," Gonzales said. "What did you have in the hole?"

Harriet flipped the three cards over slowly showing three aces and two queens. She had an Ace high full house. She quickly went down her list, and asked, "Did I win?"

"Yes madam, you won the hand, the money is all yours." Moving his chip tray over, he said, "You can stack the chips in my empty tray." He snapped his fingers, "I will take another tray."

The steward quickly came over with another tray with two thousand dollars' worth of chips.

"You can have some of my chips if we can do this again," Harriet said.

"We will play another hand, but you may keep my chips." Gonzales said. "You seemed to be very lucky."

"Who deals the cards next?" Harriet asked stacking her chips.

"I believe you do," Gonzales said, but you gentlemen will have to be patient, this is her first time dealing the cards."

"Let her deal," the man across from her said, "As long as I get to cut them."

Harriet brought her chips in close and stopped stacking them. She took the cards, tried to move them with her hands until finally, she placed them on the table, and moved them around. Then bringing them all together, she stacked them, and handed them to the man across the table.

He smiled, cut them three times, satisfied, he handed her the cards.

She placed a chip in the middle of table as the others threw out a chip. She began dealing the cards. She dealt Gonzales a King and herself a Queen. Being high, Gonzales placed two hundred dollars in the pot, "That's two hundred for my King."

Harriet followed with two hundred, waited until everyone had placed their bets, then she said, "The pots right." She looked back at Gonzales.

He nodded.

She dealt out the cards, one to each player giving Gonzales another King and herself another queen.

Gonzales was high, "I bet two hundred on my two Kings."

"I have two Queens, I will raise you two hundred dollars," Harriet said placing her chips into the pot.

Two of the men folded thinking this was going to be way out of their league again. The other three stayed wanting to see one more card.

When the pot was right, Harriet dealt another card around giving two of the three men a potential straight and a flush. She gave Gonzales a ten matching the suit one of his Kings. She gave herself an Ace to go with her two Queens.

Gonzales threw some chips into pot, "That's two hundred for my Kings."

Harriet followed, "I will raise it two hundred dollars." She carefully placed her chips into the pot. She still stacked her chips in between the bets. The three other players stayed and placed their chips into the pot. They all had potentially good hands developing.

Gonzales placed his additional two hundred into the pot, "I call."

Harriet saw that everyone had placed his chips into the pot, "The pots right." She glanced towards Gonzales to be sure she said it right. Then she quickly dealt another card around.

The three other players seemed to be happy with what they received. Two of them had a straight going and one of them had a flush in Spades developing. Gonzales' full house developed more when he received another ten.

Harriet dealt herself another Ace giving her two Aces and two Queens showing. She had not looked at her down cards yet.

"I will bet two hundred dollars on my full house," Gonzales said knowing Harriet would raise the bet. He threw his money into the pot.

"I will raise it five hundred dollars," Harriet said, and placed seven hundred dollars in the pot.

The man with the flush remained to see if he had a straight flush on the next card. The other two quickly folded. Gonzales placed another five hundred dollars in the pot, "I call."

"The pot's right," Harriet said. She dealt the next card down. When she finished, she looked at the remaining man with the potential straight flush showing. The man looked at his card and threw it on the table. He was out. He did not get his straight flush. He knew the First Mate had his full house, and Harriet, he didn't know what she had. He folded his cards to watch the two of them battle it out.

Harriet lifted her down cards slightly, a smile developed. She tried to cover it up, but everyone at the table had seen her smile.

"I bet two hundred dollars," Gonzales said. He knew she had her full house, but maybe it wasn't in the Aces.

Harriet looked at Gonzales's cards. Again, she allowed a slight smile to come out. She looked at Gonzales chips, and said, "I will raise you all of your remaining chips." She began stacking her chips to match the number remaining on his tray.

Gonzales cleared his throat, "That will not be necessary, I bow to the better hand. The pot is yours."

Smiling big, she began taking in the chips from the table.

Looking at his depleted chips in his tray, he said, "Miss Cumming I don't think I can afford to play more poker. Why don't we continue our tour of the ship?"

Harriet finished stacking the two trays, but she still had a pile left over. "What should I do with my all my chips?"

"The steward will take care of your chips and give you credit on your tab."

Harriet stood looking out over the table, "It has been my pleasure playing with all of you. Thank you for allowing me to win. It made my first time playing very exciting."

"I have one question, Miss Cummings," The man who had the possible straight flush asked, "Did you have your full house?"

"That is a very good question, sir," Harriet said, "But I don't think a lady should tell all of her secrets." She smiled and allowed Gonzales to lead her away.

As they were leaving the casino, Gonzales said, "The man did ask you a good question."

"Yes, he did," Harriet said. "Was I supposed to tell him?"

"It is best you don't say." Gonzales said. "It is always best to keep them guessing."

"Even you?"

"Especially me!"

Harriet smiled, "Where are we going next?"

Gonzales looked at his watch, "I think the theater play starts in ten minutes. It is supposed to be a comedy."

"I did not dress for the theater," Harriet said. "I thought we would be crawling through the bilges."

"Nothing so drastic, my dear," Gonzales said. "But you will be fine as you are. This is not New York."

"I will feel better if you would let me dress up some before we go."

"How long will it take you?"

"Five minutes at the most."

"Okay, five minutes," he said, stepping into the elevator. They went to the top floor walking to her suite.

She knocked on the door as she opened it, "Nadine, we have company!" She heard someone scrambling as she led Gonzales inside.

Following behind her Gonzales said, "Nothing too fancy, we may still want to explore the bilges"

Nadine came around the corner as Harriet brushed past her. "Nadine, you know Mr. Gonzales. He is only giving me five minutes." She disappeared into the bedroom.

Nadine looked at Mr. Gonzales, "Would you like to be seated?"

He followed her to the sofa, sat back, and placed his right leg over his left leg. He looked around, "This is a very nice suite."

"Yes, it was all that was available," Nadine said. She looked at him hard, "Harriet is not used to dating men. She is quite innocent. I hope you keep this mind while you are showing her around."

"I told the young lady I would be the complete gentleman," Gonzales said. "I intend to keep my word."

"Thank you," Nadine said.

"Has Miss Cummings ever played poker before?"

"She has never played cards as far as I know."

"She has just beaten some very good poker players, one being myself for over four thousand dollars."

"I think someone was being extremely kind, sir," Nadine said.

"No, she pulled off a bluff that was beautiful to watch," Gonzales said. "She has training in something"

"She is a very resourceful young lady," Nadine said.

"Yes, she learns very fast." Gonzales said. "One should not underestimate her."

Harriet entered the room with a long dress showing bare shoulders, "Okay, I am ready. I think that was five minutes."

Gonzales stood walking towards her, "Yes, five minutes exactly."

"We're going to a play, where after that I don't know," Harriet said walking towards the door.

"Have fun," Nadine said. She had an uneasy feeling about Mr. Gonzales. He was hiding something. It was important. Maybe if she had a few more minutes with him.

Harriet led Gonzales out the door and to the elevator. Inside the elevator she did a twirl, "Will this do?"

"I told you it was not necessary for you to change."

The theater was located near the center of the ship. Gonzales led her to the Captain's box. The Captain already there sat with two young ladies dressed in formal attire. Harriet was not wearing a formal. She immediately felt out of place.

Captain Morgan saw her distress, "We don't always dress this formal on this ship, Miss Cummings. The ladies just wanted to dress up. Please be seated. I am sure you will enjoy the play."

"Thank you, sir."

She took the seat behind the ladies, and Gonzales sat behind the Captain.

The Captain turned, "I hear you did not do well in the casino, Mr. Gonzales."

"Lady Luck found a new soul tonight, sir." He replied and smiled.

The play started; the curtain opened.

The ladies in front of her began whispering loudly about Harriet's dress.

Harriet leaned forward, "The drama is on the stage ladies. We would prefer to hear it."

The young ladies looked back at her realizing she could hear them. Turning back to the play, they did not talk again until they left the booth at intermission.

Captain Morgan turned back to Harriet, "That was the first time I have heard the play. Thank you for your help. Now, would you like to play the piano during the intermission?"

"I don't think it would be appropriate, sir," Harriet said. "Besides, I may not be dressed properly."

"Nonsense, you have natural beauty that exceeds any dress," Captain Morgan said. He picked up the phone next to him, "She is here, can you bring out the piano?" He waited a second, "Good, Mr. Gonzales will bring her down." Turning to Harriet, he said, "There, they were expecting you."

Harriet turned to Gonzales, "You set me up, and you were going to have me play in my hiking clothes."

Gonzales stood, "I told him it was not a good idea, but he wanted to hear you play once more."

"And the poker game, that was suddenly cut short?"

"I couldn't afford to lose anymore," He said smiling as he led her down the steps towards the stage. "See, I am showing you places the other tourists never get to see."

"I can see why," Harriet said. She worked her way around the backstage going over and around the props. Finally reaching the stage, she saw the piano. Looking out over the audience only half of the seats were occupied.

Captain Morgan stood up from his seat, spoke into his phone, "Ladies and gentlemen, we are honored to have Miss Harriet Cummings play the piano for us during intermission." He nodded towards Harriet.

She sat down behind the piano thinking what she might play. She ran her fingers across the keys. Notes came up bringing more notes until she was playing music from her soul. It filled the theater taking her with it. It also made her weaker.

Gonzales, standing in the wings, watched her play. He noticed she became more consumed the longer she played.

The music took you to the depths of your soul as the sounds came out. It was simply light, and beautiful for a while, then it would turn to dark and heavy. People coming into the theater stood against the wall. They did not want to disturb the mood she had developed by finding their seats. Then coming out of the depths, she slowly forced the music lighter until she had it dancing on air. Finally, she brought it to a close as she collapsed over the keys.

Gonzales in the wings had tears in his eyes. When he saw her collapse, he rushed to her from the wing. He slowly lifted her from the piano keys.

Slowly she regained enough strength to allow Gonzales to help her stand. She bowed slightly to the audience and stumbled her way off the stage with Gonzales at her side.

The audience gradually realized she would be alright. They left their seats, stood, and began clapping.

They did not stop until Harriet walked back out on the stage and bowed. She felt better, smiled, then embarrassed she had almost fainted earlier, turned, and ran off the stage.

Gonzales took Harriet into his arms and held her a moment.

Embarrassed, she disengaged his arms, "I am alright now. I think that is enough piano playing for a while. I become too emotional. Let's do something calmer, like take a tour of the ship."

"What about the rest of the play?"

"That would mean I would have to endure another emotional scene. I really need something quieter,"

"I have just the thing," Gonzales said releasing her. "I had planned for this later, but we can do it now." He pulled his phone out, and said to somebody on the phone, "Let's do it now." He closed his phone, smiled, "Now you must follow me."

He took her hand, led her from the theater, and up the stairs to the elevator. When they were in the elevator, he released her hand, inserted his key, and pressed the up button. It took them to the top deck revealing a large outside patio opened on three sides. Only the forward section was blocked by the ships' superstructure. This prevented the wind created from the forward motion of the ship from reaching the area.

The large patio looked out over the back of the ship with a rail running around the outside. The sea was calm. The full moon reflected off the water taking in a hundred eighty degrees of the ocean. The deck chairs had been removed. A single table and two chairs had been placed in the middle of the deck with heat lamps on each side. Way to the side of the patio were two men standing by a portable barbecue and a table filled with food and wine.

Gonzales led her onto the deck, "I was saving this for later."

Harriet not listening, walked slowly out to the rail. She looked at the moon-lit water, "I didn't know it could be so beautiful."

Coming up beside her, Gonzales said, "She has her moments, tomorrow this will not be here. A storm is coming in tomorrow night. So, I took advantage of tonight."

"You can actually see the curvature of the Earth here. How could the people who went to sea say it was flat? Look, you can see where the moon light fades as the curvature of the Earth takes place."

"Probably those that said that never went to sea. Actually, men at sea did not venture too far from land thinking they may fall off the edge. Later, those that did venture further found they did not fall off and discovered new lands."

"Would you have been one of those?" Harriet asked.

"If the opportunity was there, I would have taken advantage of it. I have a question for you? Where did you learn to play the piano so emotionally?"

"It was my only escape from a very boring existence. I made up for it with my music."

"Your friend, Nadine, mentioned you did not get out much."

"I was very sheltered as a child. Since both of my parents have passed away, I have had to grow up very fast."

"I am glad you did not leave your music behind."

"What about you, running a ship is not your real occupation. I can feel it from the way you talk."

"What do you think my real occupation is?"

Harriet turned, looked at him a moment, and then said, "You have never been poor. Your skilled in the use of the English language even though it is not your native language suggests you are well educated and from a wealthy family. You were bored when you were younger and sought a more active life. A man in your position would not settle for a seaman's job. The fact it did not bother you to lose four thousand dollars to me earlier confirms this. Now the question is who are you? Why are you here?"

"That's not very flattering," Gonzales said. "I may have had an earlier desire to be a sea Captain and sought this course to achieve this goal."

Harriet smiled, "That's a remote possibility, but I think I will stick with my mystery guy."

"Now let's look at you," Gonzales said. "You are obviously from a wealthy family. Your clothes suggest you are not trying to impress anyone, but the distinction is there. You also were willing to lose four thousand dollars just to learn how to play a game, or to impress me. I am not sure which?"

"I have your four thousand dollars," she said smiling. "You were willing to give it to me, and I was willing to take it."

Gonzales smiled, "You are not so innocent as you would like people to believe."

"Maybe you are a very good teacher," Harriet said.

"Perhaps, but I was not through analyzing you."

"You want to continue this and ruin the evening?" Harriet asked walking back towards the table.

Yes, he wanted to know more, but he was pressing too much. She was the detective he was warned about. He did not have to throw it into her face. She also suspects him to be something more than a First Mate. He thought he had hidden it better. He followed her to the table. He would keep up the farce. Once it was out in the open, their relationship would cease, and he would have to respond in some other way. He was not ready for that to happen tonight.

Seating her, he took his chair across from her. He made sure she would face the moon.

The steward came over to the table with a bottle of champagne and two glasses. "Would you like a glass of champagne, sir?"

Gonzales looked at Harriet.

She nodded, "That would be very nice, thank you."

The steward turned the cork out and poured them each a half glass of champagne. He set the bottle into an ice bucket the chef had just brought over. They both returned to the barbeque.

Gonzales lifted his glass to Harriet as she brought hers up, "This is to a perfect evening."

Harriet smiled, "A perfect evening."

"Good, now tell me what you like to do most in the whole world?"

"I like to learn new things," Harriet said.

"Like what for instance?"

"The game of poker was extremely interesting, but I know I have much to learn. I can see luck has a lot to do with it."

"Are you going to ever play the game again?"

Christopher Charles

"Not right away, I think I was just lucky this time, and you were letting me win. Besides, I will have to learn how to deal the cards first before anyone will take me seriously."

"Believe me, they will take you seriously, but why did you say I let you win? I played very hard to beat you."

"Your hand obviously had me beat, but you folded your hand to let me win."

"Wait a minute here, I folded my hand because you had completed your hand with your down cards."

"Who told you that, I didn't?"

"You smiled when you looked at your cards. That's why everyone folded."

"I smiled because I didn't have anything."

"Then why did you bet my entire rack of chips?"

"I was trying to give you your money back. I only wanted to learn how to play not make you indebted to me. When you folded, and allowed me to win, it made you upset. You took me away from the game. I want to apologize for that. I will give you back your money."

"No, the money is yours won fairly with a very good bluff that fooled everyone at the table including me."

"What is bluffing?"

"When you try to make others believe you have the cards when you do not as in your case."

"All I did was smile."

"That's all you needed to do." Gonzales said, and smiled. "You played your hand like an expert. You fooled all of us."

"Then why did you take me away so quickly?"

"Because no one knew how you played up until then, but once they discover that last hand was a bluff, you would be hard put to bluff another time."

"Then it is best no one discovers I know how to bluff." Harriet said, taking sip of her champagne.

"Yes, you should not have told me, if you ever want to play poker with me again."

"I am not required to show everyone my cards?"

"Not if no one has paid to see them," Gonzales said.

The chef came over, "What will you be having tonight?"

Gonzales looked at Harriet, "Now as your reward for playing the piano for us, what would you like to eat? We have barbecue steak and barbecue steak?"

"Humm, let's see, I think I will have the barbecue steak cooked medium."

The chef nodded, "And you sir?"

"Make mine medium rare."

"Yes sir, medium rare." He turned and left with the order.

The steward came over bringing a salad, "What would you like for a dressing. We have blue cheese and ranch."

"Ranch," Harriet said.

"The same," Gonzales said.

The waiter produced a bottle of ranch dressing from his pocket, poured the contents over the salads and left.

They ate in silence a few minutes. Then Gonzales asked, "Do you like horseback riding?"

"I have never been on a horse," Harriet said. "It sounds like it would be fun."

"I have relatives just outside of Puerto Quetzal, Guatemala and they have horses. We will be there in a couple of days. It's an hour drive from the city, but you will like the drive. It is almost all jungle."

Christopher Charles

"Are they close relatives?"

"My grandparents on my mother's side. I spent a lot of my years there when I was growing up."

"Where do your parents live?"

"In Cartagena, Columbia."

"I assume your family is very politically involved?"

"Why would you say that?"

"Usually when parents are super busy, they have no time for their children. It is fortunate you had your grandparents."

"I didn't say I spent a great deal of time there," Gonzales said.

"Sorry, that is what I picked up."

"It sounds like you didn't see a lot of your parents," Gonzales said.

"My mother died when I was born, but Nadine has been very helpful."

"Is she related to you?"

"In a way she has been like a mother to me."

"And was your father politically inclined?"

"Not politically, but a very busy businessman. I never saw him much."

"Sorry to hear that, but you are right, I did spend a great deal time with my grandparents. It was some of my best years."

They finished eating their salads and the steaks arrived.

Harriet cut into hers and tasted it. She liked the flavor and felt it melt in her mouth. "This is so tender," she said. "Where did you get these?"

"I had them specially brought in for this occasion."

"You mean you had intended to bring someone else up here?"

"I had no idea at the time, but fortunately I brought you up here," he said with a smile.

Other people began coming and setting up their instruments.

Harriet watched them setting up, "You took the band from the main deck?"

"You have played for them long enough, now it is time for them to play for you."

By the time they had consumed their steaks the band had finished setting up. They began playing a soft melody.

Gonzales asked, "Do you feel like desert?"

"I am very full. I don't think I could eat another bite."

"Okay, how about dancing?"

"If we go slow," Harriet said, "I may not be up to a fast beat."

"How about a Waltz," Gonzales asked.

"Maybe," Harriet said.

Gonzales came around the table. He helped her with her chair. Taking her by the hand, he led her to the middle of the patio. He looked at the band, "Let's play a Waltz."

They stopped a moment, had a quick discussion, and then began playing a Waltz.

Gonzales took Harriet's right hand. He placed his right hand on her shoulder blade. Using perfect form, he took her around the patio doing pivots, spin, turns, and even a walk around.

Harriet was not sure of the walk around being on her own walking the six counts away from him. She made it. He immediately took her through several spins. He began weaving frontwards, and backwards as they moved around the deck.

She allowed him to lead going with her emotion. It was beautiful to watch as they became one with the music. Finally, ready to collapse, he led her back to the table.

The steward had cleared the table while they were dancing. He brought over a bottle of port wine and two glasses, "Would you allow me to pour you a glass?"

"Please," said Gonzales.

Harriet only nodded still trying to catch her breathe. She felt her emotions ebbing as she took the glass of wine. Breathing easier, she said, "That was a long way from slow."

"Sorry, but I became caught up in the music," Gonzales said.

"I'm not complaining, in fact it was very pleasurable."

"How about a slow one this time?"

"If you promise slow!" Harriet said standing after taking a quick sip of her wine.

Gonzales took her hand, led her to the dance floor, and said slow to the band.

The band began playing a slow foxtrot as Gonzales took Harriet into his arms. He held her close.

She liked it allowing him to move her around the deck.

The music picked up as Gonzales began taking larger steps. He began spinning and turning her taking in the whole patio area.

Harriet going with him allowing the music to guide her. She could anticipate his every move allowing the music to carry her.

All too soon the music was finished. The band began taking their instruments down.

Harriet looked up at Gonzales, "Are we losing the band?"

"Yes, the play is about over. They need to return to the ballroom."

She went over to the band, "Thank you for coming, you play beautifully."

"It is you who dance so beautifully, Miss Cummings. It was really our pleasure."

"Thank you," Harriet said as she walked back to Gonzales.

"Let me walk you back to your suite," Gonzales said, "Our fantasy world must come to a close."

"You mean my tour is over?"

"Yes, my dear. It has been very pleasurable and exciting, but duty calls. The Captain will be expecting me."

Harriet turned to the chef and steward, "Thank you for a wonderful evening."

"It was our pleasure to watch you dance again," Miss Cummings.

"Thank you," Harriet said, taking Gonzales's arm.

Gonzales led her up a flight of stairs to her suite.

Reaching her room, Harriet knocked at the door letting Nadine know she was there. She turned to say goodnight, when Gonzales took her into his arms. He kissed her on the mouth.

She felt her feet leave the deck slightly as she felt the emotions flowing through her. She kissed him passionately back as the door behind her opened. Then falling back from him, she landed in Nadine's arms.

Smiling, Gonzales said, "Thank you for a very nice evening, I will always remember it." Turning, he walked back to the elevator, pressed the down button. He watched the door close. Now to see to the Captain, he said to himself.

Nadine eased Harriet into the suite. She allowed her to fall on the couch in the middle of the room. Once she was settled, Nadine said, "I want to hear all about it."

Harriet looked at her, "I can't think straight around him. He is the bad guy here, and I've allowed my emotion to control me."

"Did you have fun?"

"Yes," Harriet said quietly, "He taught me how to play poker."

"You can lose a lot of money playing poker, dear."

"I didn't lose, I won over six thousand dollars."

"He must have let you win," Nadine said.

"That's what I said, but he insisted I won the money on my own, something about a bluff."

"What did you discover about him?"

"He's a great dancer," Harriet said.

"Other than he is sexy, and a good dancer, what did you learn?"

"He is involved in something far more complex than being the First Mate. He is from a wealthy family that hold high political offices. He did not mind losing four thousand dollars to me. He invited me to his grandparent's home for horseback riding. I should find out more then."

"One does not invite one to meet his family unless he is very interested in possible marriage."

"He's never said he loves me."

"That passionate kiss said a lot more," Nadine said. "And your response to it says you better go slower."

"He's a good kisser."

"And?"

"Okay he gets my emotions going especially when we're dancing."

"You didn't say anything about dancing."

"Oh, after they had me play the piano for them at the theater, he took me to the outside patio where we had dinner and danced."

"Where did all that come from?"

"The food and wine from the chef and steward, and the band from the ballroom."

"He brought that up for just you?"

"There was no one else, except the moon. Did you know you can see the curvature of the Earth when there is a full moon?"

"Girl, he more than likes you, or he is up to something."

Harriet stared at her a moment, then softly, "I hope he's not up to something."

"You like him a great deal?"

"He makes my heart beat faster. I can hardly breathe sometimes when we are dancing."

"Yes, you are infected. I hope he's clean too."

Ballroom

Captain Morgan took his usual table as he watched the band set up. He wondered why they had not been set up, when his First Mate walked in, and took the chair next to him.

"Where is our Miss Cummings?"

"I took her back to her suite."

"That's too bad, I would have loved to hear her play again."

"I believe she is going into Acapulco tomorrow, sir."

"Then we should allow her to rest." Captain Morgan said. He allowed that to settle, and then said, "You seem to be quite taken by her ignoring the other passengers."

"She is a fascinating woman, but she is also our private detective aboard."

"You found her then?"

"I thought it best I keep her off balance."

"Yes, by all means, but she does not act or look like a private detective. She appears to be way too sensitive."

"That's what Mr. O'Brian told me before we left."

"Then I can see why you have given her so much attention, but we have a problem that needs to be addressed."

"I can handle her, sir. She will not interfere with our plans."

"I still cannot believe she is a detective."

"She only appears to have the lady Nadine with her, and she does not seem to be a threat."

"You say they are going into Acapulco tomorrow?"

"She didn't say, I did not make any other plans with her."

Captain Morgan allowed that to settle. His mind worked rapidly. He had to take her off his ship.

6 Acapulco Mexico

Captain Morgan called a man he knew from his previous trips, Mr. Rivus. He owned a taxicab in Acapulco.

Phone:

"Mr. Rivus, this is Captain Morgan, Yes, you used to be my First Mate, remember?"

Pause:

"I want you to pick up a couple of women from my ship and keep them awhile."

Pause:

"The Norsewegian Cruise Lines, yes, they gave me command of a ship again."

Pause:

"I know after our last incident, I didn't think I would ever command again, but things have a way of turning around. Look, I have a problem. I've got a private detective on board I need to unload for a while."

Pause:

"Yes, but not so drastic, only delay them long enough for them to miss departure tomorrow."

Pause:

"Yes, we will be docking at six tomorrow morning."

Pause:

"When they leave the ship, I will blow the horn, otherwise look for a young lady with an older woman companion." He proceeded to give him their description.

Pause:

"Yes, take both of them, otherwise I will have problems leaving."

Pause:

"I will pay you two thousand dollars when you have them secured. There will be a steward waiting at the dock with your money after I receive the phone call you have them."

Pause:

"Of course, she's rich. She has the best suite on the ship, but I said to let them go after the ship leaves. I don't want a kidnapping."

Pause:

"Then you want another two thousand for your friend."

Pause:

"Okay, but handle them gently," Captain Morgan said.

Pause:

"Yes, leave them their phones. They will need to call someone to pick them up."

Pause:

"Yes, you can take their money. It will slow them up a bit."

Pause:

"Yes, this reminds me of old times. We will have to get together on my next trip down." Captain Morgan said closing his phone, thinking, "That should solve his problem."

At six in the morning the ship pulled up to the dock and tied down. The lower hatch opened, and the gangplank was shoved into place. At eight o'clock people began leaving.

Harriet slept in until eleven. She looked around the room to see Nadine patiently waiting for her sitting at the table with a cup of coffee in her hand. Harriet stumbled out of bed, she headed for the shower. An hour later she was ready. All girl, she wore a dress and high heel shoes. She swallowed a piece of toast and sipped some of Nadine's coffee.

Heading for the door, she yelled, "We're going to miss Acapulco unless we get a move on."

Nadine already dressed sat at the bar, "I have only been waiting for you."

Harriet slipped her pointed high heels shoes on at the door.

"Those are not going to be comfortable walking in," Nadine said.

"They go with my dress," Harriet said, as they headed for the elevator. Reaching the lower main deck, they proceeded out the lower hatch and crossed the gangplank. She could see the city's tall buildings in the distance.

"You want to walk," Nadine asked. "It's only five minutes into the city."

"I have heels on, remember," Harriet said, as they walked through the terminal.

Suddenly the ship's horn blew.

Harriet stopped, looked back, "Did we miss something?" Thinking the ship was calling the passengers back to the boat.

"I don't think so," Nadine said. "It's not time yet."

Coming out of the terminal, they saw a lone taxi waiting by the docks, and walked that direction.

"Then why did the ship's horn blow?" Harriet asked.

"I can't answer that, but let's get that taxi."

The taxi driver opened the door for the ladies allowing Harriet to enter first. As soon as they entered the taxi, Nadine felt something was not right. Tying it in with the ship's horn, she became very nervous. Leaning over closer to Harriet, she whispered in her ear, "Something is not right here."

Harriet looked around. They were heading towards the city. Seeing a hotel on the next block, she said, "Drop us off at that hotel."

The driver continued to drive. He passed the hotel and slowed the car down to pick up a man on the corner waving them down.

Harriet leaned over, whispered to Nadine, "When I yell, open the car door hard and make a run for the hotel back there."

Nadine had her hand on the handle. When the cab pulled up to the curb, the man on the corner opened the door. When he backed some to get in, Harriet yelled, "Now!"

Nadine's door struck the man's behind. It sent him hard into dashboard. She jumped from the taxi and started running for the hotel.

Harriet opened her door. She started to run. She made it to the sidewalk, when the driver reached her. He grabbed her arms and held her close.

"Let me go!" She yelled.

The man held her tighter to keep her from struggling.

Harriet raised her feet up, forcing the driver to hold her weight. Then she came down hard driving both heels into the taxi driver's feet. The sharp tips went through the thin leather driving a half inch into his feet. He screamed as he released her. Free, Harriet, running on her toes, caught up with Nadine as they continued into the hotel.

Inside, they entered the restaurant, and quickly found a table. Breathing hard, they took a seat across from each other.

"What just happened?" Harriet asked. Her hands were shaking.

"We were almost kidnapped," Nadine said breathing hard.

"I think we need some help," Harriet said dialing Rose. When Rose answered, "Where are you?"

"I'm on the deck drinking a cool lemonade."

"Nadine and I were almost kidnapped. We are presently in a hotel restaurant, but I do not think we are out of it yet. Where are the boys?" Her voice was shaky coming out fast.

"They're in town."

"Find them and track them to us."

"Okay, just when I was relaxing on this trip." She went down to her stateroom below deck and opened the compartment with her equipment. She brought up the screen, inserted the tracking number of the GPS inserts in the back of Youngsu's and Harriet's neck that she had placed several months ago. In a moment she had them.

Picking up the phone, she said, "Okay I have both of you. You are not that far apart. They are within a mile of you."

"Then direct them here," Harriet said. "We will wait for them."

Rose called Mc Craw, "There has been an attempted kidnapping of Harriet and Nadine. They are waiting for you at a hotel. I will give you directions."

"We are on our way," Mc Craw said. He motioned to Youngsu, "The girls are being threatened by some bad people. Are you ready for some fun?" He lifted his phone back to his ear, "Which way?"

"A mile west of you," Rose said looking at the screen. "You will need transportation."

Mc Craw and Youngsu left the store and hailed down a taxi.

At the hotel restaurant Harriet turned towards Nadine, "We were set up. We were no accidental pick up for the taxi driver. He was waiting for us."

"Someone on the ship told him we were coming."

"Yes, the ship's horn," Harriet said, "That means someone knows who we really are."

"It has to be the captain or your boyfriend. Who else would be allowed to blow the ship's horn?"

"There is one way to find out," Harriet said.

"You want to capture them?"

"We will see what happens. If they have left, we go back to the ship. If they wish to pursue us, then we will have the boys take them." Harriet's phone rang. Opening it, "Yes."

"We are outside the hotel. There is a taxi waiting for a pick up. Youngsu tried to climb in, but the man driving it, said he already had a passenger. There is also another guy standing not far from the taxi waiting for someone."

"They know we have to get back to the ship. If they keep us here long enough, we will miss it."

"Okay, there is an alley a half a block east of the hotel meaning you are to walk there fast. I will be waiting in the alley. Youngsu will take command of the taxi and pick you up. Give me five minutes to get into position."

"Okay, but we do not want to do anything that will place us in a jail cell. This is not our country."

"I will do my best." Mc Craw said as he nodded towards the door and walked inside.

Youngsu waited a few seconds. Then he followed a couple of people inside. Once inside, he found Mc Craw.

"Okay here is the plan," Mc Craw said. "You're to take over the taxi when the girls come out of the hotel and head for the alley. The girls will enter the alley, where I will be waiting for the other guy following them. Bring the taxi into the alley to pick us up."

Youngsu nodded, walked back out of the hotel, and stood near the taxi like he was waiting for one.

Mc Craw left the hotel a few seconds later. He walked down the street towards the alley. When he reached it, he turned into it quickly, and positioned himself behind a trash container.

Harriet and Nadine came out of the hotel. They walked fast towards the alley.

The man waiting for them quickly followed at a fast pace.

The doorman noticed the girls were nervous coming out of the hotel. He saw the man who had been waiting around the entrance going after them and the girls running into the alley.

The taxi driver's feet were in immense pain. He had not been able to take his shoes off to check the damage. He saw the girls come out of the hotel and his man following them. He had to time this just right. "God, his feet hurt!"

Christopher Charles

He did not see Youngsu come up to his door. Suddenly, he felt his door being jerked open. He could not move his injured feet. He found himself flying towards the cement driveway. He struck his head, and everything went blank.

Youngsu stepped into the taxi, drove it out of the hotel driveway, and into the alley as the doorman watched.

In the alley the man ran hard after the girls as they passed the trash bin. He was almost on them, when he found himself flying in air and ending up against the concrete wall of the hotel building. He felt something hard hit him in the stomach. He could not say a word. Survival was only on his mind. He felt another blow to his stomach as he heard a voice asked, "Who hired you!" He thought about lying, but he was too frightened, and softly said, "Captain Morgan!"

He felt himself slide to the pavement as the taxi pulled into the alley. He felt relieved knowing his partner had arrived. He knew he had at least three broken ribs. The taxi passed him and stopped fifty feet further into the alley.

Mc Craw jumped into the front passenger side. The girls were already inside. Youngsu drove the taxi on through the alley and headed back towards the ship.

Fearing for the girls' lives, the doorman called the police. Being close in the area, they pulled into the hotel drive. The doorman pointed to the man lying on the pavement and pointed towards the alley.

One of the policemen jumped from the patrol car. He ran back to the man recovering. The other one drove the patrol car to the alley. He saw a man moving slowing towards the far end. He drove up to him quickly, stopped the patrol car in front of him, and quickly handcuffed the man. He placed him in the backseat. Coming out of the alley, he drove around to the hotel, picked up his partner, and the other prisoner.

In the taxi going back to the ship, Harriet turned to Mc Craw, "What did you find out?"

"Captain Morgan sent them."

"That means he is on to me," Harriet said. "He may not be aware of you two yet, but after today that may change."

"Then something is really going to happen," Nadine said.

"Yes, I would suspect it to be just before we enter the canal," Harriet said. "Now, Nadine and I will enter the boat first, then you and Youngsu find a place to park the taxi and walk back to the ship. We will pretend nothing has happened and let our Captain Morgan believe they attacked the wrong people."

The taxi pulled up to the dock. Harriet and Nadine disembarked. They walked slowly to the ship. Both of them still shaking. Youngsu drove the taxi back toward the city a few blocks until he found a deserted old building. After parking the taxi, they walked back to the ship.

First Mate Gonzales was on the Bridge when the call came in from the police department an hour later. The ship was ready to sail in ten minutes.

Phone Conversation:

"This is First Mate Gonzales"

"This is Chief Ramon of the Acapulco police department. Do you have any missing passengers?"

Gonzales went to his list of passengers, checked those that went ashore, and returned a second time, "No sir, they are all accounted for."

"We had an incident downtown that involved the kidnapping of two American women. We have two men badly beaten up as a result of it, but we believe they were involved. One of them has a concussion and a hole drilled into each foot. The holes could be from a high heeled shoe. The other one has three broken ribs.

Christopher Charles

We also found the missing taxicab that they were either rescued or abducted in, we are not sure which, parked within a few blocks of your ship. One of the men rescuing the ladies was a large black man, and the other one we are not sure of. We are only concerned, that none of your passengers were missing. We will handle things here otherwise."

"All of our passengers are aboard, sir," Gonzales said. "Thank you for your concern."

"We want to be sure our friends from America are well taken care of. We do not want anything to discourage your ship from docking in our port."

"I will take care of things aboard, sir. You do not need to be concerned. We feel Acapulco is a good port of call."

"Thank you, I am relieved."

The phone went dead. Gonzales placed a call to O'Brian's office.

Phone Conversation:

"Mr. O' Brian, this is First Mate Gonzales."

"Yes, how may I help you?"

"You mentioned a detective was coming aboard when we met, is that correct?"

"Yes, is there a problem?"

"No sir, no problem, but I believe I have located her on the ship, she goes by the name of Harriet Cummings."

"I am not sure what name she is using, but the private detective we hired is named Miss Harriet Brown."

"How many are in her party?"

"Five I believe, two are in the upper deck suite, and three are in two cabins in the crew's quarters. Does that help you?"

"Yes sir, would you know if someone of her team is a large black man?"

"I do not know who makes up her team. I probably have already told you too much."

"Sorry sir, we had an incident, and I am trying to close up loose ends."

"Has something happened to her?"

"There was a kidnapping attempt in Acapulco, and I was wondering if it may have involved our Miss Brown."

"I would appreciate it if this did not become public knowledge."

"The Acapulco police have been very cooperative, sir. I don't believe there is a worry there."

"Good!"

"I will update you if anything more comes of it, sir."

"Thank you."

Gonzales closed his phone. Looked at his passenger list. There were only three passengers located in the crew's quarters, a Mr. Thompson, and a Mr. Lee in one cabin, and Miss Rose Bennet in the one next to it. He would have to give those three special-attention.

Rose had all of the spyware working recording conversations especially those on the Bridge after she received the call of the kidnapped attempted on Harriet and Nadine.

When Harriet returned to her cabin, Rose played the recordings of the phone conversations over Harriet's ear pod, "I think our First Mate is on to us."

"Yes, but it is also obvious he was not in on the kidnapping," Harriet said, "That was Captain Morgan's idea."

"What do we do now?"

"We will have to play this through. Our boss has sold us out. We cannot rely on anything from that direction. In fact, we should assume he is our enemy until this cruise is finished."

"What about the First Mate?"

"I will see where he takes this. I don't believe he would actually hurt me. I need to keep this feeling alive. A confrontation would place us in more danger. We will continue as if nothing has happened and let them figure how they will handle us. This will all be over in a few days."

Bridge

Gonzales allowed the information he received from O' Brian to settle. He had already assumed it was Captain Morgan's idea to have Harriet and her friend Nadine kidnapped. He gave him some information and the man responded radically. He did not dare tell him her real name, and the fact there are five of them aboard. She can take care of herself it appears. He would have to take this into account later.

If she is willing to continue playing the game, he would participate until he was ready. He could not have her taking control over the ship before then. He sent a messenger to invite her and her companion to the Captain's table for dinner. He would see if she was going to continue the charade. He hoped she would.

He needed to talk with the Captain to coordinate future actions. This one obviously backfired from lack of knowledge, but first they needed another lifeboat drill. He picked up the phone and called Chief Myers.

Phone Conversation:

"Chief, Gonzales here, I want you to lower my boat and take it around the ship during the next lifeboat drill. We will be lowering the boats again."

"Yes sir, only the one boat in the water?"

"Correct," he closed his phone, waited a half hour, then had the ship slow to a stop. He pushed the abandon ship drill horn. Everyone expected it. They responded quickly. Harriet made it to her boat. It lowered to just above the water line. She could feel the swells lapping again the boat. She saw the other boats being lowered until all of them were down. She heard the First Mate's boat moving around the ship inspecting the lowered boats.

Twenty minutes later the boats were taken back up to the ship. The passengers and crew disembarked back to their activities.

Over the loudspeaker system, she heard the First Mate say, "Very good everyone. It was ten minutes to the water. There are still a few stragglers that need to move faster. The crew will see what they can do to move this along easier, especially those having difficulty walking up or down the steps. If you are one of these people, please contact a crew member. Thank you again for participating in our lifeboat drill."

When Harriet returned to her suite, she found the invitation waiting for her. She looked at Nadine, "I guess we are continuing this."

"Let's keep it there," Nadine said. "I am anxious to see how our Captain is going to react."

"He will behave and probably be very apologetic," Harriet said. "We will not be leaving the ship unescorted again. That means all of you stay on board. It will be more difficult for him to attack you on the ship without upsetting the passengers."

Christopher Charles

"Are you still going out with our First Mate tomorrow?"

"Yes, we still do not know what they plan to do. The more I am with him, the more likely he will let something slip or tell me too much. If for some reason I am not able to return back to the ship, you are still here, and can function to stop whatever it is."

Ballroom

Captain Morgan was at his table alone. He did not participate in the drill. He was drinking a glass of wine when the First Mate Gonzales arrived. He raised his glass, "Another successful lifeboat exercise."

"Yes sir," Gonzales said taking a chair next to him. "I have invited Miss Cummings, and her companion to dinner, sir."

"I don't think she made it aboard. I fear she will not be coming to dinner."

"She's aboard, and participated in the lifeboat drill, sir. I think your information is wrong."

Captain Morgan looked at him hard, "Have you actually seen her?"

"I also received a call from Chief Ramon of the Acapulco police department. Seems they have two men in custody who tried to kidnap two of our passengers."

"Is that all he asked?"

"He was apologetic, but it should not have happened," Gonzales said looking at him straight on.

"You know who she is," Captain Morgan said. "We have to get her off this boat. She could upset things."

"Yes, but now you have her very suspicious of any moves in that direction. You could have gotten her killed. I will take care of it my own way and no one will get hurt."

"As long as she is off my ship."

The band suddenly began playing a Waltz as Harriet and Nadine arrived.

Harriet had a long dress that twirled when she spun around on her toes keeping her spiked heels off the floor. She smiled at the band leader as she began twirling with the music going across the dance floor. She remembered doing this when she was a child allowing her arms and legs to flow with the music accentuating the third count. There were only the Captain and the First Mate besides the band in the room. The other stragglers were slowly coming in recovering from the lifeboat drill. They stopped at the entrance to watch her.

When the music stopped, she was at the Captain's table. She did a polite bow, "Thank you for inviting us to your table, sir."

Gonzales immediately stood. He pulled a chair out for Harriet as Nadine walked towards the table.

The small crowd coming in clapped as they moved to their tables.

Gonzales helped Nadine with her chair. He looked at the Captain who remained seated.

Harriet noticed the Captain's mood, "I thought we were invited, sir. You will have to excuse me for being presumptive." She started to stand.

Gonzales still standing gently pushed her back to her seat, "It was I who invited you to dinner. The Captain was not aware of the invitation."

Captain Morgan could see he made a bad impression, "You will have to excuse me, I have had a very bad day." He knew his friend was in jail for the attempted kidnapping. He was responsible. They would not go easy on him. To kidnap a tourist would carry a very hard retribution. There would be torture. The man would confess, his name would be mentioned. How long before O'Brian knew? Yes, he made a mistake. He did not think she would escape. This would be his last cruise.

"I have had a very bad day myself, sir," Harriet said. "Two men tried to kidnap Nadine and myself. One of them was a taxi driver waiting for us to come off the ship."

"Maybe it was just the luck of the draw," Captain Morgan said.

"No, he waited for us specifically. Someone on the ship sounded the horn as we stepped off the gang plank."

"That is serious, I will look into the matter, but how did you escape?"

"We were rescued by two undercover policemen, I think. They took the two out very professionally and brought us back to the ship. It makes one not want to go ashore."

"You will like Puerto Quetzal," Gonzales said, "It is very peaceful, it has a very rich history, and I personally will guarantee your safety."

"Then we will not speak of your kidnapping again," Captain Morgan said. "We do not want to scare the passengers."

"Yes, I suppose that is important, if their safety can be guaranteed, but I will make a report to the company when I return to Los Angeles."

"Maybe we can make it up to you," Captain Morgan said. "Then perhaps you will give the company a different report."

"Perhaps," Harriet said as she turned to Gonzales, and smiled.

Captain Morgan was amazed how well she recovered from the kidnapping. Most people would be shaking for days from the stress with some going into deep depression. Yes, she has seen more than she is letting on in her life.

The waiter brought over a bottle of champagne. He began distributing glasses and pouring as the other guests began to arrive taking their places around the table.

The music turned to a slow foxtrot, Captain Morgan stood, "Will you allow me the first dance Miss Cummings to make up for my bad behavior."

"This will be my first dance with you, sir. It will be my pleasure." Harriet said as Gonzales pulled her chair out for her. He saw a look in her eye that said something more.

Captain Morgan took her into his arms, keeping his shoulders straight, taking long steps, he took her around the dance floor. Then he became rougher in his leads, jerking her one way and then another way. It was not smooth. He no longer was dancing in time with the music.

He flung her out, brought her back hard, handling her breast in the process. Harriet had enough! She tried to break free, but the restraint of his strong arms prevented it. She turned into him bringing her back to his chest. He took a firmer grip as she leaped up and brought her left foot down sending her spiked heel into the soft shoe leather penetrating his foot a half-inch, and loudly yelled, "I said let me go!"

The Captain released her. He fell to the floor in wrenching pain.

She looked down at him, and loudly said, "Now you know how I actually escaped being kidnapped." She turned towards Nadine at the table, "I think we have overstayed our welcome. I think it best if we had dinner in our room."

Nadine stood beside the awe-struck Gonzales. She quickly followed Harriet from the room.

Gonzales, recovering quickly, ran to his Captain on the floor. The man was in extreme pain. He called the ship's doctor, turned back to the Captain, "Can you walk?" Then returning to the phone, he said, "No!"

Captain Morgan looked up at him, "You see why I wanted her off my ship!"

"You pushed her, sir. Maybe that was not a good idea." His mind remembering what the Acapulco police had said regarding one of the kidnappers being spiked on both feet.

The doctor came running in with two men carrying a stretcher. They dropped down beside the Captain still in pain and helped him to the stretcher. He was taken to the infirmary where his shoe was cut off and his foot X-rayed. There were no broken bones, but the tissue was badly damaged going in a full half-inch. The doctor dressed the foot the best he could. He gave him a pill for the pain.

"You need to stay off your foot, sir," the doctor said, "And it is going to be painful for a few days."

When the doctor left, Gonzales walked in, "She took out two feet on her assailant. You're lucky she did not go for your other foot too."

"I want her out of here!"

"She will be going, but in due time," Gonzales said. "Maybe it is better you remain in your cabin resting your foot. It needs to be functional in a few days."

"I know what I've got to do. I will be ready."

"Good, now I will see what I can do to repair the damage," Gonzales said, "A note of apology from you would be helpful to show you no longer harbor a grudge."

"You going to take her off my ship, then?"

"I need to gain her confidence to accomplish this. Your note will allow this to happen." He handed the captain a pen, and a piece of notepaper from the physician's desk.

The Captain quickly wrote his note, handed it to Gonzales, "I think this will do it."

Gonzales quickly read it, "Good!" He placed the note in his pocket and left the room. Now that emotions have been expressed, maybe he can calm the situation.

Harriet's Suite

Harriet walked into her suite, "I think we have blown any rudiments of our cover, but the man needed to feel there are consequences to one's actions."

"He was mishandling you," Nadine said. "He deserved anything he received."

Harriet flipped her shoes off, "I guess I will have to wash off his DNA."

"Maybe we should tell the FBI we were almost kidnapped."

"We might need some backup," Harriet said, and picked up her phone. She dialed via satellite the Assistant Director of the FBI James Clark. She waited a few seconds, then she heard his voice, "Harriet Brown, sir. I was just checking to see how successful you were in placing a naval ship down here?"

"They do not see a pending emergency that would call for a naval ship. As I said before it is very expensive to move a vessel into the region."

"How about an attempted kidnapping of an American Citizen?"

"Who was almost kidnapped?"

"Nadine and myself."

"If you remained kidnapped it would have more leverage, but I will give it a try. I don't think you should rely on help from that direction. You say kidnapping, that means something is seriously going on. Are you in any danger at the present time?"

"No, it was Captain Morgan trying to remove us from his ship. He found out I am a private detective from our Mr. O' Brian who hired us. He has really made everything very difficult for us. If something does happen, he should be your first suspect."

"You are alright now?"

"Yes, I just stomped on our Captain's foot with my high heeled shoe. He may take some action, but he had it coming. He tried to manhandle me after his failed attempt to have me kidnapped."

"I probably could get him removed," Clark said.

"No, it is too early. I think he will allow it to slide, realizing he had it coming, and he does not want to disturb what is coming later."

"What do you want me to do?"

"Try and convince the navy to place a ship near here."

"Other than that?"

"I will call you as things develop," Harriet said. "I am just thankful you are there."

"Call me anytime."

"Thank you," she said as she closed the phone. She dialed a second number. This one was to the Chief of Detectives, Paul Ramos of the Los Angeles Police Department. When she heard his voice, she said, "Hi, this is Harriet.

"We should be in Panama in two days."

"How many men?"

"Four counting myself."

"Thank you," Harriet said. "I am fortunate to have a good friend."

"One that is taking a vacation in Panama City," Ramos said. "Anything happening yet?"

"I was almost kidnapped, but it was a local thing with the Captain after he discovered I was a private detective."

"That's rather drastic for that."

"It means something is going to happen. I am glad you are going to be nearby." Harriet heard a knock at the door. "I need to go," Harriet whispered, "Someone is here." She closed her phone and walked barefoot to the door. When she opened it, she looked up to see Raul Gonzales. She stepped back.

"May I come in," Raul asked.

"Are you here to arrest me for stepping on the Captain's foot? He was jerking me around on the dance floor. It caused me to have difficulty finding my footing."

"That's why you stomped your heel into his foot?" Raul asked smiling.

Harriet put her two hands out, "Guilty, put the cuffs on, but I want a public hearing."

"Nothing so drastic," Raul said. "I really came to apologize for his misbehavior. He would have come himself, but his doctor said he needs to stay off his foot for a while."

"Did you bring a note to that effect?"

"You are a tough taskmaster," Raul said, and reached into his pocket to withdraw the note from Captain Morgan. He handed it to her, "I pray you will accept his apology."

Harriet read the note:

> "I overreacted when I was informed you were
> on my ship to spy and take command at your

convenience. Now that I realize you are here to protect my ship in light of the recent murders, I would like to apologize for my actions. The kidnapping was a farce. The man was my former First Mate. He would not have harmed you in anyway. He was instructed to only delay you and then allow you to go free after the ship sailed. I hold no grudges for my injured foot, I believe I deserved it for my deplorable behavior. Please allow my Frist Mate to make my apologies."

———————

After Harriet read the letter, she looked up at Raul, "The apology is accepted, you may come in."

Nadine stood as Gonzales entered the suite, "I was about to order dinner."

"No need, I have taken the liberty to have it brought up here. I pray you like lobster and steak."

"But…"

"Consider it a peace offering." Gonzales said.

Right on cue, a knock on the door.

Gonzales opened the door to reveal the steward standing with a cart of food in front of him.

Gonzales waved him in, pointed towards the table, "Please set everything up on the table."

Harriet and Nadine watched as the steward prepared the table. When he finished, he gathered up his things, and rolled his cart from the room.

Gonzales pulled the chairs out for Harriet and Nadine, "It may not be as elegant as the ballroom, but we will have our privacy here."

"Thank you," Harriet said, taking her chair. "Are you the steward now?"

"I am many things, my dear," Gonzales said working the cork on the champagne bottle, "Would you like a glass?"

"How could we refuse someone working so hard," Harriet said.

Suddenly the cork came loose, and the champagne flowed from the bottle. Quickly taking a glass, he had it full. Still coming, he filled the second glass. The third glass reached a third full before the foam stopped.

"Now that's what I call perfect timing," Harriet said, "And I will take the third glass."

Gonzales handed Nadine a full glass, held his glass high, "This is for the acceptance of the apology and the enjoyment during the rest of the cruise." He touched the ladies' glasses and took a big sip from his glass.

The steaks were on a hot pad still being cooked. Gonzales took the lid off, "If you like medium steak, you need to take your steak now."

"Then I will have mine now," Harriet said as she handed him her plate.

He flopped a large steak on her plate and looked at Nadine.

"I will take the last one. I like mine more on the done side."

"Then I will take mine now," Gonzales said as he placed the second steak on his plate.

He waited a few second. Lifted the last one off the heat plate. "I think this one is more on the done side."

"Thank you," Nadine said taking the plate.

He passed the vegetables around, "Does anyone want their lobster now?"

"No, I think I will eat my steak first," Harriet said. "It may just be enough for me."

"Harriet tells me you have grandparents in Puerto Quetzal."

"Yes, they have a five-thousand-acre plantation, but most of it is jungle now."

"Do you have cattle on your plantation?" Nadine asked.

"Some, but the coffee bean was the main crop, but now it is probably all jungle. It takes a great deal of effort to keep the jungle out. Now they enjoy the land, but they still keep a few horses to get around on the plantation."

"Where do your parents live?"

"My mother and father moved to Cartagena, Columbia, and left me with my grandparents until I was twelve. They brought me to Cartagena to see to my education. They expected great things from me, but I have been reluctant to move that direction. I wanted to see what else was in the world before I settle on a profession."

"What do they want you to become?" Harriet asked.

"They want me to go into politics, but there is a lot I have to do before I can consider that."

"Do the drug cartels more or less run the country?" Harriet asked. "I mean it is your major cash product."

"As I said, we have a lot of cleaning up to do, but yes, we have a problem with the drug cartel," Gonzales said, "But it's not only evident in my country. I think I heard of a recent drug bust in the Los Angeles that amounted to over eight hundred million in cash and product."

Harriet immediately picked up the term 'product' instead of cocaine, "Yes, we have our own drug problem, and I feel we probably support the drug cartels in Columbia."

"Then you see there is no simple answer."

"We made a start in Los Angeles by taking eight hundred million dollars plus cocaine off the market."

"You did not pay for the drug," Gonzales said. "You just took the eight hundred million dollars-worth of product and left the cartels unable to pay their people depending on it to live."

"That was the idea," Harriet said. "It was forcing the people producing cocaine to find a new occupation."

"There is no other occupation. It has caused many to suffer. The cartel bosses are still okay. They have enough money to live very comfortably anywhere in the world. It is the people who are suffering. It is like taking eight hundred million dollars out of the marketplace and expect it to survive."

Harriet did not dare say she was responsible for taking the eight hundred million dollars-worth of cocaine off the market. He already knew her real name, but he may not have made the connection. Finally, she said, "I don't agree with you. It is like saying it is good to continue to make atomic weapons because to stop would place millions of people out of work."

"I think you said it correctly. You cannot just shut a bad thing down until you can replace it with something else."

"You can, because no one is going to shut it down otherwise. No one will be interested in shutting it down as long as they are making money. It is when they don't make a profit and are forced to find another one does it happen."

"The drug cartel is not going to let this lie without a fight. They see this as your government attacking them by stealing their product. They could have taken the product and left them the money, or at the very least, sent the product back to them. There will be payback, that I can assure you." Gonzales stopped to clear his throat realizing he had said too much. He would have to control his emotions better.

Seeing no more was going to said, Harriet worked on her steak, "I feel sorry for the people who must suffer, but I would think most of the people producing the cocaine know of the damage it does to people. They probably take home some of the cocaine themselves. So, when efforts are being applied to stop the cocaine from reaching the innocents, it is part of the risk they accept."

"You are forgetting who runs the operation," Gonzales said. "They have to keep face with their workers who have families. If they lose the product and cannot pay their employees, they will lose their employees or worse, the employees may seek other ways to get paid. This placed a great deal of pressure on the cartel bosses. It is the bosses that keep the people in check. It works as long as the people are being fed and taken care of. When this stops, they will rebel and seek another leader. It is more this than the money. You do not stay with a failed business."

"You said the cartel bosses will probably do something to retaliate for the loss of their cocaine. I assume do something to recapture their money." Harriet said trying to dig for more information.

"I don't think that is possible. I was only giving you a possibility." He turned to lobster beside him, and asked, "Is anyone ready?"

"I will take a little piece," Harriet said. "The steak filled me up, but someone went to a lot of trouble to prepare it."

Gonzales took another plate, cut off a small portion of the lobster tail, and handed the plate to her, "It is quite good, I think you will like it."

Gonzales changed the topic to something lighter. He knew he was giving out too much information. He also knew the cartel bosses would love to get their hands on the one who was responsible for them losing their product. He would have to make sure she was safe.

He opened a bottle of port wine, poured each of them a half glass, sitting back in his chair, he said, "I must thank you for the lively discussion. It is not often one gets to discuss politics with young ladies."

"I think you would make a very good politician," Harriet said. "You seem to have a passion for it."

"Thank you, but my responsibility is running this ship, which reminds me, I have a watch to relieve." Standing, he continued, "If you young ladies will excuse me." He started for the door, turned, "Thank you for a lovely evening. Don't worry about anything, I will send the steward back."

Harriet stood, walked quickly to the door, "Let me walk out with you."

Outside the partially closed door, "Harriet asked, "What time tomorrow to you want me ready?"

"How about nine o' clock at the lower hatch if that is not too early."

"Nine will be fine. You know I was never angry at you."

"You made that clear when you spiked the Captain," Gonzales said with a smile.

She gave him a hug, "You remember that."

He kissed her lightly on the lips, "Yes, I will remember." He turned and headed for the elevator.

Harriet returned inside and closed the door. She started to settle down when she heard a knock on the door. Opening it, she allowed the steward to pick up the dinner and dishes. They had left most of the lobster and salad. Someone was going to eat good in the kitchen. In minutes the steward had the cart moving out of the suite.

Finally, Harriet turned to Nadine, "What did you pick up?"

"I think this is becoming way too dangerous for you. If the cartel bosses ever found you, your life would be measured in seconds."

"You suggesting we pull out of this?"

"I think 'You' should pull out of this," Nadine said emphasizing the word 'You'. "If we are boarded, which is a distinct possibility, you would be their most valuable prize. You are walking right into a den of wolves."

"I am not going to quit because of some cartel boss. One of them ordered the killing of my father."

"I believe that is what this is all about," Nadine said. "There is going to be payback, and I feel this ship is involved somehow. That means you are very vulnerable."

"Okay, what did you pick up on Gonzales?"

"He seems to believe what he says, but he is hiding something much more serious. You are right, being First Mate is not his goal in life. He is here for some other reasons. When we find out, it may be too late for you."

"Stop it! Stop it now, you are trying to frighten me," Harriet said. "I plan on seeing this through. I am not going to desert you in the middle of this thing. Only Gonzales knows my real name. I don't think he will let anyone kill me."

Gonzales walked onto the Bridge. He checked their heading. They were on course. The radar did not show any other vessels within twenty miles of the ship. He felt secure, "Wake me before we enter port."

The officer on Bridge nodded, "Have a good night's sleep, sir. If anything comes up, I will have someone wake you."

Gonzales nodded and left the Bridge. Tired, the food, wine, and champagne were taking their toll.

7 Puerto Quetzal, Guatemala

Gonzales woke up on his own. He was on the bridge at 5:30 to take the ship into the harbor. He watched the Second Officer anchor the boat two thousand meters offshore. He used the thrusters to lay out the anchor. He was impressed.

The lower hatch opened, two tenders were lowered and brought up to the hatch. He smiled as he made his way to his quarters. He still had time for a quick nap.

Harriet, going over the conversation of the night before was more certain than ever something was going to happen on this cruise. She had to look at the facts. The Captain wanted her off the ship. Raul has had a lifeboat drill every day at sea. He also said the cartels bosses would seek revenge for the loss of the product and money. Now she knew who, and approximately when, but she did not know what or how. Maybe she could get Raul to reveal more.

Then how much was Raul involved? He defended them yesterday. Did his family have connections with cartel bosses? She would have Rose try another background check. She should have done it long ago. She needs to think better. Raul has her confused on many fronts. He seems like he is a decent person, but if he is involved with the drug cartel, then he is as guilty as they are.

Her alarm went off. Again, a night without much sleep. She rolled out of bed and worked her way to the shower. Nadine was still sleeping. She punched in the coffee maker on her way.

Nadine was awake when she stepped out of the shower. She quickly slipped on a pair of Levi's and a light blouse over her undergarments. It was going to be hot.

Nadine had breakfast going.

Harriet took a cup of coffee and a piece of toast.

"You will need more than that today."

"I think we will be eating with his grandparents."

"That won't happen until later today."

Taking another piece of toast, she said, "There, now I am full."

"You should still think about getting off this ship and going home."

"Let's see how today turns out," Harriet said slipping her ID and passport into her fanny pack. She would not be taking her purse. Heading for the door, she said, "I will see you tonight."

On the lower deck next to the open hatch, First Mate Gonzales watched the tenders loading the passengers. He saw his red private boat waiting behind it.

All smiles, Harriet came bouncing down the steps in a very good mood as she took Raul's hand.

"Our boat is next," Raul said as he looked out the hatch.

The tender pulled away. Raul Gonzales' red boat pulled up to the ramp.

The Chief climbed out taking the line with him. He helped Harriet aboard the boat. He threw Harriet the line as she took the driver's chair, "Where to, Captain?"

"Away from the ship to start with," Raul said. "Then we will follow the tender in and dock somewhere beside it."

"Aye, aye, Captain," She swung the boat out wide to avoid the ship. Then she slowed the boat to match the speed of the tender.

When they reached the dock, Raul pointed to a spot further down the dock, "Pull into that slot."

Harriet expertly worked the engines until the boat was in the slot. Taking the line, she placed her foot on the gunwale, and leaped to the dock. She took the line, wrapped it around one of the cleats, and held it until Raul stepped on the dock.

Taking the line, he said, "You make a figure eight with the top portion of the figure eight flipped over. This locks the line to the cleat." He removed the line and showed her again.

She took the line from him and proceeded to make the figure eight with it. "It's not all that hard when you know how to do it." Then looking up she asked, "Where to now Captain?"

"We need a car," Raul said, "That means we rent one." He found a car rental. Ten minutes later they were on the road driving a Mercedes 230 SLK. It was an old model, but the roof folded down into the trunk. It still had some spunk in her, as he drove it into downtown Puerto Quetzal.

He pointed out the central plaza, museums, and churches. "This is a very old city. It goes back to the Spanish Conquistadores. It even has a five-star hotel, the Casa Santa Domingo. If we have time, we will stop by for a drink on our way back. It is beautiful inside."

They drove on through the city, entered the dirt roads going back into the jungle. Harriet began memorizing the turns and landmarks thinking she might have to come back alone.

They rode in silence a while until Raul asked, "Are you going to tell me your real name?"

She knew he already knew, but she did not want him to know about their spyware, "How do you know Harriet Cummings is not my real name?"

"Mr. O'Brian informed me you were on the ship."

"What else did he tell you?"

"That you were a detective."

"Hmm, it seems our Mr. O' Brian talks too much."

"I've known for some time you were a detective."

"Is that why I have received all of this attention?"

"At first, but now it is more personal."

"Then you are not going you throw me off the ship"

"Mr. O' Brian would lose his insurance coverage. You are the token protector of the ship."

"It does not appear I am all that good at it."

"I don't know, you taught the Captain a lesson he will not forget soon, Miss Harriet Brown."

"I kind of liked Cummings."

Raul smiled, "Harriet Brown fits you very well."

"It might be best to keep my cover a while longer."

"That is probably a good idea."

A half hour later they pulled into a long narrow dirt road that led to a large house. On both sides of the road were rows of bushes. Three laborers were in the fields working between the rows of bushes that ranged in size from two-foot to six-foot. The rows of the larger ones had white flowers on them. These were also sprouting reddish orange seeds.

Noticing Harriet looking at the fields, Raul said, "Coffee bean bushes at different levels of growth. They don't sell beans anymore. There was not enough profit in it. Now, they sell the coffee bushes to the other coffee growers. The market is guaranteed, and they don't have all the stress."

"How many acres in coffee bushes?"

"Functional, maybe a hundred acres, nonfunctional five thousand acres," Raul said as they pulled up beside the old styled adobe house. Further from the house was a barn with a large fenced in field coming off from it. Four horses were grazing in the field.

An older lady, Mrs. Hanna Gonzales, came out of the house dressed in an older Spanish dress and high heels. When she saw the car pull up, she smiled, and waited on the porch.

Harriet noticed the long dress. She mmediately felt out of place dressed in her Levi's. She put on a good front and waited for Raul.

He gave his grandmother a big hug first, then he came around the car, opened her door, "And now I want you to meet a very special person, Miss Harriet Cummings."

Harriet worked her way out of the car, walked beside Raul as she approached Mrs. Gonzales. Taking the hand offered, she said, "It is my pleasure to finally meet you. Raul has told me how much he enjoyed staying here when he was a child."

"The pleasure is all mine," Hanna said. "We have not seen him for some time. Thank you for bringing him to us. You must be very special." She gave Harriet a hug, "You are always welcome to our house."

An older big man walked out of the barn. When he saw Raul, he smiled, and shouted, "You finally decided to come and see us." When he reached Raul, he grabbed him, and gave him a big man size hug. "We missed you son." He quickly wiped a tear developing, turned to Harriet, "And who is this beauty you have brought us?"

"This is Miss Harriet Cummings from my ship. We're in port today. I thought I would take her out for a horseback ride in the country."

Harriet shook his hand as he lifted it to his lips. He kissed the back of it, "She is welcome here anytime. My name is Raul also."

"Please come in for something to drink," Hanna said. "It is very hot today."

They all followed Hanna inside. The house was cool. The walls were made out of straw and mud that has been covered with a vinyl substance making it very cool inside. The floor was covered with expensive tile, and the kitchen looked modern. She led them to a table in the living room with four chairs.

Raul pulled a chair out for Harriet and Hanna went to the kitchen.

"What brings you to Puerto Quetzal?" Senor Raul asked.

"I volunteered for a First Mate position on the Norsewegian Cruise line going through the Panama Canal. They were making a port-of-call here, so I took advantage of it."

"And the young lady?"

"I promised her a horseback ride, so I brought her here," Raul said.

Hanna brought in four glasses of lemonade, "I want to hear all of it. You have been away so long." She looked at Harriet, "What do you do?"

"She is a Detective," Raul said quickly. "The ship lost its Captain and First Mate under mysterious circumstances. The company hired on a token detective per the insurance company's requests."

"You do not look like a detective, my dear," Hanna said. "You should be playing the piano or getting married."

"I play the piano," Harriet said. "But it is very hard to make a living playing the piano."

"You should hear her play," Raul said trying to take the questioning another direction.

"We have a piano," Hanna said. "I play at it when I have the time. It relaxes me."

"Would you like me to play for you?"

Hanna smiled, "If it would not be imposing. You are a guest in our house."

"It would be my honor."

"The piano is in the other room," Hanna said standing. They all followed her into the living room.

Harriet saw the grand piano. It was a beautiful Steinway. It did not match the house. She sat down, looked the keys over, "You play this?"

"Not very well," Hanna said. "It is very hard to find someone to give me lessons."

Harriet ran her fingers over the keys. She listened to the notes. They all seemed to be in tune, "You have taken very good care of your Steinway."

"Go ahead, and play something, Harriet," Senor Raul said.

"What would you like to hear?" Harriet asked. "Something dramatic, light, opera…"

"Give us a mixture like you did on the ship," Raul said.

Christopher Charles

Harriet began working her fingers on the piano keys. She started off light using the higher keys, then took it deeper. She touched the emotions deep inside allowing the music to carry it. She thought of her father's death. The music accentuated it. Then she took it lighter. She went into the near-death experiences she had been through allowing the music to carry it. Then she thought of Raul allowing her emotions to surface carrying those feelings higher and higher until she collapsed over the piano keys.

The audience stunned, had tears in their eyes. No one could move for a moment to help her. Finally, Raul went to her. He helped her off the keys. She allowed him to lift her away to a chair.

She looked up at him as he seated her, "Maybe I should not play for a while."

"It was beautiful, but we will not impose on you again."

"I am okay, really, I should have played something lighter." She stood slowly, walked back to the piano. She began playing something lighter thinking about her snorkel adventure. Her mind visualizing the fish swimming in front of her. She played for another fifteen minutes. The scene finished, she turned around, "Thank you for allowing me to play on your beautiful piano. I did not mean to upset you earlier."

"That was the most beautiful music I have ever heard," Senor Raul said. "You have nothing to be sorry for. I would not have missed a second of it."

Hanna gave her a hug, "You have shown me what this piano can do. I have never heard such beautiful music."

Harriet looked up at Raul, he beamed.

"Thank you," Harriet said. "I did not mean to get all emotional. I play what I feel."

"You haven't eaten yet," Hanna said. "Let me fix you something" She ran off to the kitchen wiping a tear.

Walking towards the dining room, Raul asked, "How are the horses doing?"

"They need riding," Senor Raul said. "I can only ride one at a time. They are getting a little frisky."

"I thought we would exercise them a bit for you."

"Be my guest but remember they haven't been ridden for a while especially that black stallion. I only keep him around for you. He's too wild for me."

Raul helped Harriet with her chair as they all took a chair around the table.

Hanna walked in with a plate full of chicken tamales, "I made these yesterday, but they are still good."

Senor Raul brought out a bottle of wine, "I have been saving this for the right time." He worked the cork out, smelled it, "This one came from my own vineyard."

"I didn't know you were into wine making," Raul said.

"I just started three years ago," Senor Raul said. "This is one of my first bottles. I am very proud of it. Let me pour you a glass." He began filling four glasses half full handing them around the table.

When everyone had a glass, He raised his, "Here's to Harriet Cummings who brought our grandson to us today, and who allowed us to hear very beautiful music."

Harriet blushed as they all clicked their glasses. The tamales were served.

Harriet bit into her tamale. Her tongue was suddenly on fire. She took a quick drink of her wine to cool it. It didn't help. Her eyes watered, but she held it down. She took another bite and swallowed the other half of her wine. She still had half of a tamale to go, but no more wine. She looked up at Senor Raul, "I love the taste of your wine, sir."

Noticing her glass was empty, he smiled, "Please allow me to fill your glass again." He was proud she enjoyed his creation.

She managed the rest of the tamale and drank the wine slowly as she recovered.

"Now tell us what you have been doing," Hanna said. "We have not heard from you in a long time."

"Presently I am just the First Mate on a cruise ship. The next step up is Captain."

"Are you going to pursue this?"

"We will see how this trip works out."

Standing, Senor Raul said, "I think we should be giving our guest what she came for, horses," He could tell his grandson was becoming uneasy with the questions in front of his girlfriend.

Standing, Raul said, "Yes, we only have a few hours." He helped Harriet with her chair.

Harriet blushed, "You don't have to stop asking him questions on account of me. I have never been on a horse."

"Then it is time you were learning," Senor Raul said leading her to the door.

Harriet turned, "Thank you for the tamales." She was a little unstable from the two glasses of wine.

"You are very sweet dear," Hanna said. She knew they were too hot for her, but once the hot sauce was in the tamales, you could not take it back out. This was her rationale, but she also wanted to see how she would react. She smiled to herself when Harriet took her second glass of wine. It pleased her husband.

Senor Raul led them to the corral outside the barn. He opened the gate to the open pasture, banged the feed bin, the four horses came running expecting the bin to be full of oats. As they came running in, he asked, "Which one do you want to ride?"

Raul took the big black stallion's head into his arms, rubbed its nose, "I think he still remembers me."

"How about, Lizzy, the small mare for Harriet," Senor Raul said slipping the halter over her nose. "She is gentle when she is away from the others. She will go well with her weight."

"I'll take Thunder here," Raul said. "It will be like old times." He reached for the halter and slipped it on.

The horses were led into the corral and tied to the fence post. Senor Raul saddled Lizzy, and Raul saddled his big horse, Thunder.

Harriet watched the western saddles being placed on the horses. She still felt very relaxed from the wine. She smiled when Senor Raul called her to the climb up on Lizzy.

When she lifted her left foot up, he placed it into the stirrup, "Take hold of the horn and pull yourself up on the saddle. Now swing your right leg up over the horse."

Harriet pulled, lifted herself up on the horse. She could not find the other dangling stirrup. It was too low for her. Senor Raul adjusted it for her. She put her foot in, stood a moment, the left one was off. He adjusted it, handed her the reins as she looked around. She was high off the ground. She stood again and sat down.

"Okay, let's try this again," Harriet said. Taking hold of the saddle horn, she swung her leg back over the horse, and dropped quickly to the ground. She almost fell, but she managed to catch herself.

Without assistance, she kept the reins in her hand, stepped up on the left stirrup, took hold of the horn, and pulled herself up on the horse. Swinging her right foot over, she was in the right stirrup.

Christopher Charles

Feeling more confident, she did it four more times until she could pull and leap at the same time. Then looking back at Senor Raul, she said, "I think I have it. What's next?"

To move the horse, you push your heels into her ribs, and give some slack on the reins. To turn her right lay the reins on her right shoulder and pull towards the right. To turn left lay the rains on her left shoulder and pull left. To back up pull the reins evenly towards you."

"Okay," Harriet said. She was already aimed out towards the middle of the corral. Kicking her heels into the mare's ribs, the horse suddenly shot forward catching Harriet off guard. She hung onto the saddle horn until the horse reached the other fence. Unable to go any further, it reared up, sending Harriet off the back of it. She landed on her bottom. The soft muck enclosing her Levi's.

She quickly stood brushing herself off the best she could, "You left out an important detail. How do you stop it?"

"You pull back on the reins," Raul said.

"That's how you make it go backward," Harriet said.

"If you are stopped, you pull back on the reins, and the horse will go backwards. Once you are moving, you stop it by reining up or pulling the reins back."

Harriet took the reins into her left hand and swung back up on the horse. She leaned the reins to the left and kicked the horse with her heels. It moved to the left. She turned right by laying and pulling the reins to the right. Then she kicked it harder, going across the corral, bouncing on top of the saddle. Pulling the reins back, the horse stopped.

She started the horse up again, turning it right then left, but all the time bouncing hard on the saddle. Finally, she stopped, "I am still missing something."

Raul was up on his horse riding around the corral. She noticed he did not bounce. He brought his horse up next to hers, "You have to go with the horse. Allow your body to become one with it. Go with her movements."

Harriet started the horse up again, rode around the corral, but the stride of the horse was still too sharp for her to coordinate with. She did manage to turn and stop it. Then she began picking up speed. Sitting straight, she felt herself falling to the right side as her bottom struck the saddle. She lowered her head, kicked herself back into the saddle. Soon she found the rhythm of the horse, and had it moving fast around the corral. She still bumped, but not as hard.

"You better let her out," Senor Raul yelled, "Or she will be going over the fence."

"Open the gate!" Raul yelled.

Senor Raul pulled the gate open. Raul took his large black horse out.

Harriet followed on the smaller horse. Suddenly free, the little horse took off after the larger one with Harriet bouncing up and down on the saddle. She fell one way, and then the other way, trying to stay on top, when she came down from a bounce.

Hanna stood on the porch watching them leave. She smiled, and yelled to Senor Raul in Spanish, "She's going to be very sore by the time she returns."

"Maybe not, she learns very fast."

Harriet noticed how Raul moved with the horse. He was not bouncing up and down. He was also going faster leaving her behind. She kicked her heels into her horse. It did not like to run, but it did after she kicked it a second time with her heels. The rhythm of the horse changed. It no longer trotted and bounced her up and down.

Smoothing out her rhythm, she found she could move with it. No longer bouncing, she learned to use her legs and knees to hold herself on. Balancing herself, it was much like playing the piano. She allowed her body to follow her emotions, or in this case the horse's rhythm. She kicked her horse to go faster, and easily caught up with Raul's stallion. She came up beside him.

He was amazed how fast she learned to ride. She did not seem to show any fear. He pulled his black stallion back to ride at the slower pace beside the little horse.

They rode across a large open area in the jungle where the trees had been removed. It was probably the five thousand acres they were not working, Harriet thought. She noticed some of the overgrowth had the same white flowers and seeds as the other field. The coffee plants were trying to grow back.

The black stallion, suddenly free of the enclosure, didn't want to slow down. He took the bit into his mouth and took off running across the field. He headed straight into the jungle following a dirt path, leaving Harriet far behind.

Raul knew the horse needed to work off its energy and decided to slow him up some. He turned him up a steep path that led to the top of a plateau.

Harriet on her smaller horse followed. She could not keep up with the stallion, but she saw which trail the stallion took up the hill.

When the black stallion reached the top, the land flattened. Still holding the bit in his mouth, it picked up speed, and headed for the edge of the cliff six hundred feet above the valley and ranch below.

Raul jerked the bit free. He pulled the reins back hard, and to the left yanking the horse's head around.

The stallion reared up and came down hard taking Raul with him. When its front feet touched the ground, Raul's body was already loose from the saddle. The stallion immediately bucked bringing his hind legs up, it sent Raul to the ground.

Harriet came up on the plateau as Raul came off the saddle. She watched him strike the ground. He kept sliding right on over the cliff.

Raul felt himself going over. He looked quickly for something to grab on to. His right hand found a bush fifteen feet down that stopped his descent. He kicked around quickly trying to find something to catch his foot. His left foot found a small rock sticking out. Resting it there, he tried to find another one for his right foot, but it forced him further from the face of the cliff. It started his bush to move. He stopped and held on to the bush with both hands.

Harriet brought her horse to a stop beside the stallion. She slid off her horse and dropped the reins. She ran to the edge of the cliff, dropped to her stomach. Edging out, she yelled, "Raul! Raul!" She knew it was useless gesture. The sudden loss filled her heart. She was in tears yelling again, "Raul! Raul!"

"I'm down here," He yelled up. Thankful she was there.

"Are you okay?" Harriet suddenly felt relieved.

"If you call hanging over a cliff holding onto a bush okay," Raul yelled up. "I will need a rope to get out of here. There's one in the barn."

"If you're okay, I'll go get it," Harriet yelled back.

"Hurry, this bush is starting to give some."

Harriet worked herself back from the cliff. She stood, looked at her horse, it was tired from the steep climb up the hill. She knew it would have to be the stallion. She tied her horse to a bush.

Walking back to the stallion, she took the reins. The stallion reared some trying to free itself. Harriet pulled the reins down hard bringing the stallion's head close to her. Then grabbing it ears with both hands, she squeezed very hard.

Christopher Charles

The stallion reared, but Harriet went up with it, squeezing harder as her weight added to the pressure. When the stallion came back down, Harriet's feet touched the ground. She squeezed harder as it tried to shake its head. "Do you want to die?" She yelled.

The horse, his head in pain, stopped resisting, and remained still.

Feeling the horse was under control, she took the reins, and leaped up on the saddle. It was higher than her horse, but she managed to bring her right leg up, and over it. Her feet did not reach the stirrups.

Leaning forward, she kicked the horse in the ribs with her heels as hard as she could. The horse immediately took off over the plateau back towards the trail. Going down the trail, she kept her head back, and allowed the horse to find his own way down.

The stallion did not try to buck her off. She was his master. He did what she demanded. He went down the trail at a fast clip. A few branches hit his legs. They would be leaving some bruises.

When they reached the jungle trail, Harriet kicked him again. The horse picked up speed. Harriet, going with his rhythm, stayed with him.

Hanna heard them approaching. They were coming way too fast. Feeling something might have happened, she stepped the door. Coming across the open field in front of the house, she saw Harriet on top of the stallion.

Harriet pulled the horse up hard in front of the corral causing it to rear some as she slid off taking the reins with her. She quickly tied the reins to the fence and ran into the barn. She saw the rope hanging on the wall, and quickly retrieved it. She slipped her head into middle of the loop allowing the rope to lay on her right shoulder and left hip.

Hanna made it to the corral as Harriet leaped up on the stallion. She looked down, and yelled, "Raul is hanging over a cliff at the top of the plateau. He needs the rope!"

She pulled the reins back hard and to the right, causing the stallion to rear, and turn at the same time. Coming down, Harriet kicked her heels hard into its side, the stallion hit a quick gallop immediately.

Hanna watched the two of them race back across the open field and into the jungle. She matched his rhythm perfectly. The two were in perfect synch.

Senor Raul came out of the house as Harriet entered the jungle at the other end of the open area. "What's going on?" He asked in Spanish.

"Raul is hanging over a cliff on the plateau. That was Harriet coming back for the rope."

"She's riding thunder! That girl is going to get hurt!" Senor Raul yelled running to the corral. "Raul hanging from a cliff?"

"That's what she said," Hanna yelled at Senor Raul. "Hurry before something dreadful happens."

Senor Raul was saddling another horse, "It's probably that stallion."

Moving up the trail, Harriet kept pushing the stallion by kicking it every time it started to slow. Coming out on the plateau, she pulled to a stop twenty feet from the edge. She slid down from the horse and dropped the reins. The horse was exhausted. He no longer was resistant to her.

Harriet took the rope, ran to the cliff, and yelled, "You still there?"

Raul, not doing well, his arms were tired, he could barely move, and managed to say, "I'm still here. Tie the line to the horn of the saddle, then throw the other end to me."

Christopher Charles

Harriet threw the rope to the ground, picked up the end of it, and wrapped it around the stallion's saddle horn. She used the figure eight where you loop the horn and flipped another loop over upside down causing the pull on the line to tighten the line on itself much like tying the line from a boat to the cleat. That was the only knot she knew.

She threw the other end over the cliff. She could not see Raul. She estimated his location and threw the rope.

"Swing it to your left about ten feet," Raul yelled from below.

She picked up the rope, tried again. This time it landed right beside his left arm.

"Do you have it tied up? I'm going to put my weight on it."

Harriet ran back to the stallion, took the remaining end of the line, wrapped her hand into it, and yelled, "Okay, we're ready!"

Raul wrapped the rope around his waist and placed two half hitches into it. It was the only knot he could tie with one hand. "Okay, move the horse out slowly."

Harriet took the reins and led the stallion away from the cliff.

"Not so fast," Raul shouted. He wanted to use the rope to climb up the face of the cliff, but his strength was gone from holding the bush. He had to allow the horse to bring him up. Straightening himself, he was away from the cliff. "Okay, take her up!" He shouted.

Harriet moved the stallion forward again. The horse seemed to know the seriousness of the situation. He responded exactly as Harriet directed.

Slowly Raul appeared over the ridge, "Hold!" he yelled. His body was halfway over, and his feet were dangling. "A few more feet!"

Harriet took the horse forward two feet and stopped.

Raul on the ridge slowly crawled forward until he was far enough away from the ridge.

Slowly he stood, his body exhausted, he began removing the rope. He looked up to see it was his black stallion that rescued him. He started to say something, when he found Harriet leaping on him with tears streaming down her face.

She pulled him close and kissed his neck. Her tears were really flowing. She could not stop them. "You almost died!"

"Yes, but thanks to you, I am still alive." He gave her another hug and released her as Senor Raul rode out onto the plateau.

When Senor Raul saw the line still attached to the black stallion, he yelled, "You used that black devil for the rescue."

Harriet released Raul, turned, "He was the stronger of the two."

Raul, still a bit shaken, tried to brush some of the dust off. He held onto Harriet for support. His legs and arms, weak, were not doing well. He walked to the black stallion, removed the rope from the saddle, "I should be mad at you for dumping me over the cliff, but if it wasn't for you, I would not be here." He rubbed the stallion's nose.

"If you are up to it, we should be getting you back to the house," Senor Raul said.

"Yes, it's getting late," Raul said. He put his foot into the stirrup, and tried to lift himself up, but his muscles would not respond. Senor Raul gave him a push sending him up and on the saddle.

Harriet placed her foot into the small mare's stirrup. Suddenly she found herself going up over the saddle. She turned and saw Senor Raul below her. He winked and walked back to his horse.

They rode down the steep hill slowly with Harriet riding behind them on her mare. They walked the horses through the jungle. Harriet noticed the beautiful white flowered trees. The flowers looked like a white lily. She reached up, and picked one taking a seed with it. She slipped the flower and seed into fanny pack to look up later.

The stallion was giving Raul a very smooth ride. Puzzled, he asked, "What happened to Thunder? It looks like all the fight has left him."

"Maybe he is sorry for bucking you off his back," Harriet said.

"It's something more than that," Raul said. "He's as gentle as lamb."

Harriet did not say a word.

"Maybe you wore him out," Senor Raul said.

"Maybe," Raul said.

They rode the trail across the overgrown cultivated field of white flowers and reddish yellow seeds.

The horses picked up speed. Ahead meant the pasture and food for them. Harriet had to hold the reins tighter to keep her mare from running out ahead of them.

Coming to the corral, Senor Raul slipped from his horse, and helped Harriet from the mare. Taking her waist as she swung her right leg over the horse, he lowered her to the ground.

"Thank you, sir." Harriet said. "These horses are high off the ground."

Raul allowed himself to slip off. He rubbed the nose of his horse again. He turned to Harriet, "Go on into the house, we'll take care of the horses."

"You are alright?"

"Yes, a little weak, but I am feeling better moving around."

Harriet walked into the house.

Hanna handed her a towel, led her to the bathroom, "Go ahead, and clean yourself up, I'll have something laid out for you to wear."

Harriet felt herself being pushed into the bathroom, and the door closed. She quickly allowed her soiled clothes to drop and climbed into bathtub. The water was already drawn and steaming hot. She eased herself into the hot water, leaned back, allowing the water to flow over her body.

One of the workers came out from the field and took the horses. He removed the saddles and bridles and sent the horses into the enclosed field.

Leaning on the rail, watching the man with his grandfather, Raul said, "I need a package, sir, business!"

Senor Raul turned to his grandson, "I have some stored out in the greenhouse. How much do you need?"

Following, Raul said, "One package will be enough."

Reaching the green house, Senor Raul unlocked a cabinet revealing a hundred plus envelopes. He took one, handed it Raul, "The Scopolamine drug is very dangerous. It kills very easily."

"It also makes one tell the truth," Raul said, "I have used it before." Slipping the envelope into his pocket, they both headed for the house.

They entered the kitchen. Senor Raul poured him a glass of wine and took one himself. In Spanish, he said, "That is some girl you have there."

"She saved my life, but I think she was lucky using Thunder to pull me out."

"Then you don't know she rode Thunder back here for the rope."

"No, that horse would be too much for her."

"Ask your grandmother, she saw her come in like a bat out of hell. She had complete control and rode it like she has been riding for years."

"She's never been riding before," Raul said. He turned to his grandmother. "You saw her ride him?"

"She came riding in here fast, reared him to a stop, and leaped down to the ground. After she retrieved the rope, she leaped back up on him, reared him high, and turned him at the same time. Then she kicked him hard causing him to leap out into a gallop. She had complete control of the horse. She played him like she played the piano, perfectly."

Raul shook his head, "That horse is too wild. Even I had a hard time controlling him."

"If it wasn't for the emergency aspect of it," Hanna said, "It was beautiful to watch."

Harriet came out of the bathroom wearing a beautiful Spanish dress that accentuated her better parts. She had her dirty clothes folded and carried them in her hands, "These are much too nice for me to wear," Harriet said. "You will have to give me your address, and I will mail it back to you."

"No, no," Hanna said in English, "The dress is yours for bringing our Raul back to us and stirring the hearts of two old people. It is our pleasure."

Raul excused himself and headed for the bathroom.

Hanna followed him to the bedroom where she looked for some clothes for him to wear.

Senor Raul started for the door, "I need to be feeding the horses."

"Do you mind if I come along?" Harriet asked

"It will be my pleasure."

The horses were in the pasture grazing on the grass. Senor Raul went into the barn to pick up a sack of oats.

Harriet walked up to the fence.

When the black stallion saw her, he came running over. He placed his head over the fence rail.

Harriet reached up to stroke his head when he pulled it back quickly. Harriet smiled, "I am not going to pull your ears this time."

Slowly the horse placed his head back over the fence. He allowed her to stroke his nose. She worked her hand up between his eyes, then she rubbed his ears affectionately.

The horse whinnied as Senor Raul walked out of the barn. He saw her stroking the black stallion's head, shook his head, "What kind of spell did you place on that horse?"

"No spell, sir." Harriet said, watching the horse leave the fence, and head towards the corral and food. "We have an understanding. I will not squeeze his ears, and he will behave nicely to me."

Opening the sack, and filling the pails, Senor Raul asked, "That's how you made him behave?"

"Sorry, sir, I didn't have time to do otherwise. Your grandson was hanging from the cliff."

"Didn't he buck you off?"

"I did it standing in front of him. He took me straight into the air, but that only placed my weight on his ears also. He came down very obedient after that. Please don't tell Raul. I know how much he loves his horse. It was an emergency, you know that."

"Don't worry, your secret is safe with me," Senor Raul said smiling. "But I'll keep that ear method in mind. It could come in handy."

Raul came out the door, "We need to be leaving to catch our ship."

Senor Raul put the oat sack down, and came out of the corral, "You cannot go without a hug." He took Harriet into his arms, whispering, "Thank you for livening up the place. You are welcome back here anytime." He released her and sought out Raul. Shaking his hand and then pulling him close, he said, "You better not let this one go. She is very special."

"I will do my best," Raul said being released.

Harriet hugged Hanna, "Thank you for your wonderful hospitality, and my new dress."

"It was our pleasure," Hanna said, "You are very beautiful. Please come again."

Raul gave his grandmother a hug, "I will see you again soon."

In Spanish Hanna said, "You keep this one, and bring her back to see us, and always remember we love you."

Raul broke the hug, "I love you too." Then turning to Harriet waiting by the car, "We better be going if we are going to make the ship."

He started to open the door for her, when she said, "Maybe I should drive. Your legs took quite a beating."

Relieved, "Maybe you are right." He handed her the keys and opened the driver's side. She climbed in. He started to walk back around the car when his grandmother took hold of him, pulled him close, and said in Spanish, "We almost lost you today. Please be careful. I could not handle losing you."

"I'll be careful," Raul said ducking out of the hug, and climbing into the car. Harriet had already started the car. When the door closed, she slowly drove the car down the dirt road.

Senor Raul walked up to his wife, and said in Spanish, "Do you know how she tamed the black stallion?"

She looked up at him and waited.

"She stood in front of him and squeezed his ears very hard."

"Didn't he react?"

"She said, he lifted her off the ground, but she didn't let go. Her weight added to the pressure, and he became hers."

"Amazing, but what about his hooves?"

"She went up between his legs. He could not reach her."

"Okay, then how did she ride so expertly?"

"Probably from her piano training," Senor Raul said. "She plays the piano with her emotions. She just moved that principle to riding a horse. She allowed her emotions to go with the horse's movement. They became one motion."

"You go with that belief, and I will go with she has been riding since she was a child," Hanna said. "But it was beautiful watching her ride that black devil."

In the Car

Harriet was paying close attention to her driving. This was the first time she had driven a car since she passed her driving test. The top was still down allowing the wind and dust to reach them inside the car. She was following a dirt one lane road going twenty miles an hour.

"You may have to speed it up if we are going to make the ship," Raul said.

She pressed the accelerator down, the car moved fifty miles an hour leaving behind a cloud of dust. Ahead she noticed a fork in the road. She slowed the car, "Which one?"

Raul pointed to the right fork, "Take that one."

She immediately took the left one, then asked, "How long have you lived here?"

"I make that mistake all the time," Raul said. "So, you memorized the road coming here."

"It is probably good I did."

"Yes, it would have cost us another ten miles, and made us late for our ship." He was impressed how well she had memorized the route. He would have to keep this in mind later. She also learns very quickly. He will have to be careful what he teaches her.

She saw a slick spot ahead and stepped on her brakes to slow the car. The car suddenly spun taking them completely around. She saw the car moving in slow motion. When they were facing ahead again, she stepped on the accelerator, the car drove out of the spin. The left tire hit the puddle of water spraying the car and them. She continued on down the now dry road wiping the dirty water from her face with her left hand.

"You can slow us up a bit," Raul yelled trying to wipe the water from his face. His heart was still beating fast from the sudden spin in the road. Swallowing, he relaxed himself, and said, "My grandparents were very impressed with your horseback riding."

"You teach very well, and then you have to find the rhythm. That took a while, but it was fun once I learned that."

"How did you manage Thunder after he bucked me off?"

"I think he was sorry he did that," Harriet said. "He knew I was trying to rescue you."

"Well my grandparents liked you. That is a first."

"You have brought other women to meet your grandparents?"

Raul smiled, "Some, but none of them could ride a horse, let alone Thunder."

"You think that is why she gave me this beautiful dress?"

"She does not impress easily. You did very well."

They entered the city and moved on through.

She saw the hotel ahead, "Are we stopping for our drink at the hotel?"

"We'll miss our ship if we do. I'll treat you to dinner, and a drink once the ship is underway."

Ten minutes later Harriet pulled the car into the rental lot. Her hair had been blown dry. She pushed the red button beside her, the top came out of the trunk, and fell into place. The windows came up, and the top was secured. She turned the engine off and handed the keys to Raul.

Raul returned the keys. They walked down the dock looking for his red boat.

"It is right over there behind that large boat." Harriet said, pulling Raul along.

There's never a dull moment with her, he thought. He allowed her to take him to the boat. Climbing in, he asked, "You going to drive again?"

"If I can," Harriet said smiling. She untied the line from the cleat on the deck and stepped into the boat. Turning the ignition key, she started the boat. Using the forward and backward levers, she had the boat out of the dock, and heading for the ship. She did not stand this time wanting to keep her new dress dry. She sat on her other clothes.

Coming up fast to the ship, she slowed as they approached the opened hatch on the lower deck. Working the throttle, she had the boat up against the bumpers. She threw the line to one of the security officers.

He tied it to the cleat and waited for the stern line coming from Raul.

Catching it, he quickly tied it down. Another security officer helped her aboard the ship. She walked through the X-ray machine and waited for Raul.

Raul climbed up behind her and walked through the X-ray machine. He looked at his watch. The ship needs to sail in five minutes. He took Harriet up the stairs to the Bridge. Walking in, he asked, "Is everyone aboard?"

"Yes sir, we were only waiting for you," the First Officer Bitterman, a short slender man said. His uniform was a size too large for him.

"I need to change." Raul said. "Weigh-anchor and take her out."

"Yes sir."

Turning to Harriet, "Wait for me here. I'll be back in a few minutes."

"There is no hurry," Harriet said. She watched him disappear down the steps. She turned to the First Officer, "May I watch you weigh-anchor while I am waiting?"

"Yes, of course," The First Officer Bitterman said. "I'll explain as we do it." He blew the ship's horn, telling everyone aboard, the ship was pulling anchor. He walked to the thruster station. The chain motors control switches were located inside it along with the thruster levers.

"We are in a hundred feet of water. The forward anchor has five times that much chain out, but we must put more chain out to release the stern anchor, that also had five hundred feet of chain out."

The ships electric motors have been on idle. The Second Officer pulled the thruster reverse lever slightly back and released the bow chain at the same time.

She could hear the chain being dropped into the ocean.

He began the stern chains coming into the ship as it passed over it.

"Look at the gauge," The First Officer said. "It will tell you how much chain is out. You can see the chain coming in from the stern, and you can see the chain going out from the bow. There, see the end of the stern chain. When the ship is right over the anchor the fluke will straighten out, allowing the anchor to be brought in."

Harriet watched the screen. It showed the stern chain coming in, and the anchor coming up to the ship. A red line indicated the anchor was all the way up.

"Now we will bring in the bow chain," The First Officer said. "We are out close to a thousand feet now." He shifted the thruster lever forward slightly, the ship edged forward. Slowly the chain came in until the red line was reached. He reached up, blew the horn twice indicating they were getting underway.

The Second Officer had the wheel.

Harriet move up beside him, looked at the screen in front of him, "Is that line the course you have set?"

"It is only temporary until the Captain or the First Mate decide to change it which will probably happen. There is a storm coming in where we are heading. That dot on the screen is the ship. As long as I keep the dot on the line, we will stay on course."

"The line behind the ship shows where the ship has been, correct?" Harriet asked.

"That is correct," the Second Officer said. "Sometimes it is important to know where the ship has been."

The First Officer watched another screen.

Harriet walked over beside him. She saw the radar screen showing the boats around them, but he was looking at another screen. It showed a mass moving across it. "Is that a Doppler Radar map?" She asked.

"Yes, it's telling us the direction of the storm coming in. I am trying to find a way around or through it, but it doesn't look good at the moment."

Harriet moved on around the Bridge. She stopped at a bank of switches the Third Officer of the Bridge was looking at, "Do those switches control the lights, and communication aboard the ship?"

He knew she was close to the First Mate, "We can control the lighting and the communication from this board. Different sections of the ship have their own lights run by a separate generator. We can also shift power from one section of the ship to another. So, if we lose one generator, we can quickly back it up with another one waiting to come online."

"How about communication?"

"It has its own separate generator. The antenna on the ship is connected to a satellite passing over. This allows the passengers and crew to use their cell phones."

"If this should be shut off, then all communication would be lost to the outside world?"

"Correct, they would not know where we are, and we would not be able to communicate with anyone."

"This would not affect satellite telephones?"

"If you had a direct line to the satellite by standing on deck, it could work."

"Thank you," Harriet said, and wandered to the front of the Bridge. She could see the clouds now. They were hiding the last of the sunset. She felt very alone compared to the immense ocean she was looking at. There were no lights out in the blackness that developed rapidly leaving only the sound of the ship moving through the water. She knew that would change soon when the clouds reached them. She watched the life-giving sun slowly losing to the eternal darkness, the taker of all energy. The last glimmer of energy grasping for its last breath of life. Then it was over. The light was gone.

The blackness slowly took on a life of its own. The dark clouds began to grow, sweeping over the clear sky. It brought with it a very heavy energy that thundered, threatening all those beneath it. It built in volume and intensity as the swells grew with the whitecaps cresting them.

The First Officer came up beside her, "The First Mate will not be coming back to the Bridge. He said he would see you tomorrow morning at 9 AM on the lower deck."

Harriet, coming out of her trance-like state, turned, looked around, "Oh, tomorrow, yes, thank you."

The storm made her feel alive, but she was emotionally exhausted. It had been quite a day.

She passed Captain Morgan coming up the steps slowly favoring his right foot. He glanced at Harriet, nodded slightly, and walked slowly onto the Bridge.

The pain still in his right foot made him angry every time he stepped on it. He had not been staying off it like the doctor said. It may be infected. He came up to the First Officer, "What is she doing here?"

"She was waiting for the First Mate, sir."

"Don't let her on my Bridge, and that's an order!"

"Yes sir," The First Officer Bitterman said.

"Now, what's this storm all about?" Captain Morgan asked moving to the Doppler Radar Screen.

"I've been following it," First Officer Bitterman said. "It is going to hang in over Corinto for the next two days."

"Then take us through it and move on to Puntarenas. We will tender there. Their docks are too small for us."

"Yes sir."

Captain Morgan turned, headed for the stairs, and yelled over his shoulder, "Tell the First Mate to meet me in my cabin."

"Yes sir."

The Captain hobbled off the Bridge.

A few minutes later Raul arrived decked out in his uniform. He walked onto the Bridge, went to the First Officer, "Was the Captain here?"

"Yes sir, we are heading straight for Puntarenas. A storm is settling in on Corinto. He said to sail through the storm."

"Okay, remember it is a tender anchorage."

"Yes sir, the Captain has already advised us."

"Then carry on," Raul said.

"The Captain also said to keep Miss Cummings off the Bridge, sir. I am only passing on the order."

"Very well, we will observe the order."

He turned, started to leave, when the First Officer said, "The Captain wants you to meet him in his cabin, sir."

"Very well," Gonzales said leaving the Bridge. He went directly to the Captain's cabin, knocked at the door. He heard the come in, opened the door. Inside he saw the Captain at his desk staring at the map.

The Captain looked up, "You heard we're moving onto Puntarenas?"

"Yes sir, the storm is settling into Corinto. It is best to by-pass it."

"Then after Puntarenas it's a straight course south staying twenty miles off the coast with my lights out."

"I rather not discuss more, sir." Gonzales said. "We don't know where the ears are."

"Probably a good idea."

"Did you want me for anything else, sir?"

"How is the romance with our Miss Cummings coming along?"

Gonzales did not smile. He knew what he was asking, "I believe that is a personal question, sir, but things are coming along very well."

"That is good to hear. Then that will be all, Mr. Gonzales."

"Thank you, sir." Gonzales said moving back out the door.

"If you plan on leaving the ship, remember the ship leaves at 6 PM sharp. I would recommend being back by 4 PM."

"Yes sir. I will keep it in mind." Gonzales said ducking out the door. He was sure there was spyware set up somewhere around the Captain's quarters. He did not want to reveal too much. He also knew the Captain was becoming nervous. How reliable was he?

Harriet unlocked her cabin door. Nadine was inside waiting for her. She closed the door and placed her dirty clothes on the chair. Nadine started to say something when she heard a voice in her earpiece.

Nadine pointed to Harriet to put her earpiece on. She had left it on the ship since it was not effective off the ship.

Slipping it on, she heard Rose's voice, who said, "Listen to this:" She played the recording back she had just received from the Captain's quarters.

When it was finished, Harriet said, "It sounds like something is going to happen when we leave Puntarenas." Then thinking out loud, she said, "Why would the Captain be taking the ship south along the coast of Columbia?" Then turning back to Rose, she said, "Thank you, Rose, now, move around the ship to see if you can pick up anything on the other locations."

"I have been, but nothing of interest yet."

"Thank you, Rose," Harriet said. She turned to Nadine and swung around in her Spanish dress in front of her, "Hanna Gonzales, Raul grandmother, gave it to me."

"You must have made an impression," Nadine said.

"I saved her grandson's life," Harriet said.

"That's a good enough reason."

"She insisted I keep it. They seem like very nice people."

"Did you learn anything?"

"I don't know, maybe," Harriet said walking to the computer. "He definitely knows I am Harriet Brown Detective." She began working the computer. She was curious about the flower in her fanny pack. Pulling it out along with the nut, she went through the computer pictures of flowers.

Nadine came over, looked down, "What are you doing?"

"I found this flower and nut on a grove of trees on the ranch. They didn't seem to have a purpose. So, I brought one of the flowers, and one of the seeds back with me to look up on the computer."

Nadine stood beside her.

"Let's see, a lot of trees have flowers, but what kind of tree would have white lily-like flower and big seeds."

Then she found it, "The Borrachero tree," she shouted. "It says here, the seeds are used to make the Scopolamine drug. Just sniffing the flower will affect you. The drug is chemically made from the seed. A whiff of the powder will leave you helpless to someone's command. You will act normally, but you will not remember a thing six hours later when you finally wake up.

The CIA has used it to obtain information. It would be impossible for you to withhold it. You would willing give up everything you have and do whatever the person in command tells you to do. It is administered by inhalation, or by spiking a drink with it. If too much is given, the heart will stop, and the person will die, a very dangerous drug to control."

Harriet sat back in the chair, "Senor Raul had a hill full of these trees. He was in the business of making the Scopolamine drug."

Then thinking a moment, she decided to look up the coffee bean plant. The picture of a coffee bean plant came up. It showed the flowers and beans to be in clusters, and the leaves to be ridged. "Look," she said, "That is the coffee bean and flower!"

She tried to remember how the coffee plants looked on Senor Raul's ranchero. She didn't remember them being clustered. She decided to look up the coca plant.

She located it in the computer and looked at it. "Okay this is the Coca flower." It was single white flowers similar to the coffee bean flowers, but they were separated not clustered. She remembered riding through the field they were allowing to seed over. She remembered those flowers. They were single white flowers with single seeds or small bunches of seeds. The leaves were smooth like the coca plant. There were five thousand acres of the plant. He was in the cocaine business. So where does this leave Raul, who grew up on the ranch.

Her head was spinning when she turned to Nadine, "His family is in the cocaine business. At least his grandfather is. The whole ranch is full of the plant."

"A lot of people are in the cocaine business in this area. It's not illegal down here," Nadine said, "But it is if they try to ship it to the United States."

"They were such nice people," Harriet said. "Yet, here he is growing cocaine, and making a deadly drug used for only one purpose, and that is to control someone's mind or kill them."

Her mind was trying to comprehend the concept. Then looking at Rose, she yelled, "Rose, have you been listening?"

"Yes, are you still going out with him tomorrow?"

"I think something is going to happen tomorrow after we leave Puntarenas, but we do not know what that is yet."

"So, you are going out with him?" Rose asked again

"We have not made any definite plans, but I am almost sure he will take me ashore. It will be up to the rest of you to stop him if I do not make it back tomorrow."

"Do you think he will do you harm?" Rose asked.

"I saved his life today," Harriet said. "I do not believe he would do me harm now."

There was a knock at the door.

Harriet opened the door to see a young man standing in front of her. He handed her an envelope, tipped his hat, and left. She closed the door. She took the note inside out.

"What does it say?" Nadine asked.

"He is asking us to come down to the skylight lounge in thirty minutes for dinner, and a drink he promised."

"He doesn't really want me?" Nadine asked.

"Yes, he wanted to take both of us earlier, but I need another shower to wash out the dirt driving back to the ship."

"You drove?"

"Yes, I tried to brake the car when we hit a slippery area, and the car spun. I managed to straighten it out, but we hit a large mud puddle that splattered the car, and us inside."

"Is that how you saved his life?"

"No, that was something else. I'll tell you later." She said running to the shower.

Nadine set out a dress and shoes for Harriet. Next, she plugged in the hairdryer, and laid out the makeup and brushes. She was ready when Harriet came out of the shower.

Working Harriet's hair with the blow dryer, she began to look normal. Makeup, dress, and shoes, she was ready to go.

Exactly thirty minutes later Nadine and Harriet walked into the Skylight lounge. It was relatively empty because of the incoming weather moving the ship around. The overhead ceiling was also closed that had previously been open to the night sky.

They found Raul sitting at a large booth in the middle of the room. He saw them come in and stood to allow them to sit across from him.

"It is very nice of you young ladies coming to dine with a lonely bachelor."

"We received an invitation," Harriet said. "How could we refuse?"

After they were seated, he asked, "What would you like to drink?"

They both said red wine, and he gave the order to the steward. A moment later the steward arrived with a bottle of port wine.

Raul tasted the wine and nodded for the ladies' glasses to be filled. When they were filled, he raised his glass, "This is for Harriet who saved my life today."

"She never did say how she accomplished that," Nadine said.

Raul went into the details of how the stallion bucked him off sending him over the cliff.

Continuing: "When Harriet arrived, and leaned over ledge. I told her I needed the rope hanging up in the barn to pull myself up. This is the most amazing part. Harriet had never been on a horse before." Looking hard at Nadine, he asked, "That is correct?"

"She had never been near a horse before let alone ride one," Nadine said.

"She calmed the black stallion, climbed up on his back, and rode down the hill to the barn. She retrieved the rope, leaped up on the stallion's saddle, and raced back up the hill. It was not a moment too soon. My bush I was holding on to was slipping, and my right foot had numbed up. It was a good five-hundred-foot drop. She threw the rope over the ledge and used the stallion to pull me up. An amazing feat knowing this was her first time on a horse, a wild one at that."

Nadine looked at Harriet, "Are you going to tell us how you really did it?"

"That was about it," Harriet said. "He left out some details. The horse was wild at first, but he calmed-down after I squeezed his ears."

"You squeezed his ears," Raul shouted.

Nadine looked at Harriet, "How did the stallion respond to having his ears squeezed?"

"He reared up taking me with him," Harriet said, "I just squeezed harder. He brought me back to the ground and behaved himself after that."

"Did he try to kick you?" Raul asked.

"I went up between his legs," Harriet said. "He could not reach me. Believe me, I was hanging onto his ears for dear life."

"Why didn't you just take the mare?" Raul asked.

"The mare was exhausted from the climb up the hill. It probably would have gone down the hill okay but coming back it would have been a different story. I simply needed the stronger stallion."

"You say she has never ridden a horse before?"

"She has never been near a horse before," Nadine said, "I am quite certain of that."

"According to my grandmother, Hanna, she came charging into the yard like a professional. When she left, she reared the horse, and turned him the same time to cut the time down. Then she charged out towards the hill. My grandmother was very impressed."

"It was an emergency," Harriet said. "People do strange things in an emergency. Women have been known to lift a two-ton vehicle when her child's life was at stake. I didn't think about anything. I just did it. Can we talk about something else? You are embarrassing me."

"Then a toast to the amazing Harriet," Raul said, raising his glass to Nadine's glass. "Now we will let it go with a thank you for saving my life."

The steward came over with a menu, "What will you be having tonight?"

Raul looked it over, "I will have your twelve-ounce prime rib medium rare."

The steward turned to the ladies and waited.

"I will have the six-once prime rib," Harriet said.

Nadine nodded, "The same, but make mine well done."

The steward left, Raul continued, "Where did she learn to drive?"

"She doesn't drive," Nadine said. "She's only driven once to get her driver's license, but that was more out of fear on the agent's part. He did not want to test her again. She was almost in three accidents taking the test or was it four. I think he quit after he passed her."

"You sure," Raul asked. "She took us out of a spin expertly. She knew just when to hit the accelerator. That's expert driving."

"Unless she has been going out at night driving, she has only experienced the one driving lesson I gave her."

"You taught her to drive?"

"Yes, but at home she has a chauffeur," Nadine said. "He drives her everywhere."

"Then we do have a mystery here," Raul said.

"It's no mystery," Harriet said. "The whole thing was in slow motion. I saw we were straight and pushed on the accelerator. Unfortunately, we were headed straight for a water puddle, the reason I tried to stop the car. We hit the water puddle straight on soaking the both of us. I don't call that good driving."

The steward brought them their food, passed it around, "Will you be wanting more wine, sir?"

"No, I think we have enough," Raul said as the steward poured the last of it into their glasses.

Harriet began eating. She did not realize she was so hungry. Of course, the tamales helped earlier, but she used up that energy long ago, and the prime rib did not have any hot sauce on it. She ate all of the vegetables and bread.

Eating her prime rib, Nadine said, "I understand your family lives in Cartagena, Columbia. Are you going to visit them, when we dock there?"

"They are expecting me to visit them," Raul said. "It would disappoint them if I didn't."

"This cruise has allowed you to visit your grandparents, and your parents," Nadine said.

"Yes, it was one of the reasons I hired on."

"What is Corinto like?" Harriet asked after she devoured her prime rib.

"We are not stopping at Corinto. The Captain decided to move on to Puntarenas. The storm we are entering will settle in Corinto making a stop there miserable. It will give us an extra day we can spend in Cartagena, a large Columbia city."

"It will also give you an extra day to spend with parents," Nadine said.

"See, it already has its advantages."

"What is Puntarenas like?" Harriet asked.

"It is surrounded by jungles, but it is very beautiful. The snorkeling is some of the best in the world. They have many other tours you can go on, but I would recommend the snorkeling."

"Is that where you are taking me tomorrow?" Harriet asked.

"Yes, you enjoyed it so much last time. I will even let you drive the boat again."

Christopher Charles

Harriet smiled. She wanted to ask him about the cocaine on his grandfather's ranch, and the Borrachero tree, but the game would be over. "Okay, if I can drive the boat?"

"Then nine sharp on the lower deck hatch, we may have lunch at a hotel on our way back, so bring something you can slip over your bathing suit."

"You are promising another lunch," Harriet said, remembering they didn't have time earlier in the day.

"Yes, this time we will have lunch. I promise this unless I drown or something." He smiled.

The steward came back, "Will there be any desert tonight?"

"Not for me," Raul said, and looked at Nadine and Harriet.

"I think I have already overdone it but thank you."

Nadine shook her head, "I am fine, thank you."

"It is time we were getting to bed:" Harriet said, "I am very tired." She stood slowly, worked herself out of the booth, as Nadine followed her.

Raul stood, brought Harriet close, and kissed her on the lips.

It caught her by surprise. It lasted only a few seconds, but it did affect her. She stumbled backwards until she was caught by Nadine behind her. She mumbled out, "I will see you tomorrow."

Nadine placed her arm around her and led her from the Skylight saloon.

Raul watched them leave, smiled, pleased with himself he had that much effect on her. She will be no problem tomorrow.

Harriet entered the suite with Nadine behind her. She felt foolish coming apart when he kissed her. When she was inside her suite, she pushed her speed dial number, and put her phone to her ear. Ramos answered. "Paul, where are you now?"

"We are in Panama City. I have a helicopter reserved for tomorrow. Two of us can fly it. It has a 450-mile range. We are tracking your cell phone by satellite. We will stay within a hundred miles of you making you an hour out from us at any time."

"Good, I expect something to happen tomorrow. We overheard the Captain saying he was going to sail the ship south staying within twenty miles of the Columbian shore. There has also been a change of plans, we are skipping Corinto, and going directly to Puntarenas, Costa Rica. I expect something to happen then because we are supposed to go through the canal after that."

"Have you apprised Clark?"

"No, but he is limited what he can do, but put him in the loop. I am depending on you for support."

"I'll take care of it."

"Thank you, Paul," She said flipping her phone closed.

First Mate's Cabin:

Raul was in his cabin when there was knock on the door. He opened to see the below deck Petty Officer Molina standing with ten-pound bomb with an antenna and pulsating blue light.

"May I come in, sir?"

"By all means, where did you find this?"

"I found it beneath the forward deck plates. I thought I should bring it to you." He brought it inside and placed it on the table.

"Do you know what this is?"

"It looks like a bomb, sir. I am bringing it to you, since you are in charge of security."

"Yes, thank you," Raul said, looking it over. "You did the right thing. This should stay between us."

"Yes sir, I understand."

"If you find anymore, bring them to me immediately," Raul said moving him towards the door.

"Yes sir," Molina said looking at him. He was not sure of the First Mate's reaction to the bomb.

When the door closed, Raul looked the device over. It was obviously a bomb. It had an antenna sticking up from the top communicating to somewhere. There had to be more of these on the ship. Now he knew how they were going to sink it. He decided to keep the information to himself. The Captain was not very reliable at the moment, especially since he would have to take the ship south along the Columbian coast alone.

He placed the ten-pound bomb into his overhead cabinet, and carefully closed it. Now he would have to learn how to sleep with a ten-pound bomb above his head.

8 Puntarenas, Costa Rica

At six in the morning the ship entered the Tarcoles River, pulled into the Port of Caldera, and anchored off from Pantarenas, Costa Rica. The storm had moved inland. The sun was coming out.

Raul Gonzales, on the Bridge when they anchored, had his boat brought down to the lower deck hatch. He boarded it and headed back towards the mouth of the river. He pulled into the docks near the Si Como No Resort and walked up the hill to the hotel.

The hotel was a series of bungalows that allowed each to have a semblance of privacy. It was for this very reason he selected this hotel. The bungalow ranged from a single resident to multi residences that include a two-story structure. It had the normal pool and viewpoints of the beach below.

He approached the desk and asked for a single bungalow away from the main section of the hotel.

"We only have the one bungalow, sir. One guest has taken the rest of them, and this one is only for the one night."

"I'll take it," Raul said. He gave the clerk five hundred dollars cash and a false ID.

The clerk gave him the key card, "Enjoy your stay senor…" He looked at the registration card, and continued, "Senor Antonio Manuel."

Raul nodded, "Have them place some fruit in the room." He took the key card, walked back into the resort, and located the bungalow. Secluded, it lay towards the back of the main part of the resort. He tried the key card, it worked. He entered, looked around. It had a large king size bed in the middle of the room with a kitchenette off to one side. It also had a view of the beach. He opened the window to allow the slight breeze to fill the room, and to drive out the musk odor. Satisfied, he left, walking back to his boat. It was easier walking downhill.

He drove the boat back to the ship further upriver. It took fifteen minutes. He could see the tenders being lowered. He was right on time.

Harriet woke up at eight, and quickly dressed. She slipped into her bathing suit first, then her light pants and blouse. She found her tennis shoes when Nadine woke up.

Staggering out of bed, Nadine said, "Be careful, dear, this is the time we suspect something is going to happen."

"I think it won't happen until after we weigh-anchor," Harriet said checking her fanny pack. She had her phone, ID, and some money. A girl should always have a little money, she thought.

Nadine handed her a slice of toast as she headed for the door.

"I expect to see you this afternoon," Nadine yelled after her as the door closed. She felt something would happen sooner than after the ship left port. She had nothing to base these fears on, she only felt it.

Nine O' clock Harriet was at the lower hatch waiting for Raul Gonzales, the First Mate. She checked everything again. She was ready for an adventure snorkeling.

She watched the security officer take the fins and snorkels from the locker beside her. Bringing them to the hatch, he looked at Harriet, "It appears you are going snorkeling."

"Yes, it should be fun."

The two tenders had already come to the hatch and left full of passengers. She started to ask the security officer about Raul when she saw his red boat come along side. Raul was driving it. He threw the lines to the security man who quickly tied it to the cleat inside the ship.

"Welcome aboard," Raul said. "I thought I would take it out for a spin, since you will be driving it from now on as agreed."

Harriet entered the boat. The security officer handed the snorkel equipment aboard, and threw the line to Raul, as she asked, "Where did you go?"

"I checked out the best reef area. It is down around the river opening. I think you will enjoy it. Normally reefs are 60 to 90 feet down, and some are 300 hundred feet down, but this one is forty-five feet, and still in excellent condition."

Harriet turned the boat out away from the ship before she pushed the thrusters forward all the way. The smooth water of the river allowed them to go very fast.

"It supposed to be five miles an hour while you are in the river," Raul cautioned her.

"It is so wide here, how can you tell when you are out of the river," Harriet asked.

"You have a point. That may only pertain to the area around the docks."

Christopher Charles

Harriet stood as the front end of the boat came out of the water creating a large wake behind it. Fifteen minutes later, they passed the Si Como No Resort, but they continued out to sea. Rounding the Tarcoles River opening, she turned south, going another ten miles.

"Pull into that small inlet. They have a reef a hundred yards offshore. We'll be exploring it."

"Aye, Aye Captain," Harriet said as she entered the inlet dropping her speed. "Anywhere particularly?"

"Let's drop anchor in the center of the inlet. We'll work around the boat in that area. If it is not good, we'll move further in."

Harriet brought the boat to the center of the inlet, Raul dropped the anchor, and broke out the swimming gear.

Harriet began peeling off her clothes revealing her swimming suit. She made sure her fanny pack was secure with her clothes. Her heart racing, she was going into the unknown underwater world.

She remembered the last time when she almost drowned. She felt a shutter run its course, then she slipped on the fins, and the head plate with the snorkel attached. She sat on the side of the boat waiting for Raul. She wondered if he might leave her here while she was underwater. She put the fear aside and decided she would enjoy the day.

Raul slipped his gear on, "Are you ready?"

Harriet flipped over the side of the boat and struck the water with her back and shoulders. She went underwater a moment and came back up blowing out the water in her snorkel.

Raul went off the other side and worked his way around the boat. Seeing Harriet was okay, he pointed towards shore, and moved that direction.

Harriet followed him with her head in the water face first. She blew out the water to take in a breath. A sudden panic tried to enter, but she held it down, and kept her head in the water breathing through the tube.

The reef began to appear. It was down about forty feet. She saw Raul dive in front of her. She blew-out her air tube and took in a deep breath. Dropping her head, she went underwater. Kicking her fins, she moved down thirty feet, but the reef seemed to be going deeper.

Raul followed it down with her twenty feet behind him. Thousands of different colors were coming up from the fish moving over the coral. It was simply beautiful. She saw a couple of snakes working their way through the holes in the coral looking for small fish.

She was fascinated until she felt something was not right. Looking around, Raul was not there. He had gone to the surface. She kicked hard moving upward. She did not realize how deep she had gone. More than forty feet, it took her time to reach the surface.

Coming up fast, she came up out of the water, and blew her tube at the same time. Taking in a deep breath, she quickly looked around for Raul.

She saw him diving again twenty yards from her. She felt a little foolish thinking he was leaving her. She took in another deep breath and dived again.

This time going down forty-five feet before she leveled out, she saw Raul in the distance. The water was very clear. She swam that direction and dove lower to the reef sixty feet down. She began examining the different colors and the small animals occupying it.

She felt something very large pass over her blocking out the overhead sunlight. Looking up, she saw a very large white shark swimming slowly towards Raul twenty yards up, and in front of her.

Christopher Charles

She kicked her feet harder. She could not warn him unless he surfaced. The shark and her were going to meet Raul at the same time. The shark did not see her coming up from the bottom. The closer she came the larger it appeared. It was a good fifteen feet or longer.

Raul was looking the other direction kicking his feet slowly. He did not see the white shark approaching.

At any moment the shark could kick in, and charge, but it was more curious at the moment. It would take a bite first to test the swimming animal in front of it.

Harriet wanted to yell, but all she could do was swim hard closing the distance fast. She looked for a weak point on the shark. The only thing she saw was its eye. She clasped her hands together forming a fist with protruded knuckles. Kicking hard, she charged the white shark.

The shark turned its head to take a bite out of Raul with its mouth, when something hard struck its left eye temporarily blinding it. The shark did not see what it was, but it hurt. Jerking off to his right hoping to escape his attacker, he kicked his tail hard striking Raul in the side and chest sending him flying to the surface.

Harriet bounced from the white shark's eye. She found herself moving upward behind Raul. When she surfaced, she saw him floating with his face down in the water. She knew his breathing tube was probably full of water.

She took her mask off pushing her left arm through the straps. She took a deep breath and allowed it to ease out. Pushing herself to Raul, she took a handful of his hair, and brought his head up. Taking his mask and snorkel off, she placed her left hand and arm through the straps.

Pulling him back using his hair, she straightened his body to a floating position on his back. Kicking hard beside him, she raised herself high to breath into his mouth. It was all she could do to raise herself high enough. After two breaths, he coughed up the water in his bronchial tubes breathing through his mouth.

Raul found himself looking up in the sky with his mask off. He felt someone pulling hard on his hair and turned over quickly.

Harriet released her hair hold, "You were attacked by a white shark. He hit you so hard, it knocked you unconscious."

Raul looked around quickly. He did not see any shark, but his hair and chest hurt. He may have a few cracked ribs. He remembered seeing Harriet coming towards him a brief second, then blackness.

"You ran into me!" Raul shouted feeling his side and chest.

"No, the shark hit you with his tail. I got part of it, but you took the brunt of it." She handed him back his mask and snorkel.

He looked around for the boat. It was a good two hundred yards towards the beach. Placing his mask on, he really didn't believe her, but he said, "I didn't know we had swum so far. We should be getting back to the boat if there is a white shark around here." Putting his head into the water, he took off swimming for it.

Harriet slipped her mask on following him. She managed to stay up with him, pulling hard with her arms, or maybe his chest hurt.

Coming to the boat, Raul worked himself in first. He could barely pull himself inside.

She waited to see if he would help her as she took off her fins and threw them into the boat. When she saw him pulling in the anchor, she pulled herself up over the gunwale, and fell inside. She started to stand when she felt her left leg cramp up. A large knot formed. She immediately sat down and massaged the muscle.

When the anchor was aboard, Raul turned, "Let's go look for your shark."

She didn't tell him about her muscle cramp. The fins were heavy, and she had been placing an extra strain on her leg muscles. She did not need to go back into the water at the moment.

Starting the motor, she said, "You still don't' believe me."

"When I see the shark, I will believe you."

Harriet moved the throttle forward, and the boat moved back to where they had encountered the shark. She circled the boat a few times, and then headed the direction she had seen it move off to. Four hundred yards further out from shore, she saw the dorsal fin of a large shark.

She brought the boat in close, "Would you like to swim with it again?"

"No thank you," Raul said looking at the shark.

The white shark was fifteen feet long. It dove when it felt the boat closing in.

Harriet took the boat out away from it, "Where to now?"

"I think it is time to head back to the resort, and I again apologize for doubting you."

Harriet smiled, "You should never doubt me." She turned the boat back towards the river. They had come down the coast some distance from it. Thirty minutes later they entered the mouth of the river.

"Stay on this side. There is a small cove that leads up to the Si Como No Resort. It has a docking facility there we can pull the boat into."

"Aye, Aye, Captain." She stood allowing the wind to dry off her bathing suit. She kept her weight on her right leg to prevent her left leg from cramping again.

She took the boat into the mouth of the Tarcoles River. She could barely see the resort among the jungle growth. She saw the dock, looked over at Raul.

He nodded, "Find any empty spot."

She slowed the boat, eased it up to the dock beside a sixty-foot red and white yacht that was made for speed and entertainment.

A man working on the dock saw them coming in. He waited, took the line Raul threw to him, and tied it to a cleat on the dock. He helped Harriet up.

She carried her clothes and fanny pack.

"Thank you, sir," Harriet said.

Raul climbed onto the dock on his own, handed the man ten dollars, "We will be back in a couple of hours. Will you watch our boat for us?"

The man nodded, "Si Senor, no problem."

Harriet slipped her pants and blouse on over her now dry bathing suit. She worked her feet into her tennis shoes, looked up, "I think I am ready to go."

Raul had his clothes on. He led the way off the dock.

Harriet tried to keep up hobbling on one leg.

The dock man watched, and said to himself, "A shameful way to handle the beautiful lady."

At the end of the dock, Raul found himself way ahead of her, and waited.

Harriet noticed him watching. She slowed her walk, turned, and looked the jungle over as she casually walked up the dock enduring the pain in her left leg. She would have to get off of it soon.

Raul realized he was not treating her well, took her arm when she reached him.

Harriet put her left leg weight on his arm. She managed the walk up the hill.

"You okay?" He asked.

"I think I over worked my leg muscle. It wants to cramp up."

"Can you manage the stair climb?"

"I think so," She said, leaning on him more.

He took her to an outside bar, and restaurant that overlooked the water on the lower level of the hotel.

She was thankful to be able to sit down. All she needed was some rest. She overdid it when she had to kick very hard to raise herself high enough to breathe into Raul's mouth.

"What would you like to drink?"

"A cold glass of lemonade would be nice."

The waiter came over, handed them a menu, and asked in Spanish, "What would you like to drink?"

"The lady will have a lemonade. I will have a cold beer."

"Yes sir, we only have tap beer." The waiter said in Spanish.

"That will be good."

The waiter nodded and left.

Harriet looked the menu over. She did not understand most of it, turned to Raul. "What would you suggest? Something that's not spicy would be good."

Raul looked at the menu, "How about a salad with some chicken in it?"

"If that is my only choice, I will take it."

"I'm going to have the local fish," Raul said. "It is supposed to be delicious."

"I will stay with the salad."

The waiter arrived with the drinks, and asked in Spanish, "What have you decided upon?"

Raul gave him the order in Spanish, and the waiter left.

Raul stretched his chest muscles trying to relieve the pain developing. "That shark really hit me hard." He still did not believe the white shark struck him. The shark would not do that. Take a bite out of him, yes, but run away, no.

"I think when he realized there were two of us, he backed-off," Harriet said.

"How long was I unconscious?"

"Maybe two minutes," Harriet said.

He began working his hair into place, "Why were you pulling my hair?"

"Your head was in the water face down, and your breathing tube was probably full of water not allowing you to breath. I jerked your head back to clear your mouth. I gave you mouth to mouth breaths about three times before you came around."

"How did you manage that?"

"I pulled your head back and kicked very hard taking me high enough to breathe into your mouth."

"I'm lucky to have any hair left," Raul said.

"It was the only thing available." Harriet said. Then looking around, "Can you excuse me, I need to seek out the bano."

Raul stood, helped her from her chair.

She hobbled off into the hotel and disappeared.

Raul watched her leave. Then he took a small package of white powder from his shirt pocket and poured half of the contents into Harriet's lemonade. He was not sure of the amount. She may be resistant to the drug. She would also be eating food with the drink diluting the effects even more.

Harriet found the bathroom, flipped her phone opened, speed-dialed Ramos. "Hello, Paul, you are still in Panama City?"

"Yes, we have a helicopter for three days. We are staying near the airport. We can be in the air in thirty minutes."

"The ship leaves at 6 PM and goes south. We're 600 miles from Columbia or 21 hours. That's three O' Clock tomorrow. I would be ready any time after that. I would encourage extra fuel. There's only jungle down here."

"3 PM, got it. How about Clark?"

"You could check at 3 tomorrow and see if there has been any action anywhere down here."

"Is there anything else?"

"Call Nadine and give her the timetable if I do not call you at six tonight."

"You think something may happen to you?"

"I am only trying to think of everything," Harriet said. "Now, I've got to go. Thank you again for being there for me."

"It is my pleasure," Paul said.

She closed her phone and used the bathroom.

At the table the food arrived. Raul's fish was a large filet, and Harriet's was a large bowl of salad.

Raul removed his packet of white powder. He sprinkled a portion of his filet with it and placed the remaining amount onto the chicken in the large bowl of salad.

When she came back to the table, she noticed the food had already arrived. Raul was waiting for her. He helped her with her chair.

She saw her salad. It was full of chicken. Something told her not to eat it. Why did she leave him alone with her food and drink? She remembered his grandfather's Borrachero tree and the Scopolamine drug.

Raul raised his glass, "Salute for saving my life again."

She raised hers and touched his glass slightly. She took a slight touch of the liquid and put the lemonade glass down in front of her. It had a bitter taste.

She placed the salad dressing on her salad and mixed it thoroughly. She watched him eat his fish slowly.

"This is very delicious," Raul said as he took another bite. "Would you like to try it?"

She did not trust her salad, and the lemonade had a bitter taste. She was hungry, and he had been eating his fish. It was probably safe, "I'll try a piece."

He cut off a piece of the powder portion of the fish with his fork, lifted it to her mouth.

She took the portion of fish, chewed, and swallowed it. It had a slightly bitter taste. She wanted the taste out, but it was too late. She took a large drink of her lemonade, and immediately felt slightly dizzy.

She could not remember why she was apprehensive about eating her salad. She took a big mouth full and began chewing it.

Now Raul tried to prevent her from taking too much of the drug. She had almost emptied her glass of lemonade. He picked up her salad, "This will not do!"

He snapped his fingers the waiter came running. "This is not what we ordered." He handed him the salad and his fish plate. He quickly took Harriet's lemonade from her hand, and continued, "The young lady wants a beer instead. We will both have an order of enchiladas with red sauce."

"Yes sir," the waiter said, and took the three items away shaking his head. Walking into the kitchen, he gave the fish and chicken to his cat, and threw the salad into a container for his animals.

Harriet looked up at him, "Why did you take away my salad?"

"Because you will like the enchiladas better."

"Thank you, I am sure you are right."

The waiter brought back two drafts of beers.

Harriet looked up, smiled, "Thank you."

"Was I really hit with a white shark?" Raul asked.

"Yes, but it wanted to take a bite out of you."

Curious, he asked, "What stopped it?"

"I did. I was much lower in the water than you. I saw his shadow go over me very slowly heading straight for you. I doubled my fist and kicked as hard as I could with my arms straight. I aimed for his left eye. He was almost on you with his huge mouth open when my fist struck his eye. I completely blindsided him. He kicked his tail hard in response striking you in the side and chest.

His body sent me to the surface, where I found you floating with your face in the water. I pulled your head back with your hair and took off your mask. Then it was a matter of getting high enough to breathe into your mouth. I think that is where I strained the muscle in my left leg."

Raul was feeling really low. She risked her life to save him. He repaid her by drugging her, but he needed information. "Thank you for saving my life again."

He took a sip of his beer, "The beer tastes very good. I believe it is a local brew."

Harriet took a large drink, "It is very good."

She seemed to be under enough, he thought, "What is your name?"

She looked at him like he was a dunce, "Harriet Brown."

"What was your father's name?"

"George Brown, but he is dead now. They killed him." A tear started to develop.

"Who killed him?"

"The drug cartel ordered it, but the Los Angeles police chief, Don Morales actually killed him."

"He was working for the Paniagua cartel?"

"I don't know who Paniagua is, but Morales along with the head of DEA, and the Los Angeles Homeland Security are all dead now."

"You did not say why they killed your father," Raul said.

"He hid 800 million dollars from them until he could figure out who he could trust. They killed him thinking he would tell me somehow. There's been six attempts on my life because of it."

"Where's the money now?"

"I gave it to the FBI after the bad guys were removed."

"Then he did give the money to you?"

Christopher Charles

"Sort of, I found a code saying where it was, and told the FBI."

"What about the product?"

"You mean the cocaine?" Harriet asked loudly.

"Not so loud, we don't want others hearing our conversation."

"Quiet, yes we must be quiet," Harriet whispered.

"What about the product?" Raul asked again.

"I found it, and gave it to the FBI? There were 30 tons of the stuff hidden in three containers located at the Los Angeles docks."

"How did you come about all of this information?"

Harriet leaned over closer, "Spyware, we had our bugs everywhere, even in the FBI office. We just listen to what people say."

"I suppose you have your spyware on board the ship?" Raul asked.

Harriet looked around to be sure no one was listening, "We have a bug on the bridge, the Captain's cabin, and even your cabin. You are not supposed to tell anyone."

"You mean Nadine is recording everything?"

"No, not Nadine, she is my nanny. Rose does the recording with her receiver in her cabin."

"You have a spyware network working in the ship?"

"She hides it in her cabin behind the false partition."

"How many people are in your team?"

"Five on the ship. There's Youngsu, Mc Craw, Rose, and Nadine." Then pausing a second, "And myself."

"Do you have any outside help?"

"Yes, Detective Ramos is standing by with three of his men at the Panama Airport. He has a helicopter waiting there."

"What have you learned so far?" Raul asked.'

"We are not going through the Panama Canal, but south along the Columbian coast staying within twenty miles of shore. We are not sure what you have in mind down there. You are supposed to tell me."

"The waiter came out with the enchiladas, "Is there anything else, sir?"

Raul handed him a hundred-dollar bill, "No, I think we will be fine now."

Taking the hundred dollars, the waiter said, "I am sorry for the mix up, please come again."

Raul began eating his enchiladas. They were hot from the red sauce.

Harriet looked at hers, "Are they very hot?"

"Go ahead and eat them, you will like the taste."

Harriet took a big bite. Her eyes watered, and her tongue burned, "These are very hot."

"But you will enjoy them."

Harriet ate the second one. Her mouth burned, and she drank half of her beer trying to reduce the burning on her tongue and lips.

When they were finished, Raul said, "It is time to take you to our room."

"We have a room?" Harriet asked.

"Yes," Raul said helping her with her chair.

Harriet stood, moved closer to Raul, and whispered, "Are we going to have sex?"

"Let's not discuss it here, dear," Raul said, and led her from the patio. He took her to the far end of the resort and unlocked the door to the bungalow. He allowed Harriet to walk in first. He noticed the fruit had been sent over.

Harriet went over to the bed, turned, and fell straight back on it. She bounced some, looked up at Raul, and asked, "Are we going to have sex now?"

"No, you are going to sleep here. Now close your eyes and sleep."

Harriet closed her eyes. In moments she was fast asleep.

Raul took off her fanny pack, opened it, and pulled the contents out on the bed. He saw the money and her cell phone. It was a satellite phone. He placed the phone in his pocket. He did not want her calling anyone, when she woke up. He checked her ID and passport. It said Harriet Brown. Next, he placed ten hundred-dollar bills beside the fanny pack, "That should be enough to pay for an airplane ticket and take you home."

He leaned over. Kissed her lightly on her lips.

She opened her eyes, "Do you love me?"

Shocked, then realizing she will not remember anything later, he said, "I love you very much, and I am sorry I have to do this to you. If there was any other way, I would do it. There is a price on your head here. If anyone discovers your real name, you will be killed. Now go back to sleep."

He turned and quickly left the room. He walked back through the resort, and past the desk. He went down the hill and walked out on the dock.

The deck man saw him coming, jumped to his feet, "I watch boat good."

Raul did not say anything. His mind was still on Harriet back in the room.

"Is nice woman coming too?"

"She is staying at the resort," Raul said as he climbed into the boat.

The deck man threw him the line, and watched the boat leave the dock. "Him leave nice lady by herself."

The cat finished eating the fish and chicken. It suddenly ran out of the kitchen towards the docks right after Raul's boat had pulled away. The dock man recognized the cat and called to it. He knew who it belonged to.

The cat obediently ran out on the dock. Jumping into the man's hands, it purred a few seconds, and then died. The man was shocked thinking he somehow killed the cat.

He took it back up the hill to the waiter in the kitchen. Quietly he entered with the cat in his hands.

The waiter came, saw his cat in the man's hands, and asked in Spanish, "What happened to him?"

"I don't know," the dock man said in Spanish. "He jumped into my hands, purred a few seconds, and died."

"He doesn't like you that much. Why would he just jump into your hands?"

"I don't know. What did he eat?"

"I gave him the food the gentleman did not want thirty minutes ago," the Waiter said looking around for any leftovers. The fish was gone, but he found the salad in the leftovers for his animals. He picked it up, sniffed it. He noticed a light white powder sprinkle though out it, "The man spiked the young lady's food."

"He left without the nice lady."

"I'll check it out," the waiter said. "The man killed my cat! There's no telling what he did to her."

Christopher Charles

The waiter left the kitchen, walked to the front desk, "I believe a woman may be in trouble. I need to check her room."

"There's only one room rented today, but it was to a Senor not a woman."

"I think you better check out the room," the waiter said. "There may be a dead woman inside."

"Okay, I'll check it out, you wait here." He located the key card and walked across the resort to the bungalow. He knocked on the door, no one answered. He put his ear to the door and listened. He could hear snoring softly inside. Someone was asleep. He was not about to interrupt someone sleeping and left. Coming back to the front desk, he said, "She's sleeping. Now go back to your kitchen and leave me alone."

The waiter quietly slipped back to the kitchen. When he saw the dock man he yelled, "Go back to your docks. The woman is sleeping."

9 Ship Abduction

Raul took his boat back to the ship. It was after four by the time he had his boat lifted back in place. He placed his phone to his ear, "Sergeant Fuentas, meet me at the fantail now." He walked from the lower hatch up the stairs to the fantail and waited.

Sergeant Fuentas approached Raul, "Do I salute now, sir."

"No, we will remain undercover for a few more hours. For now, I want you to go below deck, find one Youngsu, a Mc Craw, and a Rose. They are using false names but check the ships passenger list. They are located near the engine room. They should be grouped together.

You are to remove any sources of communication that includes cell phones, and in Rose's cabin you will find spyware behind a false partition. Take all of that for storage, and place all of the occupants in Miss Cummings suite. These people are very dangerous. Please take the proper precautions. I want no one hurt. Take the men you need to accomplish this, but I do not want to alarm the passengers. I would do this all at once because they probably are in communication with one another. To make it easier, tell them I wish to speak to them. Call me when you have them in custody."

"Yes sir." The Sergeant said. "We are very close?"

"When we do our next lifeboat drill, I want you to organize the men to be sure all of the decks are clear of people. If you find anyone holding back, take them with you on the last raft off the ship. I want no one left behind."

"Yes sir, when will that be?"

3 PM tomorrow afternoon. It has to go off without a hitch. That means controlling our detectives, and their spyware."

"Yes sir, it is good to be finally getting some action."

"Patience is the key word here to have success," Raul Gonzales said.

"Yes sir."

"Dismissed!"

Sergeant Fuentes nodded, turned, and left.

Raul turned back to the rail. He looked out over the water. Tomorrow was the show. He removed one problem, now to neutralize the other problem.

Rose was in her cabin listening to her recording when she heard a knock at her door. She quickly turned the recorder off and replaced the false partition. "Who is it?" She asked.

"Steward, madam. I have a message from Miss Cummings. You are to come to her suite."

Rose knew Harriet probably just came aboard. She would have information about tomorrow. She opened the door, and said, "Tell her I am on my way up."

"Yes madam." The steward said and left.

She closed her door, secured the partition, and left the cabin. She followed the steward up the stairs.

Sergeant Fuentes came out from below, unlocked the door, removed the partition, and closed up the two suitcases with the spyware. He turned and headed out the door.

Rose noticed her earphone was suddenly off. Thinking she must have turned it off when she answered the door, she continued to follow the steward.

Mc Craw and Youngsu came in on the last tender. They were met with security as they came through the X ray machine. Their cell phones were taken and told Miss Cummings wanted to see them immediately in her suite. There had been an accident. The policemen remained back allowing the deception to work. They had already entered Nadine's suite.

Rose knocked at the door as the steward left. It was opened, allowing her inside, and closed again. She did not see the policeman behind the door at first. Two policemen came out from the other room. They took her into the bedroom.

There was another knock at the door.

Another policeman opened the door to reveal Youngsu and Mc Craw. Two more policemen came up behind them pushing guns into their ribs. One of them was Sergeant Fuentes.

"Please enter the cabin gentlemen," he said. "We would not like to create unpleasantness here."

Youngsu and Mc Craw entered the cabin along with the police officers, and the door was closed.

"You are to wait here, Senor Gonzales wishes to speak to you," Sergeant Fuentes said, "He will be here in a few minutes." He raised his phone to his ear, "They are all in Miss Cummings' cabin, sir." He did not wait for an answer and closed the phone.

Mc Craw looked around, "Where is Miss Brown?"

Rose and Nadine came out of the bedroom.

"She has not come back yet," Nadine said.

Mc Craw turned to Sergeant Fuentes, "I suppose you guys have something to do with that?"

"We have not harmed Miss Cummings," Sergeant Fuentes said. "You will have to wait for Senor Gonzales for more information. He is on his way here."

"She has some friends in very high places," Mc Craw said. "I would not do her harm."

Ignoring him, they were moved to the couch in the living room.

"Please sit down," Sergeant Fuentes said. He knew they would be less of a threat to Senor Gonzales sitting down.

As they all dropped to the couch a knock was heard at the door. An officer opened it. Raul Gonzales walked in.

He looked around, saw the spy group on the couch, "Well done Sergeant Fuentes."

Nadine started to rise from the couch when she was forced back. "What did you do with Harriet?" She yelled.

"Miss Harriet Brown is on her way home," Raul said.

When they heard him say, 'Brown', they all knew the man had too much information. He was on to them.

Looking from one to the other, he said, "I sent her back because her life is in danger down here. There is a price on her head. If Paniagua, the cartel boss, knew she was here, her life would be measured in minutes."

Mc Craw suddenly realized Raul was more than the First Mate, "Who are you? You don't sound like any ship officer."

Raul took out his wallet, opened it to reveal an ID card, "I am Colonel Raul Jimenez Morales of the Colombian National Police. We have learned Emilio Paniagua of the Columbian Cartel is planning on controlling a cruise ship, then holding it for ransom until the ship lines or the US government replaced the 800 hundred million dollars he lost. They had his product, and they took his money was the rationale. He also knows who was responsible for his loss. That is why Harriet had to leave the area immediately.

This is a desperate attempt to keep himself in business and alive. He has a lot of people to pay. Some are threatening him with his life. When we learned Captain Waverly and First Mate Williamson were suddenly killed, we knew which ship and cruise line he was targeting.

Captain Waverly was replaced with Captain Morgan, an obvious plant by the cartel. I saw to it I became the First Mate, and had my men replace the other police officers coming on the cruise.

I brought Captain Morgan over to our side, but they have his daughter and grandson. He is cooperating, but he doesn't know very much. They told him to inform them when he was going past the Panama Canal and heading south along the Columbian coast staying twenty miles out. That's all he knows. They may be boarding after that or sending a missile to blow it up. We don't know.

The plan is to unload the passengers and crew at a village I am aware of on the coast off Columbia near the Emilio Paniagua hacienda. I believe he is there, and probably why he wants the ship to sail south along the coast. I will take my men there to capture him, and the boat continues on south as if nothing has happened."

"Who's driving the ship?" Mc Craw asked.

"Captain Morgan as instructed by Paniagua, but we will leave him a life raft. It is essential Paniagua does not know we have removed the passengers and crew from the ship until after we have captured him."

"Then Harriet is safely on her way home?" Nadine asked.

"Yes, but you cannot call her because I have her phone here. I could not risk her calling in this Detective Ramos. I don't want him barging in here. This is a very delicate operation. It requires perfect timing. Do you have any questions?"

"Do we get our equipment back?" Rose asked.

"No, your equipment will be left on the ship along with your satellite phones. I cannot have you contacting this Detective Ramos or telling your government anything until we have Paniagua in custody. The lives of the passengers and crew are at stake. Once we get them off the ship, he will no longer have that leverage. He will almost certainly fulfill his threat once he sees us coming for him. The man has nothing to lose."

"We are to just sit here, and watch?" Mc Craw asked.

"I think your place is the sideline on this one, sir." Sergeant Fuentes said.

Morales (Gonzales) smiled, "If you interfere in any way, it will be dealt with quickly and severely. I will not risk the lives of the passengers and the crew because of the actions of one man. You may have the use of this cabin, but I will have my men inside and outside until the lifeboat drill is announced at 3PM tomorrow. Then you will be escorted to the rafts as quickly as possible. Please do not try and stay aboard. It will only delay our departure, and give Paniagua more time to escape, or worse destroy the ship."

"What do you think he will use?" Mc Craw asked.

"I would guess a guided missile," Morales (Gonzales) said. "If he learns we are taking the passengers and crew off the ship, he will probably send it. The man is desperate." He knew there were bombs on the ship, but that information he was keeping to himself. He did not want everyone to panic.

"Why don't you just sail straight out to sea?" Mc Craw asked.

Detective Harriet Brown

"That might be a good idea if we knew exactly what he is sending. It would have little effect on a missile, but it would stop a boarding."

"Okay, we'll do it your way," Mc Craw said.

"When do we get our phones and equipment back?" Rose asked.

"After we have captured Paniagua," Morales (Gonzales) said. "Now, I must get this ship underway. Relax, and sit this one out please." He turned and left the cabin.

Outside were five policemen. One of them had Rose's two suitcases.

"Put the spyware in Miss Cummings' cabin," Morales (Gonzales) said, "Let's keep everything together." He turned and walked fast towards the Bridge. Entering, he saw Captain Morgan waiting for him.

"Did you take care of the problem?" Captain Morgan asked.

"Yes, everything is under control, Morales (Gonzales) said, "Let's weigh-anchor!"

Si Como No Resort

Harriet slowly opened her eyes. They were blurry. She had a hard time focusing. At first, she thought she was laying on her bed on the ship, but the noises were different. She heard birds chirping and the sound of wind blowing through the trees.

Suddenly realizing she was not on the boat. She raised her head from the pillow. Her stomach felt terrible, she wanted to throw up, and stumbled out of the bed. She saw an unfamiliar bathroom. She managed to reach it, but nothing would come up. She could feel her stomach turning.

Christopher Charles

Her head pounding, she tried to make sense of where she was, and what happened to her. There was also something important she needed to remember. Her stomach tried again, but nothing would come. Finally, she gave it up.

Gradually she was able to stand by holding onto the sink. She looked into the mirror. She looked terrible. Her hair was a mess, her clothes were crumbled. She had her bathing suit on. Why would she have a bathing suit? She was trying to remember where she was.

She sat on the bed a moment with her hands holding her head trying to think. What was the last thing she did? The bathing suit told her she was in the water at some point. It was coming back some. She was on the ship, boarded Raul's boat. They went snorkeling, the shark, they had come to the resort to eat.

She tried for more, but that was it. She could not remember anything else. She looked outside. It was dark. The ship, it was leaving at 6PM. She had to get back to the ship.

She started to stand when her hand felt her fanny pack beside her. Looking down, she saw the contents of her pack on the bed, and money scattered beside it. She looked at the money. There was her money and another thousand dollars beside it. Did she provide the services for someone, and this is his payment?

"Oh my gosh! Oh my gosh, was I raped?" She checked her bathing suit again, and thought, "No, if he raped me, he would not have put my bathing suit on again. Maybe I am okay there. But why the money?"

Raul, yes, she had lunch with Raul. She ate part of his fish. That's all she remembers.

"Oh my god!" She suddenly remembered Senor Raul's Borrachero tree. "He gave her the Scopolamine drug! What time is it? It was daylight when she ate the fish."

She struggled to her feet and replaced the items in her bag. She looked in the mirror to straighten her hair the best she could and left the room. Still unstable, a bit dizzy, she started across the resort. She was about to enter a walkway that seemed to lead out when she was stopped by two men in black suits.

"Did Senor Paniagua ask for you?" The larger of the two men asked.

Harriet heard the name Paniagua. It did not register. She said, "The front desk please. I appear to be lost."

"That way!" the man said in English. He pointed the other way.

Harriet stumbled the direction the man pointed.

"She has a real hang over," The big man said.

"Yeah, someone already had fun with her."

They watched her disappear around the pool, and into another section of the resort.

Harriet worked herself to the front desk, "What time is it?"

The man looked at his watch, "Eleven ten! You alright Miss?"

"I think I missed my ship," Harriet said. "I need a boat."

The Clerk knew she was the woman asleep in the room. The man had left her stranded. "Check the dock, you might find one there."

Harriet was slowly recovering. She could stand straighter. "Thank you," she said stumbling towards the door. She reached the stairs. Using the rail, she worked her way down the steps.

Reaching the bottom, she walked faster to the docks. She saw a man sitting on a box out on the dock. She remembered him as being the man that helped her out of the boat earlier. She walked up to him, "I need a very fast boat. My ship has left me stranded."

"You nice lady man left in room?"

"Yes," Harriet said. Reaching into her purse. She pulled out the thousand dollars, "I need the fastest boat here to catch my ship and the man who left me here."

The dock man looked at the money. He remembered the dead kitty. Taking the money, he said, "The big red boat end of the dock is fastest boat."

Harriet's head was still spinning, when she turned it slightly, "How do you start it without a key?"

"Start by self," the dock man said. "No need key."

"Thank you," Harriet said turning and walking slowly further out on the dock with the dock man following her.

"I'll throw you rope," the dock man said.

"Thank you," Harriet said working her way over the gunwale (rail).

She climbed the stairs to the wheelhouse and looked around. Everything was compact compared to the ship, but it had almost all of the same equipment. She saw the button to start the boat. She pushed it. The engines came alive. She checked the fuel gauge, it was full. She also noticed it carried an extra tank. The thrusters were beside the wheelhouse, and the screens were laid out in front of her. They all came alive when she started the engines.

The dock man untied the lines and threw them onto the boat. He watched the boat head out for the open water at full throttle. He smiled. "That's one angry lady." He counted his money as he walked down the dock. He would have to seek employment somewhere else after tonight, but the thousand dollars will see him through until his next job. Maybe he will go over to Puntarenas for a while.

On the Boat

Harriet figured the time to be after eight somewhere, but she picked up fifteen minutes on the ship by leaving from the mouth of the river. She looked at the scopes. One had the coastline on it showing the boat moving along it. She moved the curser, and drew a line giving her the shortest distance to the Columbian west shore at ten miles out. The course set in; she locked the wheel that direction.

She knew the radar scope had a twenty miles radius, but the ship had a two plus hours head start. She pushed the throttles to maximum. She was going thirty-five knots plus or about thirty miles per hour. Doing the math, she would not catch the ship until tomorrow about this time. That's saying the ship is going south along the Columbian coast. If all of this is wrong, and the ship goes through the Panama Canal, she will be a fugitive running from the law until her fuel runs out somewhere in southern Columbia.

The wheel had a clicker on it, that prevented the wheel from turning. One had to place a little pressure to move it. She had her course set in. She could settle back to relax.

She tried to think how she came to be in this position. It was all very hazy. She must have told Raul everything. He probably knows about Ramos and his helicopter. That's why he took her phone. He will have her people in custody by now.

She has ruined everything. She needs to get back on that ship. She saw the phone beside the wheel, but she was not sure who would be on the other side of it. If she calls someone, they will know she took their boat. More, if it is a radio, it would not be a private line. Anyone within a twenty-mile radius would hear her. She needed to keep this quiet until she was ready.

Christopher Charles

She watched the swells in front of her. The moon was out allowing her to see clearly out into the night. She also had her lights on, but it was her radar she relied on. It would tell of any other boats in the twenty-mile area before the curvature of the Earth sent the pulse into space.

She was not sleepy. She had a good nine hours of sleep, but she did not know how she would be tomorrow. Looking out over the vastness of the ocean. She could no longer see any shore lights only the black water going on forever. The course indicator was her only reality telling her where she was going.

Before she reached the ship, she would have to contact Ramos. Someone had to know what was happening before she boarded. They could take her into custody immediately.

On the Ship

The guards in Harriet's cabin and outside the cabin were changed every two hours. The captives were allowed to move around, but not leave the cabin. All of their phones and spyware were in the suitcases by the door.

They whispered between each other.

"Should we make a breakout of here?" Mc Craw asked.

"And go where?" Rose asked. "If the man is right, we need to protect the passengers and crew, the reason for coming aboard."

"He is a Columbian policeman, and rather high ranked," Nadine said. "What he says sounds reasonable, but I do not believe Harriet just went home. She's the one I am worried about. I feel the man lied on that part."

"We do not even know where she is," Rose said. "He took her phone, so we cannot communicate with her."

"I don't like just sitting here doing nothing like this whole trip," Mc Craw said.

"Miss Brown come back," Youngsu said, "You see."

"She better before three tomorrow," Nadine said, "Once we are in the jungle, no one will find us."

"Maybe she found Ramos," Mc Craw said. "He could fly her in with his helicopter."

Captain's Cabin

Captain Morgan was laying on his bed when he heard the knock on his door.

"Come in!" He yelled.

Morales (Gonzales) opened the door, entered the cabin, "I thought I would check in on you before turning in, sir."

"You still playing the game, Senor Gonzales?"

"Yes, we will continue the game as you call it until the passengers and crew are safely ashore."

"What about me?"

"You have the life raft," Morales (Gonzales) said.

"If they board the ship?"

"Then you become their prisoner much like you were before when they took your daughter and grandson. I cannot change that until I capture him. You have to keep up the pretense until then."

"What about my family?"

"They can be saved if we are fast enough, and Paniagua does not become aware we are coming for him."

"It he sends a missile, then what?"

Christopher Charles

"He's going to bargain with the US Government. That may give us enough time to reach him before he does anything."

"How about if we bring the FBI in on this?"

"And do what? Go where? Get your family killed?" Morales asked. "They do not know anymore, nor can they do more than what we are doing, protecting the people."

On the Boat

Harriet could not see anything for hours now. The radar revealed a few blips, but they were too small, and too early to be the ship. She followed the course she had set in. The wheelhouse had a high stool. She took advantage of this at times to rest her legs. Her cramped left leg seemed to be better.

She was analyzing her feelings for Raul. He intentionally drugged and left her stranded. Where was she to go? The resort was good thirty miles from Puntarenas. The other guests at the resort did not seem too friendly. The men in the black suits were carrying guns. She did not see them, but you can always tell by their look. They were protecting someone important.

If she did make it to Puntarenas, she would have to figure a way to leave there. No, he left her in a bad position. She knew it was coming, yet she walked right into it. Maybe she trusted him again because she believed he owed her for saving his life.

That was foolish thinking. If the shark had taken a bite out of him, she would not be in this position. He would be in a hospital if he survived, and she would be by his side. Maybe she would be deserting him? No, it was not in her nature. She would stay with him.

Did she love him? Did she even know what that means? She's never been in love before. Could anyone who loves you desert you in this fashion? She couldn't. She would sacrifice her life to save him. She has already done it twice. Does that mean she loves him? Has he shown any real love other than wanting her sexually?

He didn't take advantage of her when he had her in the room barely conscious willing to do anything he asked. Yes, he could have taken advantage of her, but he didn't. Does that mean he loves her, or does it mean he just did not have time to take advantage of her? Worse yet, he didn't think she was worth taking advantage of.

No, he liked her when he danced with her. She felt it. He could not hide it, but maybe that was only sex making its move. Their energy flowed so well as they danced, it left her weak. She knew he was affected the same way. That must mean he loves her, but he left her stranded.

Maybe he really was protecting her by taking her out of the action, but he could have done that in a better location where she might have contacted someone for help.

No, Mr. Harold O' Brian set her up. He told Raul who she was. All of Raul actions from that point on were related to that information. He was giving her attention to get information. Boy did she give it to him. Their whole operation blown giving Raul full control.

When he learned she was kidnapped by Captain Morgan's people, she could very easily have been stranded in Acapulco. What did her hero do? Did he come to her rescue? Did he defend her or his Captain? She should have known then not to trust him.

Nadine told her not go ashore with him this close to the event, but she was so sure of herself. She could handle him. Besides, he loved her, right? Yeah, that's why he deserted her in the middle of nowhere.

The sun peeked. She could see the light fill the horizon before the bright light appeared. It filled the whole half of the sky. It was beautiful. She checked her course. She was good. The fuel tank showed a fourth down. She would have enough fuel to reach the ship saying she found it in the thousands of miles around her. Yes, the sunrise was beautiful.

She looked at the phone beside her. It had a switch. She pushed it. She heard noise and people speaking over it. It was alive. It was like she thought, it was radio not a phone. Anyone could hear your voice. She did not want to warn the ship of her approach.

Ship Bridge

The boat had passed the Panama Canal. Some of the passengers started to complain. They were told they would see the canal in the daylight as advertised. It was already approaching 3PM. They had moved to within two miles of shore. The trees could be seen in the distance.

Morales (Gonzales) nodded to Captain Morgan, "It is time, sir." He opened his phone, waited a moment, "Sergeant Fuentes, put your men into position. Call me back when you are ready."

"Yes sir."

Ten minutes later Morales' phone rang. "Yes, good, standby." He turned to the First Officer, "Stop the Ship!"

The ships engines went into reverse as Morales sounded the lifeboat drill, "This is not a drill. Everyone enter your lifeboats immediately. We have practiced this many times. There is no need to panic, just move along rapidly to your boat."

People quickly grabbed their life jackets. They had been keeping them close at hand from all their previous drills. The crew ran to their stations. The first boat down was Morales' (Gonzales's) boat with Chief Myers at the wheel and another security officer. They moved in close to the opened lower hatch waiting for a raft to come out. Three other hatches opened on the side of the ship as the rafts were moved into place. The supplies were right behind each one.

The first four rafts struck the water. The lines were tied to the cleats. The lever was pulled to inflate it. In seconds four huge rafts filled the openings of the lower hatches. Two men at each hatch jumped aboard as the others came in behind them with the supplies. Those assigned to each raft climbed aboard. The security officers untied the lines, threw them aboard the raft, and sent them adrift.

Morales' boat came in. It pulled away any raft not moving from the ship.

The boats were being lowered. The first one was thrown the line, and the raft was theirs. Moving fast, Chief Myers picked up another raft now floating free from the ship.

Most of the boats were down looking for rafts to tow. Rafts were filled and sent loose from the ship. Chief Myers kept the boats coming in to collect their rafts. When one raft drifted too far or was too close to the ship, he would take the line, towing it to a boat.

The boats were down in the ten minutes, but the rafts were slower since they had only four openings.

Morales walked to Harriet's cabin. When he entered, he saw them all standing looking out over the balcony. "Ready to go?" He asked.

They all turned his direction and moved inside.

"Follow the officers to your raft," Morales said, "We need to get this ship moving again before our Mr. Paniagua figures out, we stopped to unload the passengers. Please don't try any heroics, it will only delay our departure, and place the passengers and crew in more danger."

Harriet's people followed the officers to the raft below.

Christopher Charles

Morales looked around the suite. He threw Harriet's phone on the couch. He saw the two suitcases with the spyware next to the door. Satisfied, he closed the door, and walked back to the Bridge. He met the nervous Captain Morgan.

"Are they all off," Morgan asked looking out the window at the all the boats in the water.

"There were a few stragglers, but they will all be off shortly." Morales said.

"What about my raft?"

"It will be at the first hatch waiting for you. You can handle this?"

"They have my daughter and grandson."

"Sorry, but I need to leave," Morales said. His phone buzzed in his pocket.

Opening it, he said, "On my way down now." He turned back to Captain Morgan, and continued, "The ship is empty. It is all yours, Captain, good luck."

"Thanks, you should be safe enough," Captain Morgan said.

"You know what I need to do, and you know what you need to do. If we do this right, we will both come out of this along with your family."

"It doesn't mean I have to like it."

"No one likes it," Morales said leaving the Bridge. He walked down to the lower deck. His boat was waiting for him. All of the davits had been raised back into position. Only this last hatch waited to be closed. He released the line, stepped aboard his boat with Chief Myers and the security officer. Raising his arm high, he brought it down, shouting, "Let's move them out!"

Detective Harriet Brown

Captain Morgan watched the Morales (Gonzales') boat pull away and pressed the button to close the hatch. He felt deserted. He knew he was on a doomed ship. Automatically he pushed the thrusters to full forward. The ship left the passengers and crew behind. He took the ship straight out to sea fifteen miles, and then headed down the coast.

He picked up his phone, pushed the speed dial, and a voice came on the line.

Phone:

"We are in Columbian waters moving down the coast fifteen miles out."

Pause:

Yes, I have all the power on. What do you want me to do now?"

The phone hung up. They didn't tell him anything, except to turn the lights out. He still did not know what they were going to do. A picture came in over the computer. It revealed his daughter and grandson bound laying on the floor.

He didn't have to ask any more questions.

Emilio Paniagua Board Room

Paniagua with eight other men making up his cartel were sitting around a rectangle table looking at a large screen hanging at the end of the room.

A man, Peter Walsh, a computer expert, was sitting behind a computer halfway down the table.

"We have the call, send the message," Paniagua said. He smiled as he held up his switch. It was a two-piece lever that was connected at one end and held apart at the other end with a spring. A small button would connect with another one when the lever closed completing the switch.

"Now let them sweat." He said.

Walsh pushed a few buttons on his computer. A message was sent to Harold O' Brian's computer. He received it at 4PM, but he did not read it until 6 PM.

It read:

> We have your ship and all of its three thousand plus passengers and crew. You have until tomorrow at twelve noon to place 800 million dollars in the following account, or the ship and its passengers and crew will disappear. Senor Emilio Suarez Paniagua Cartel is owed the money from the US Government for product it illegally took.

A Swiss bank account was listed on the bottom of the page.

O' Brian fell back in his chair. He reread the page again. Then he lifted his phone. He tried calling the ship. There was no answer. He tried calling Harriet's phone, but it had been turned off.

He knew by this time the ship should be through the canal. He called to see if they had gone through. They answer came back negative. Finally, he called the FBI.

The call was directed to Assistant Director Clark. He picked up the phone, placed it on speaker:

Phone Conversation:

"Yes!"

"This is Harold O' Brain. I manage the Norsewegian Cruise Line. One of our cruise ships going to the Panama Canal is missing. I just received an E-mail from a Cartel Boss named Emilio Paniagua. He threatens to sink our ship with all of its passengers and crew unless we come up with

800 million dollars before noon tomorrow. I don't know if this is real, but I cannot reach anyone on the ship."

"Do you have the note?"

"Yes, they sent it by E-mail, I will forward it to you."

Clark gave him his E-mail address and called in Special Agent Ted Brooks. He arrived as the note came in over the computer. They both read it.

"800 hundred million dollars," Brooks said. "The man does not want much.

Clark tried to call Harriet, but her phone did not answer. He dialed Detective Ramos next:

Phone: Conversation:

"Have you heard from Miss Brown?"

"I've been expecting a call," Ramos said. "She said something would happen about this time. We are ready to move out here."

"Where are you, and how many are with you?" Clark asked.

"We have one helicopter and four of us," Ramos said. "We're at the Panama City Airport. What's happened?"

"A ship is missing. I believe it is the one Miss Brown is on. We have a ransom note from a Mr. Paniagua demanding 800 million dollars by tomorrow noon, or he will sink the ship with the passengers and crew aboard."

"She told us, sir. It's too bad no one there would listen to her," Ramos said.

"We had no evidence to move on," Clark said, "We do now. Do you have any idea where the ship is?"

"It's within a two-hundred-mile radius from where I am," Ramos said, "Maybe less. She said the ship was going to head south along the coast of Columbia."

"How do you know that?"

"That's why I am down here. She's supposed to call me. I've been waiting, but now I am suspecting something has happened to her. Especially now when you have the ransom note, and she has not called."

"How many people can your helicopter carry?"

"It's a commercial helicopter," Ramos said. "We can carry eight including the pilot."

"I'll see what I can do to find you some help, and maybe get a Navy ship down there."

"If she calls, we are not waiting," Ramos said.

"I'm only trying to find you some help," Clark said. "You do what you need to do."

"Yes sir."

"Call me if you hear anything," Clark said, and closed the phone. He looked at Brooks, "You better inform the Director. I think the President should be informed also. I will see what the navy will do."

"Yes sir," Brooks said leaving the room.

Clark dialed the Commander of Pacific Fleet, Admiral Theodor Higgens:

Phone:

"Admiral, Clark here, that matter I was telling you about earlier, well now we have an incident. The Norsewegian Cruise Line has lost their Panama Canal cruise ship two hours ago. It is being held for ransom. It will be sunk unless they receive 800 million dollars by tomorrow noon."

Pause:

"Yes sir, we know, he signed it Emilio Paniagua. He's the cartel boss we confiscated the thirty tons of cocaine from. Yes, 800 million dollars was removed from the table as well. I think this is his way of getting payment."

Pause:

"We have an agent on the ship, sir, but her phone has been compromised. We have not been able to reach her."

Pause:

"Yes sir, we believe it is within a two-hundred-mile radius of Panama City, and probably heading south along the coast of Columbia. Do we have anything in that area?"

Pause:

"A frigate two-hundred-miles out from Panama City is the only thing?"

Pause:

"I know we have a treaty with Panama, sir, but is there any Navy Seals in training in the area? I have a helicopter with four empty seats at the Panama City Airport."

Pause:

"Yes, I know, any military operation will have to come from the sea, and that's the frigate. How about sending some Navy Seal helicopters down into the area?"

Pause:

"No, I don't know exactly where, but we could get them moving south to be close when I do know where."

Pause:

"Thank you, sir, I know you will do your best." Clark hung up his phone as Brooks walked in. He looked up, "Did you have any luck with the President?"

"The Director called him. He said the President was angry. I think he was ready to send the military into Columbia. He said it is not the United States policy to pay ransom. He told the Director to remind the Columbia government of what happened after 911."

"It's time to give General Ernesto Lopez a call. The ship is on his coast somewhere, and it's his people doing the blackmailing." He dialed a direct number to General Lopez.

Phone:

"This is Assistant Director Clark of the FBI. We have a problem."

Pause:

"Yes, the Los Angeles branch. It seems one of your cartel bosses, one called Emilio Paniagua is holding one of our cruise ships for 800 million-ransom. He threatens to sink the ship with all those aboard numbering over three thousand people including woman and children."

Pause:

"Yes, it was him. He signed his name. I don't have to remind you how my country will feel about this if Paniagua does sink the ship. It will be another 911."

Pause:

"I was told the ship is moving down your west coast."

Pause:

"Yes, I know we could pay the ransom, but our government has a policy not to pay ransom."

Pause:

"I know it has been done quietly in the past, but this is wide open. If we pay this one, we will have every tourist ship held for ransom. It will not be paid."

Pause:

"You could try and contact him, or you could send out some of your military ships or boats to find the ship."

Pause:

"I don't know what you should do, if you find it. It's too early for that, but you could locate it."

Pause:

"Yes, the President is very angry. You go killing thousands of Americans, you can expect retaliation to be swift and deadly."

Pause:

"Yes, contacting Senor Paniagua would be a good idea. If this gets out, you will destroy your tourist money. You should think about that."

Pause:

"Thank you, sir, I know you will do your best."

Columbian Coast Village

The boats towed the rafts towards shore with Gonzales' red boat leading the way. People from the small village came out of their homes to look at the armada approaching them.

Gonzales stood high on his boat surveying the beach ahead. Chief Myer was standing with him.

"I need you to organize the camp quickly before it gets dark. We will be staying in the tents we have brought along. They need to be organized into rows, and latrines need to be built immediately. Some of the passengers can help in the process. Those in the village have been notified. They will be cooperative, but the passengers will not be staying in their homes. They are barely existing with what they have, we are not here to make that worse."

"Yes sir. We have less than two hours to complete everything."

"Then get your lighting up first and lay out your tents second. Have the cooks make a fire pit, and start the food coming. Make this an adventure for the passengers. If any of you can play an instrument, it would be helpful."

"No one has brought any instruments as per your instructions, sir."

"See what the locals have," Morales said. "I'm sure they entertain themselves somehow. You will be in charge of setting up the camp, and of course the first and second officers will be in charge of the passengers."

"Where will you be, sir?"

"I am taking my officers, and going after the man that did this, but you are to keep this confidential. I don't need someone warning him. There is someone among the crew that is working for him. Since we don't know who that is, we will say I am leaving to find us another ship. I should be back in two days at the most."

"Yes sir, but they may wonder why we don't use the radio."

"The radios went dead on the ship, and all phones need a tower to work from. If you find anyone trying to use his phone, it is to be removed. I will not have our quarry escape."

"Yes sir."

"What's going to happen to our ship, sir?"

"If I am too late, the ship will be sunk," Morales said. "I am trying to prevent that."

"Were there explosives aboard, sir?"

"That is a possibility," Morales said. "It could also be a boarding or a drone missile, but the passengers and crew are safe."

They were approaching the shore. "Have all the officers meet me on the beach, then select your people to set up camp"

"Yes sir."

Morales' boat was carried to shore with the incoming wave. The village people quickly pulled it further up on the beach. The rafts came in first. The village people responded. They began pulling the rafts further up on the sand and helping the people out of the rafts.

Chief Myers, taking charge, had the boats brought in. They were pulled up higher to prevent the later tide taking them out to sea. The passengers were helped out of the boats and assembled into one large group for Chief Myers.

Standing on a fallen tree trunk, Chief Myers began directing people to get the camp set up before the darkness set in. He had his crew and passengers working together. The supplies were taken out of the rafts and the lighting was set up.

The police officers began the heavy work setting up the larger tents that housed the kitchen and cooking areas.

A plan was laid out for the tents and cooking facilities. Chief Myers had a latrine detail set in place. He gave the detail shovels and five of the tents.

Morales had the ship's officers in front of him numbering over a hundred. He looked them over. He wasn't going to tell them the situation, but a fabrication was not going to work. "This camp must be set up before dark. I have Chief Myers in charge of that. The police officers and myself will be leaving camp when it is dark. This will leave the First Officer in charge. Captain Morgan has taken our ship out to sea where one Emilio Paniagua plans to sink it. He has a life raft with him. Are there any questions?"

"How do you know he plans to sink the ship, sir?"

"I am Colonel Morales of the Columbian National Police. We have been aware of Senor Paniagua plans for some time. My men and myself will be leaving immediately to try and prevent the sinking. It was necessary to protect the passengers and crew first if I should fail. You are not allowed to let anyone to use his cell phone. You in the security section, this will be your responsibility. I am mainly worried about the satellite phones. We could still have some of his agents in the crew or passengers. I need absolute secrecy for us to be successful. Now, are there any more questions?"

No one said a word.

"Then let's get this camp organized. I plan on leaving immediately."

The group broke up. They began taking different sections of the camp to organize as directed by the First Officer. It was amazing how well the planning had gone into this. They had enough supplies to last them for five days. Morales (Gonzales) believed they would be rescued in two days.

The sun was setting, Morales wanted to be on his way. He didn't want to be walking through the jungle in the dark. Leading his men, they headed straight inland going through the jungle following a path he had cut earlier that month.

It was dark when they reached the dirt road. He quickly removed the brush revealing two trucks, a car, and weapons. His men quickly armed themselves and climbed aboard the two trucks. Morales had one of his men drive his car in front of the trucks. The army caravan moved out travelling over the dirt road. They had to cover a hundred miles before morning to reach the Paniagua's hacienda. He wanted surprise and that meant darkness.

Mc Craw and company watched the policemen leave following Morales.

"I wonder where he is going?" Mc Craw asked. He took a flashlight and quietly followed them. It was easy. They made a great deal of noise going through the jungle.

He watched them uncover their vehicles and pick up their weapons. He thought about following them, but he did not see how he was going to do that. When they were out of sight, he headed back to camp.

Morales' phone vibrated. He opened, and heard General Lopez's voice:

Phone Conversation:

"Yes sir."

"I received a call from the Director of the FBI. He wanted answers, and he threatened invasion. I assume you have things under control."

"Yes sir, the passengers and crew are ashore, and the ship is going south along the Columbian coast. I am presently pursuing the second phase of the plan. I should be at the Paniagua's Hacienda in three hours, then it will be over."

"Good," General Lopez said, "Call me when it is completed. I don't want the US Military coming down here."

"Yes sir, I have everything under control." Morales said.

Assistant Director Clark called Detective Ramos:

Phone Conversation:

"Ramos, I have two-helicopters filled with Navy Seals on the way down to you. That will give you the frigate and the Seals in your area at 2300 hours."

"I don't know where to send them yet, sir, but I will call before 2300 hours." Ramos replied.

On the Boat

Harriet had the boat at full throttle for sixteen plus hours now hoping to find the ship. Her back ached. Every muscle in her body was fatigued. She needed to lay down somewhere and sleep. It had been daylight for some time. She enjoyed the sunrise over the ocean, but now she was tired.

She was driving the boat hard south, but it would be only luck if she saw the ship. The ocean was a very big place. She could easily pass it. That was her biggest fear. The ship could move into any port, and she would drive the boat right past it.

It was getting late in the afternoon. This was the time she should be seeing the ship if she calculated it right. She was moving down the Columbian coast staying within ten miles of shore. That would allow her to see anything moving along the coast thirty miles out.

Then she heard a ping on the radar screen. It was big enough to be the ship, but it was not moving allowing her to gain on it rapidly. Her adrenalin kicked in. She was no longer tired.

After twenty-five minutes the ship started moving again, but now she could see it very well on the screen. She calculated she would intercept the ship a little after 5PM.

Then she realized she had another problem. How was she going to stop the ship, and how was she going to board her? They are going to think she is a pirate boat trying to board. Should she radio them? Let them know who she is?

She was sure her boat had been reported stolen by now. The description, a large red and white boat, would stand out in anyone's mind. They may allow her to board only to arrest her for stealing the boat. She had not been thinking clearly for some time. It was the drug taking away her good judgment.

She could see the ship in the distance. It had moved twenty miles out from the coast. She was on an angle to it. She still was not close enough to really identify it, but the radar said it was large.

She still wondered why it had stopped for twenty-five minutes allowing her to catch up. She was sure they could see her now trying to reach them.

Suddenly the ship slowed. It came to a stop as her boat rapidly shortened the distance. The lower deck hatch opened. All of the ships' outside lights were off. This made her even more nervous. They are now expecting her. They do not know it is her yet, they only know her boat is trying to reach them. She flipped the radio on, but no one was trying to hail her. This added to her apprehension. She did not see anyone hanging over the rails, but she allowed this to slide.

She thought about trying to hail the ship, but then they would know it was her on the boat. She pulled up beside the ship's lower hatch. She did not see anyone. Where was the security officer? She thought she should at least warrant one.

She threw the bumpers over the side and brought the boat in tight. She quickly jumped aboard the ship taking the bow line with her. She ran for the cleat to secure the boat before it drifted out. She ran back to the boat, took the stern line, securing the back half of the boat to the cleat inside the hatch.

Feeling a little better, but still very apprehensive, she entered the ship. They were allowing her to board, but where was everyone? She did not see anyone in the corridors or on the decks. The only thing she saw out of place was a large raft in the middle of the hatch. It had not been inflated.

She knew there was someone piloting the ship. That someone was on the ship's Bridge. She headed that direction. Climbing the stairs, she walked onto the Bridge.

Captain Morgan was waiting for her. He was as surprised as she was?

"Where did you come from?" He asked.

"From that boat beside the ship?"

"That's the Cartel Boss, Emilio Paniagua's boat. Is he aboard the ship?" Captain Morgan asked in a confused voice.

"Where is everyone?" Harriet asked.

"I'll answer that question, if you will answer mine," Captain Morgan shouted, "Is Paniagua on this ship?"

"I am the only one boarding the ship. There is no one else," Harriet said. "Now, where is everyone?"

"They were taken off the ship over an hour ago. Presently they are setting up camp on the beach."

"Why did you think Paniagua was aboard?"

"Because this ship is doomed! I was instructed to keep this ship moving south along the Columbian coast or he would kill my daughter and my grandson." He revealed his daughter and grandson tired up on computer screen. "That's why we evacuated everyone to the beach."

"What are you expecting?"

A missile or a boarding, but it seems the boarding is out," Captain Morgan said.

"But why?"

"You don't know?"

Harriet shook her head. She had the radio off until a few minutes ago.

"He's blackmailing the cruise shipping lines for 800 million dollars, or he sinks the ship." Captain Morgan said. "They are not going to give it to him, so you take your best guess. Now I've got to get this ship moving again, or he will blow up the ship or worse yet, kill my family." He turned, and pushed the throttles forward engaging the engines.

Harriet looked at him a moment. Her mind worked again. The Cartel Boss, Paniagua was not going to board the ship, she had his boat. There was more there, but she had to keep the thought going. That leaves blowing it up, but how. Missiles or drone would need a base. There was nothing but jungle. Then you would have to know the location of your moving target before you sent it off. That's way too chancy.

Then it struck her, bombs hidden on the ship! She remembered the car bombs. The pulsating blue light and antennas to receive the satellite signal to explode. All of this only took seconds as she was running down the steps.

The main lights were out leaving the red emergency lights working. These were battery operated and came on automatically when the main lights no longer function. It left the passageways full of shadows. Normally she would be very apprehensive descending the stairs, but she knew no one was aboard the ship except the Captain and herself, she tried to reason.

She finally found Rose's cabin, but it was empty. The partition had been removed. Someone had found the spyware. She suddenly felt guilty because she knew she was the one who told them where to look. She moved to Youngsu and Mc Claw's cabin. She looked under the bed and smiled. There was a small partition with Youngsu's bag inside. She had not known where he kept it and couldn't tell Raul.

She quickly retrieved the bag and threw the contents on his bed. Then she saw his scanner for detecting signals radiating off small transmitters. She turned it on. It worked. Carrying it, she left the cabin, moving back towards the engine room. Her mind remembering the First Mate was killed in the engine room. Maybe he had discovered someone planting a bomb there, and they killed him.

She had never been in the engine room before. It was a huge place. She missed that in her tour of the ship. It was spooky. Machines running by themselves. Concentrating on the scanner, she moved around the machinery and pipes.

Suddenly the meter came alive. Following the pointer, she had to remove the floor plates to reach the bilges. There taped to a large pipe was a four-pound bomb with a pulsating blue light with a small antenna on top of it.

Slowly she reached for the bomb removing the tape holding it. It was probably meant to go off if the antenna was removed. She placed the bomb on the deck and searched the engine room for another bomb. She found it on the other side hidden up under a pipe near the bilges. It was meant to tear out a large portion of the ship's bottom.

Disconnecting it from the pipe, she moved quickly back to the first bomb. Her arms were shaking. Picking it up, she headed for the lower hatch with the two of them. She had no plan, but it was past 6PM. The sun had gone down. If she threw them overboard, the others may go off still on board. When she reached the lower hatch, she saw the boat, and decided to place the bombs in the boat. Leaving the signal scanner behind, she leaped aboard the boat. She secured the bombs to the deck using the same tapes. She was trying to concentrate. Keep your mind busy. Don't think about the bomb, she told herself.

Picking up her signal scanner, she ran back inside, allowing her meter to work. She picked up a faint signal forward. The meter wanted to point back to the boat, but she pushed on towards the front of the ship.

She found another bomb in the one of the crew's quarters below the water line. It was against the bulkhead under the bed. It was difficult to get off, but she managed it. She looked around the room quickly before she left. In the dim light she found another bomb partially put together in one of the cabinets. It did not have an antenna, but she picked it up as she headed for the upper deck.

She took them to the boat alongside the ship. Nervous, she could feel her heart pumping hard as she taped the bombs to the deck. How much time does she have? How many bombs are there?

She leaped back aboard the ship, picked up the scanner, and move forward again. She was no longer nervous about the dark shadows in the hallways. Her time must be running out. She started to run. The pointer led her to the officer's quarters, the signal meter pointed towards Gonzales's cabin. She entered and found a ten-pound bomb stuck up inside an overhead cabinet. The antenna was sticking up out of it. The blue light filled the cabinet. Raul Gonzales had to be aware of the bomb.

She eased the large bomb out of the cabinet carrying it with the meter back to the boat. She did not see any way to secure the bomb to the deck. She took it up into the wheelhouse and placed it in the large cabinet below the wheel. She forced the cabinet close. Satisfied, she ran back to the ship. Jumping aboard, she picked up the scanner, and headed inside. Her adrenalin was pumping.

She was back in Gonzales cabin. The scanner picked up the small spyware Youngsu had planted. She moved on looking for larger signals. Nothing more was coming in.

She started up towards the Captain's cabin and the Bridge, when she heard the boat engines fire up. Someone was taking the boat. She ran back to the hatch, but the boat was moving out away from the boat. The raft in the middle of the hatch was missing. He took that too.

She was stranded again alone on the big ship. This time she did it to herself. Then remembering the bombs on the boat, she ran up to the Bridge. The radio had been destroyed. There was no way for a signal to reach her, and there was no way to send a signal out. Someone had smashed it with something heavy. Why would he do that? What about his family? He probably figures I will keep the ship moving to avoid being blown up.

The ship was dark. All of the outside lights were off.

The wheel had been locked in place. She checked the course indicator. She saw where the ship had stopped earlier. She unlocked the wheel, and turned the ship, using the two throttles to the reverse engines. The ship slowed and turned quickly. Once she was back on the course and moving towards the target, she locked the wheel in place. She needed to finish searching the ship.

Taking the signal scanner, she returned to her search for more bombs. She spent the next twenty minutes searching the ship. All she found was the spyware Youngsu had placed. She collected what she could of that to avoid confusing the scanner.

Coming up to her cabin, she threw the scanner on the couch, and saw her phone. Feeling a big relief, she picked it up. Finally, a break, she turned it on, and saw everyone had been trying to reach her.

Suddenly she felt uneasy knowing the ship was steering itself. She walked quickly back to the Bridge. Everything was okay, but the ship was off course slightly. She brought it back. Feeling better, she called Ramos.

Phone Conversation:

"Hello, Paul, sorry about not getting back to you?"

"Where have you been," Ramos almost yelled. "Do you know what is happening?"

"Some of it, but Gonzales knocked me out with the Scopolamine drug. What's going on?"

"Like you suspected, an Emilio Paniagua has threatened to blow up the ship unless he is given eight hundred million dollars by tomorrow noon. The President isn't going to give it to him, and the navy will be in the area at 2300 hours or eleven O' Clock tonight. You will be getting one frigate and two helicopters with Seals aboard. That's the best we can do. Now, what do you have?"

"I have the ship, but the passengers and crew have been dropped off on the Columbian beach. There were five bombs on the ship that I have found so far with a scanner. Now, I need you to meet me where the passengers and crew are. I am taking the ship there."

"You are on the ship alone?"

"Yes, Captain Morgan took off with my boat leaving me stranded on the ship."

"What about the bombs?"

"I placed them on Paniagua's boat."

"Are you going to tell him he is carrying the bombs?"

"I can't, he destroyed the radio," Harriet said. "Not a very nice man."

"How did you get Paniagua's boat?"

"A long story."

"Where is Gonzales?"

"Probably with the passengers. You need to inform Clark where they are and have him direct the ship there. No one is to board the ship until we have captured Paniagua. He may have a few bombs aboard I am not aware of. I can give you the coordinates, or you can follow my phone signal."

"How do I pick up your signal?"

"Have Clark give it to you. I have a satellite phone. I am on a direct line to the beach. Find my phone, take a couple of readings, and draw a line to the beach. That's where the ship, passengers, and crew will be."

"How long before you arrive?"

"I should be there in about an hour," Harriet said. "I will call you when I am."

"Okay, I will get my end going. Do you expect a problem from Gonzales?"

"Yes, that is why I want you there."

"Okay, on my way," Ramos said, "Thank god you called."

"Yes, it was nice to hear your voice too," She said softly, and felt a tear drop.

She closed her phone and began thinking how she was going to handle Raul. The ten-pound bomb in his cabinet said he knew about the bombs on board the ship. That's what prompted him to unload the passengers and crew. It was no last-minute thought. He had been practicing the lifeboat procedures all the way out here. He knew exactly what he was doing. Drugging her, he put her out of action, and neutralized her team. Then he proceeded to develop his plan. She did not see where he figured into the blackmail. What was he to gain?

Emilio Paniagua Board Room

Paniagua looked at the large screen. He could see the ship moving along the coast. The transmitter antenna on the bombs went to the ships transmitting antenna sending its signal to his receiver. He could see it stop for some reason, then it moved on. He received the call right after that. Maybe there was some discussion, but after he had Walsh send the picture of his daughter and grandson, it seemed to motivate him. The ship has been going steadily down the coast of Columbia.

There was another short stop, a slight burring of the transmission, but it disappeared. The ship was underway in a few minutes. He did not know the bombs' antenna were now using the transmitting antenna on his own boat. He felt better seeing the dot on his screen moving further south.

"Walsh, what was that burring on the screen?" He asked.

"Could be anything, sir. He may have had a power surge interfering with the transmission."

Paniagua smiled, raised the large switch in his hand, "Yes, he had the power of God in his hands. They cooperate, or they lose everything."

Detective Ramos called Assistant Director Clark:

"Assistant Director Clark, how can I help you?"

"Ramos here, sir, I have heard from Miss Brown. She has control of the ship and the passengers are on the beach."

"That girl is amazing. Where are they?"

"She said to trace her phone signal every ten minutes, and you will be directed to them. She is taking the ship to that location now. She says not to board the ship until she can neutralize Paniagua. She found bombs on board."

"Where are you going?"

"I am to meet her at the location, sir, after you give me the location. I am on my way now."

"Where is Paniagua?"

"She didn't say, but I will find out when I land, sir."

"I need to inform the Navy."

"Just direct them to the location, sir." Ramos said, "She was quite definite about that."

"Yes, the passengers and crew are the most important at the moment. I will direct the Navy frigate there. Where do you want the Helicopter Seals?"

"Just keep them coming south to the passengers' site. I'm less than an hour from there."

"Okay, thank god she is alive. You had me worried for a while."

"Yes sir, I will call you when I land."

"Good Luck!"

Ramos folded his phone. He knew Clark had deep feelings for her. I wonder how he would feel if he knew about Raul Gonzales. He already knew he didn't like the man.

10 Taking the Prize

On the ship Harriet could see the glow of the fires on the beach. Otherwise it was pitch dark. Approaching the beach, she slowed the engines. Using the sonar, she checked the depth of the water. She did not want to run aground. Her radar revealed she was 2,000 plus meters from the shoreline.

When the depth read one hundred feet, she reversed the engines. When the ship was slow enough, she placed one throttle in reverse, and the other one forward turning the ship in place. She remembered that.

He arms shook as she dropped the bow anchor allowing the chain to go out reversing the engines slightly to help it along. She prayed she was doing it correctly. When she had a thousand feet out, she dropped the stern anchor. Then she recaptured the bow chain taking in five hundred feet using the engines slightly. Finished, she shut down the engines. She left the lights off except for the red battery lights in the halls. She did not want to reveal her presence.

She went to her suite following the red emergency lights. Leaving the door open she was able to see enough to retrieve her forty-five revolver and the two clips from the vent. She still had her bathing suit on. She found some clean clothes and placed them along with her purse in a small backpack. She kept her tennis shoes on.

She worked her way to the lower hatch, opened the locker, retrieved the snorkel, face mask, and fins. She found a waterproof bag, and slipped in her clothes, shoes, purse, and revolver. Sealing it, she placed them in the backpack. Putting the pack on, she adjusted the straps. She slipped the fins and face mask with the snorkel on. She was ready to go.

Looking out over the water, she could see the fires on the beach. Closer to the water it seemed further away. Her shakes started up again as she stood on the edge of the hatch. It was a long swim. Taking a deep breath, she dropped backward into the water, holding her mask on.

Once in the water she adjusted herself placing her head into the water. She blew the tube clear of water and took off swimming for the shore. She did not have to turn her head to breathe. The snorkel allowed her to keep a forward position getting the most from each stroke. The pack on her back placed her slightly lower in the water, but it took on a buoyance of its own. This allowed her body to remain level creating less friction.

She kept one arm out in front of her at all times. This kept her body level. One arm went through the entire stroke and came to rest on the other hand. Then the hand took its turn going one full stroke coming to rest on the other hand in front of her. This allowed her to move very fast through the water taking advantage of the glide with each stroke.

She was 2,000 meters, or one mile plus from the beach. It was going to take a while. She would look up every twenty strokes to be sure she was on course. She found herself drifting with the current. She had to adjust. She would be swimming more than 2,000 meters if the current continued, she thought.

Detective Harriet Brown

At first frightened when she found herself in the dark water all alone. What was down there in the darkness? It became more profound when the ship disappeared. She had to get past the fear developing fast. She forced herself to concentrate on her breathing and her strokes. This kept her mind busy. She was not drowning. She was staying afloat and moving towards the beach.

When she looked at the lights from the ship, the beach did not seem so far, but from the water everything changed. She could only see a glow. She headed that direction.

Emilio Paniagua Hacienda

Morales (Gonzales) approached the ranchero. He could see the lights up on the hill. He had the two trucks behind him wait below the hill out of sight. He drove his car to the lower gate. One of the guards came out of the hut with his gun drawn. He looked inside the car, saw Raul Gonzales, and asked in Spanish, "Who are you?"

"I am Raul Gonzales; I have an appointment with Senor Paniagua."

"He is not here, you will have to come back another day," the guard said.

The guards did not see the four men come up behind the hut. They quickly took them into custody. Raul's car moved on up the hill followed by the two trucks. The guards and the four men remained at the guard house.

Morales' (Gonzales') car approached the house and came to a stop in front of it. The trucks moved quickly around the hacienda. The men in the trucks jumped out of the back.

Gonzales' driver stepped out of the limousine and opened the door for him. Gonzales walked up the steps slowly. He knocked on the door.

A servant opened the door, looked up at Gonzales, "What can I do for you Senor?"

"My name is Senor Gonzales. I am here to see Senor Paniagua. He is expecting me."

"Sorry sir, but Senor Paniagua is not here."

"Where is he?"

"I believe he went fishing," the servant said.

The back door smashed in. Gonzales' men moved into the house.

The servant heard them. As he turned back to the house, three men rushed past Gonzales and entered it.

Six guards were found in a small building behind the house. These were brought around to the front of the house.

Inside the hacienda three woman were collected coming out of their bedrooms, and two boys age eight and twelve were brought into the main room of the house.

After they had all settled, Raul asked again, "Where is Senor Paniagua?"

"He left several days ago," A frightened young lady of sixteen said. "We have not seen him."

"Where did he go?"

"He said he was going fishing," the young lady said. She was already shaking thinking Gonzales was going to shoot her.

"Where?"

"I don't know!" the young lady cried with her eyes pleading not to be killed. "I know he was going to take his boat. He could be anywhere."

"There's people's lives at stake here!" Gonzales shouted.

"I don't know! I don't know!"

"Is there anyone else in the house?"

"No, only the guards outside," the young lady said.

Sergeant Fuentes entered the house, "We have everything controlled outside, sir."

"Search the house! Bring anyone you find in here?"

Fuentes took the two men entering, and sent them searching the house and grounds again, but they came up with nothing. Coming back into the house, he said, "You have all that's left on the property, sir."

"What about the guards?"

"Out in front, sir."

"Secure them," Gonzales said. Walking outside, he flipped his phone open to General Lopez.

After a few seconds the General came on the line:

Phone Conversation:

"Did you get him?"

"No sir, he was not here."

"What do you mean?" Lopez yelled, "You said you would have him in custody tonight!"

"We have some of his family, sir, but they do not know where he is."

"That wasn't the plan."

"I know sir. I checked a few days ago. There were no indications he would be in any other place. I don't know what happened. He could be on his boat at sea."

Christopher Charles

"Son, you just given the country over to the US Government. They will have the excuse they have been looking for to invade and remove the cocaine operation entirely. They are already sending a Navy ship and Seals, and that is only a prelude to what's coming behind them."

"Sorry sir!"

On the Beach

Harriet felt exhausted. She was a good two hundred yards from the shore. Her arms were only going through the motions. It was her fins that moved her forward.

Above and below her was darkness. She tried hard not to think about the white shark she encountered two days ago.

She was extremely tired. Finally, she coasted moving only her legs to push her forward. She was careful to always keep air in her lungs and to blow the water out of her snorkel before she breathed in. She knew the end of her snorkel had gone under water a few times already as she blew the water out.

She began thinking how she was going to handle Gonzales. She did not want to walk into his hands again. She had her forty-five in her purse. That was in her backpack. Then she heard a helicopter go over her heading for the beach. She knew who it was. She stopped swimming a moment watching it land. Feeling a new surge of energy, she pushed forward putting more effort into her arms. Ramos was here, and he was armed.

Ten minutes later, she approached the surf. Lining herself up with the helicopter, she allowed the surf to take her in. She lay spread out on the beach in the darkness a moment recovering. It had been a long swim. Slowly she stood and took off her fins and mask. She found her legs wanting to give out.

Taking in several long deep breathes, her shakes began to settle. Finding more strength, she walked past the helicopter, and on towards some people standing by a fire. They were a short distance from the helicopter. Coming into the light from the darkness, she approached them.

Nadine was talking to Ramos, when she saw Harriet coming out of the darkness. She could only look at her a moment not believing what she saw. Finally, she yelled, "Harriet, Harriet!" She ran to her followed by Ramos.

Harriet had tears flowing as they approached her. Finally, her legs would not move any further. They were about to knot up from the hard pushing with the fins. Emotionally she was exhausted.

The rest of her crew saw Nadine running and yelling. They followed her.

Nadine hugged Harriet first followed by Ramos, and the rest of her crew. The First and Second Officers saw the commotion and wandered over. Finally, everyone was emotionally okay. Ramos was able to ask, "Where is the ship?"

"It's about 2,000 meters out there," Harriet said. "I swam in." She held up her fins and mask. "It's anchored well, but no one should board it until we find Paniagua, it may still have a bomb or two aboard." She looked around, "Where is Raul?"

"He went after Paniagua," Mc Craw said. "He took his men with him."

"What men?" Harriet asked.

"Those policemen aboard were his men. Gonzales is really Colonel Morales of the Columbian National Police. He showed us his badge."

"That explains some of his actions," Harriet said. "Did he say where he was going?"

"He headed inland," Mc Craw said. "I followed them through the jungle until they reached a dirt road. They had two trucks and a limousine hidden along with weapons. They were all heading inland the last I saw of them."

She turned to the First and Second Officers standing nearby, "Do you know where Gonzales went?"

"Senor Paniagua is known to have a hacienda about a hundred miles from here, but that is only a guess," The First Officer said.

"The bombs aboard the ship can be detonated by a satellite signal. Until we have Paniagua in our hands, I would suggest keeping everyone off the ship."

"I have two helicopters full of Navy Seal and a frigate coming here," Ramos said. "They should be here at 2300 hours. That's 11 PM." He looked at his watch, "It's eight-thirty now, so we need to be moving."

"Where are you going?" The First Officer asked.

"To find Paniagua," Harriet said. She turned to her crew. "It will be Mc Craw, Youngsu, and myself going with the helicopter. Nadine, you and Rose stay here, and wait for the frigate. Do not let them board until I call you. She turned to Ramos, "Give her one of your satellite phones, and give me the number. We need to stay in communication."

Ramos took a phone from one of his men, handed it to Rose, and then yelled, "Let's board!"

Mc Craw smiled. He was finally going to see some action. He climbed aboard the helicopter with the others filling up the seats. They all wore head gear to communicate.

The first Officer tried to protest yelling, "You cannot just leave us here. You should at least wait until Colonel Gonzales or the frigate get here."

"You can handle a few more hours," Harriet said stepping aboard.

Nadine and Rose watched them leave as the First Officer approached them, "Where are they going?"

"To find Paniagua," Rose said.

"Colonel Morales is already doing that. We need that helicopter here to help us."

"A Navy frigate will be here at 11 PM," Rose said. "We will transport the people in the morning."

Inside the Helicopter

They all had their earphones on enabling them to talk.

"So where are we going?" Ramos asked.

"Puntarenas, Costa Rica, but more specifically the Si Como No Resort on the Tarcoles River."

"How do you know he's there?"

"Because I was there," Harriet said standing, trying to dry off her swimsuit. "I took his boat and transferred the bombs from the ship to it."

"How do you know it was his boat?"

"Captain Morgan told me. They have his daughter and grandson there also I believe, because they took a picture, and sent it to him over the internet."

"So where is this Captain Morgan?"

"He took the boat loaded with the bombs and left me on the ship. It was not a hero thing. He didn't know the boat had the bombs on it. Besides, he took the only life raft with him, not a nice man."

"He left you when he knew there were bombs aboard?" Ramos asked.

"I have not been treated nice for some time," Harriet said as her tears developed. "Raul left me stranded at the hotel after he gave me the Scopolamine drug. I took Paniagua's boat and chased the ship down. I didn't know it was his boat then. When I finally caught the ship, everyone had been taken off except Captain Morgan. He thought I was Paniagua boarding and stopped the ship. When he found out it was only me, he panicked, and took the boat."

"Why would he do that?" Ramos asked

"Because if a raiding party was not coming aboard, the only remaining possibility would be a bomb on board the ship or a missile from land. The bombs on the ship would be more direct. I figured it out immediately. It took him a little longer."

"How did you find the bombs," Mc Craw asked, thinking he may have been sleeping next to one.

"I used Youngsu scanner. I found it under his bed," Harriet said. "I transferred five bombs ranging from four pounds to ten pounds to the boat, but I may have missed one or two. It's a big ship. I found the ten-pounder in Raul's cabin, and a smaller four-pounder in a crew's quarters."

"How were you able to handle a ship that sized," Ramos asked. "I mean you said you anchored it 2,000 yards out."

"I watched the Bridge crew earlier."

Ramos looked at the fuel gauge, "We will have to stop at the Panama Airport if you want to make it to Costa Rica."

"Good, it will give me a chance to call Clark." Her bathing suit was almost dry. She took her seat as the helicopter came into the airport.

It landed near the gas pumps, and the rotors slowly stopped. Harriet jumped out with her backpack. She opened the pack, took out her clothes and shoes. She quickly slipped them on as she speed-dialed the Assistant Director James Clark.

Phone Conversation:

"Clark, this is Harriet Brown."

"Harriet, are you alright?"

"I'm fine. I am with Ramos. We have the passengers, and crew as well as the cruise ship. No one is to board the ship until we have collected Paniagua. We are refueling at the Panama Airport."

Clark swallowed, "You have been a very busy girl."

"Yes sir."

"Where is Paniagua?"

"He's in Puntarenas, Costa Rica, or more precise at the mouth of the Tarcoles river in the Si Como No Resort."

"I have two helicopters full of Navy Seals coming your direction."

"Have them stop at Puntarenas until I call for them. Paniagua has two hostages, and probably a device of some sort to blow up the ship and his boat."

"This should be a naval operation," Clark said. "They are trained for these things."

"He selected the hotel to give him an advantage point. He will see the helicopters coming, and the only place to land is on the beach. He will be gone, the boat will be blown, and the hostages killed. We are in a civilian helicopter dressed in civilian clothes. Let us make the entrance, and then bring in the Navy Seals."

"You have a point," Clark said. "It sounds like you have been through this."

"They will be less suspicious of a girl walking into the resort than a group of men."

"I still don't like it."

"The fuel is loaded," Harriet said. "I need to go. Remember, have the Seals land at Puntarenas, and wait for my call. It is only a few minutes by air to the resort."

"Okay, be careful," Clark said as she closed her phone.

Paniagua's Hacienda

Gonzales secured the hacienda. He left his men with the hostages and Paniagua's family. He was ready to depart when he received a call. If was his First Officer at the beach:

Phone Conversation:

"Yes, what is it?"

"Miss Cummings just arrived and left, sir."

"What, where did she come from?"

"She swam to shore from the ship, sir."

"Ship, is the ship there?"

"Yes sir, I believe she said she anchored it 2,000 meters offshore. She said no one is to board her. She believes there might still be a bomb aboard her."

"Absolutely right, no ones to board her," Gonzales was yelling now.

"Yes sir, no one will board her."

"Now, there was a helicopter coming down into that area. Has it arrived?"

"It has come and gone, sir, taking Miss Cummings with it."

"Where is she going?"

"I believe after Paniagua, sir. That is why I called you. She should be coming your way very soon."

"Mr. Paniagua is not here!" Gonzales said. "Besides, how would she know where he is?"

"I just told her you were over a hundred miles away. That did not seem to faze her."

"Then she is not coming here. I am on my way back there."

"There may be a Navy Frigate here when you arrive sir."

Gonzales clipped his phone close. He was in his car when Sergeant Fuentes came up beside it.

"Do you want us to come with you, sir?"

"No, Senor Paniagua may come back. Hold the prisoners in the hacienda and place some men in the guard house. It needs to look natural."

"Yes sir."

"I am on my way back to the passengers. The ship is anchored off the shore 2,000 meters, and a US Navy Frigate is arriving. I need to be there to keep things calm."

"What about the bombs, sir?"

"They may be off the ship, and our luck may have turned," Gonzales said.

Paniagua's Boat

Captain Morgan looked straight out into the darkness. He felt a little guilty taking the life raft, but she had it coming. She has interfered once too often. He thought about his daughter and grandson. If she keeps the boat going straight down the coast, they should be alright.

Christopher Charles

He destroyed the radio equipment. She will not be calling anyone. She keeps it going, or they blow the ship up. It didn't take any brain to know the ship was loaded with bombs ready to detonate. When Paniagua's boat arrived with no Paniagua in it, he knew immediately it was either a missile or bombs on board the ship. It could still be a missile he reasoned. Maybe she can find something to float on. His First Mate did teach her how to swim.

The boat hit a large swell. It kicked the boat up high. He did not see it in the darkness. He should be slowing the boat down. The cabinet door had opened. He felt something on his foot. Looking down, he saw the pulsating blue light attached to a ten-pound weight. His mind immediately recognized what it was. He turned his head and looked at the deck below. There were four more pulsating blue lights scattered across the deck. She had found and placed the bombs on his boat.

Locking the wheel in place, he slowed the boat to ten knots, and climbed down from the wheelhouse. He had to get off the boat. It could blow any second. He knew if he threw even one bomb overboard, it would detonate the remaining bombs.

He pulled the heavy raft to the gunwale. Pushing hard he had it up on the edge. Then hanging onto the raft, he turned sideways. Taking the raft with him, he entered the water. The speed of the boat knocked him around. It separated him from his raft, but he quickly swam back to it.

Pulling the lever, the raft inflated into one huge raft. It was thirty-by-ten feet and had a ceiling. He set the rescue beam working. Now he waited. He had water aboard and some dry food. He could last several days. Maybe a month being by himself. The raft was made for forty people.

He could hear the sound of his boat slowly fading in the distance. He no longer felt guilty towards Harriet.

Detective Harriet Brown

<h1 align="center">Si Como No Resort</h1>

Harriet checked her purse. She felt her forty-five revolver as the helicopter landed on the beach. Stepping out of the helicopter, she stretched her legs and arms. Looking inside, she said, "Only Mc Craw and Youngsu come with me. The rest of you stay in the helicopter until I call Ramos."

She lifted her phone to her ear, punched the speed-dial to Clark. She watched Mc Craw and Youngsu climb out of the helicopter as she causally walked from the beach towards the resort. "Clark, have the Navy Seals arrived?"

"They have been waiting ten minutes. I had almost given up hearing from you. I was going to send them."

"You can send them now. Tell them to land next to our helicopter. I will keep my phone open from this point on. You need to record everything"

"I understand, be careful."

"You cannot talk, only listen, and record," Harriet said.

Inside the resort Paniagua was in his converted board room. He heard the helicopter land on the beach and sent two of his men to check it out. Then setting back in his chair, he fingered the large switch. This was his hidden ace. A moment later his phone rang.

Phone Conversation:

"It is a civilian helicopter. A woman and two men are walking up to the entrance. She's talking on her phone. She doesn't appear to be a threat."

"Send them back to their helicopter. There are no reservations here."

Christopher Charles

"Yes sir."

On the beach Harriet walked with a little skip in her walk leading Mc Craw and Youngsu up the steps. At the top of the steps two men in black coats stood waiting for them.

"You need to turn back," One of the men in a black suit yelled down. "All the reservations have been cancelled. The hotel is closed to tourists."

"I was just here the other day," Harriet said approaching the man, and taking her purse into her left hand. "I was telling the gentlemen about the cutest little restaurant where you can see the ocean and the night sky."

The two men stood firm as she took the last step between them.

They started to turn to hold her, when Mc Craw, coming up fast, took the first man, and threw him into the rail knocking him unconscious.

Youngsu, up in the air, sent his foot into the other man's side dropping the unsuspecting man to the first step. The next blow to his head sent him back onto the platform where he remained unconscious. Youngsu and Mc Craw quickly hauled them to one side of the entrance. They bound their arms with the belts taken from the prisoners' pants. Their pants were dropped, shirts taken off, and used as gags. They were ready to move along. Mc Craw took their revolvers. He placed them in his belt.

Harriet meanwhile had wandered on into the hotel. The clerk immediately recognized her from the night before. He was surprised she had returned, "What can I do for you Miss?"

Harriet touched the countertop. Immediately she fainted.

The clerk panicked. He ran out around the counter to help her only to meet Mc Craw and Youngsu coming through the door. He was quickly secured and gagged.

Youngsu went around the counter and disconnected the phone system to all of the suites.

Harriet stood, pushed her speed-dial to Ramos, "Come on in. We are heading for Paniagua's suite, try and find the hostages." She redialed Clark, "We're inside."

She moved on through the resort passing the swimming pool. She remembered there were two guards located here somewhere. She saw them leaning against the wall outside a room on the lower floor.

"Okay," Harriet whispered, "I will distract them, and try to enter the suite. You two move up quickly and remove them."

Mc Craw nodded.

Harriet, holding her purse over her shoulder, walked quickly towards the men. As she approached the door. They stepped up to her, "This section is closed to everyone."

"Senor Paniagua called for me to come. It seems I messed up the other night."

The first man on her left looked at her. Then he recognized her, "Senor Paniagua is busy tonight, maybe tomorrow."

Harriet slowly shook her head, and her tears began to flow as she said, "I know I made a mess of things the other night. I need this job. Maybe you could check with him first before I go."

The man turned, knocked on the door, and said in Spanish, "Open up, it's Karl. We have a situation here."

Harriet heard the door being unlocked and opened slightly. She quickly stepped past the man, smashed into the door, and ended up inside. The two men recovering attempted to stop her when they found themselves going up against the wall. The third man opening the door was pushed aside by Harriet coming though.

Coming in, Youngsu had him handled with a kick. Inside, Harriet opened her purse, withdrew her forty-five revolver. The men around the table could not move for a moment.

Paniagua quickly picked up his large switch, held it high, shouting, "This will blow up the ship, and kill three thousand people."

The two men were unconscious outside the door. Now Mc Craw was in the room as Harriet fired her gun sending the large switch flying to the floor taking off two of Paniagua's fingers in the progress.

The man next to Paniagua leaped from his chair landing on top of the switch. At the same time another man in the middle of the table pulled his gun.

Harriet fired a second time. The bullet struck the man in the shoulder sending him back over his chair, and his gun flying to the corner of the room.

Mc Craw withdrew the two pistols in his belt, fired into the ceiling, shouting, "Anyone else want to take a bullet."

The man on the floor turned over with the switch in his hands, squeezed the switch closed, and smiled.

Out in the Pacific Ocean Captain Morgan was floating in his raft looking out over the water when he suddenly saw a brilliant light flash in the night sky. "They did it. They actually were going to do it." He heard a helicopter in the distance.

Back in the Paniagua board room Harriet heard men coming down the hall and entering the room behind her. It was Ramos and his men. She allowed them to take over as she almost collapsed from exhaustion. She had been moving on adrenalin. Now that the excitement was finished, there was nothing left. She stumbled back to the front desk. She heard two helicopters landing on the beach and knew the Navy Seals had arrived.

She held onto the countertop as the Seals rushed by her. Two of them remained with her. One was Lieutenant Roberson.

"You're Miss Harriet Brown?"

"Yes sir," Harriet said. "We have Paniagua secured, but he has two hostages hidden somewhere in the resort."

Lieutenant Roberson put his wrist to his lips, "Look for hostages in the cottages."

The Navy Seals had reached the board room. They saw Paniagua secured, and up against the wall.

Ramos handed one of the Seals the computer, and the closed switch, "He exploded the bombs, sir."

The Seals took over the captives allowing Ramos and his men to leave the room.

At the hotel lobby Lieutenant Roberson felt a vibration on his wrist communicator. He flipped it on, and one of his men said, "We have Paniagua, sir, but he detonated the bombs. Mr. Paniagua has two blown away fingers, and another man has a blown away shoulder. He needs medical attention immediately. We also have Paniagua's computer."

Lieutenant Roberson turned to Harriet, "You should have allowed us to take him. He's blown away your ship."

Harriet took her phone out of her purse, "Clark, I need the phone a minute, I will call you back." She pressed the phone number to Rose's phone.

Phone Conversation:

"Did the ship blow up?"

Rose looked out into the night, "It doesn't appear to have blown up. I can barely make out its outline in the moon light. We did not hear any explosions."

"Thank you, Rose, we have Paniagua. We will be on our way back shortly." She closed her phone, turned to Lieutenant, "He didn't blow up the ship, but he probably did blow up his own boat, and may have killed Captain Morgan." Not waiting for him to reply, she speed-dialed Clark's phone.

Phone Conversation:

"Sorry, sir, but I needed verification the ship did not blow up. It didn't. I have a Lieutenant here with the Navy Seals."

"Thank God!" Clark said. "Let me talk with the Lieutenant."

"Yes sir." Harriet handed her phone to the Lieutenant, "The Assistant Director of the FBI wants to talk to you."

He took the phone, "Lieutenant Roberson here, sir. We have custody of Paniagua, and his computer, but not before he exploded the bombs."

"The hostages?"

"We are still looking for them, sir."

"An Airforce transport plane will be landing at the Puntarenas airport to pick up Paniagua, his computer, and his people. You are to transport them there, and then proceed to the passengers' site and connect up with the Navy Frigate. A helicopter from the Frigate spotted an emergency beacon south of there. They also saw a brilliant light indicating an explosion took place. The Navy Frigate is checking it out."

"Yes sir," Lieutenant Roberson said. "What do you want me to do with Miss Brown and the detectives?"

"Allow them to return to the passengers. I think they deserve a little rest."

"Yes sir, but they need to be debriefed."

"That can be done on the Frigate when it arrives," Clark said.

"Yes sir," Lieutenant Roberson said. His vibrator moved indicating one of his men needed to talk to him. "One moment, sir, emergency." He brought his wrist to his lips, "Yes!"

"We found the hostages, sir. There are two women and a boy. They are all well. One of the women says she is Senora Molina."

"Bring them to the entrance," Lieutenant Roberson said. "Going back to the phone, he said, "The hostages are okay, sir, but there are three of them. One of the women says she is Mrs. Molina."

"Good, transport them to the frigate as soon as you can."

"Yes sir."

"Now let me talk to Miss Brown," Clark said

Lieutenant Roberson handed Harriet back her phone, "The Assistant Director wants to talk to you." He was impressed she could call the Assistant Director directly.

Harriet took her phone back, "Yes sir. We have to go back to the ship. Youngsu needs to make sure there are no more bombs aboard with his scanner."

"You are going back to the ship," Clark said. "When the Navy Frigate arrives, they will want to debrief you. I want to be in on the debriefing."

"I will have them patch you in, sir. Now I am very tired."

"You did well Harriet, I will talk to you later."

"Thank you, sir." Harriet said, and closed the phone. She pointed to the desk clerk on the floor, "He was not connected with Paniagua. We just secured him to prevent any leakage to Paniagua."

She could see the relief in the man's eyes.

The Lieutenant pointed to the man, "Release the man."

The man beside him quickly untied the man allowing him to pull his pants up and remove the gag in his mouth.

Ramos approached the front desk with his men and her people behind him. "I think we are about done here," he said. "The Navy has arrived."

"We need to go back to the ship," Harriet said. "Youngsu needs to search the ship for any unexploded bombs."

Ramos looked at the Lieutenant, "I am Chief of Detectives Ramos of the Los Angeles division. We have been following this case since the Captain and First Mate were killed at the Los Angeles Port of Call. We're going back to the ship, is that alright with you?"

"Yes, we will clean up here, and meet you back there," Lieutenant Roberson said. "A frigate will be arriving at 2300 hours. They will want to debrief all of you."

"Yes sir," Ramos said, and led his party out the door with Harriet following behind him.

She had to hold the rail going down the steps to prevent falling. Mc Craw stayed with her ready to carry her if necessary.

Lieutenant looked at them leaving, shook his head, "Civilians should not have been in on this. They're lucky they were not killed."

They boarded the civilian helicopter. It lifted off, headed back to the ship, and its passengers and crew.

The prisoners were brought out and placed with the others standing by. Some of the earlier guards were not doing very well. They also needed medical attention. They were taken down the steps and loaded aboard the helicopters to be taken to Puntarenas and the Airforce transport plane arriving. There was a medical team on board the transport plane. Paniagua two missing fingers were found, placed in a wet napkin, and taken along.

Half of the Navy Seals remained behind to give room for the prisoners. They would be picked up on the way back to the ship. They would fuel in Puntarenas.

Lieutenant looked at the clerk, "Bring him along, he needs to be debriefed."

"But the young lady said I was innocent." The Clerk said.

"She's not military. You are coming along with me," Lieutenant Roberson said.

Ramos' helicopter landed at Panama Airport, fueled up, and headed out towards the ship.

A helicopter was dispatched from the frigate as it made a detour towards the emergency beacon further south. They would be a little late arriving to the passengers and crew site, but he also had a duty to rescue people at sea. The Assistant Director of the FBI said to pick him up believing him to be the elusive Captain Morgan.

An hour and a half later, Ramos' helicopter landed on the beach where the passengers and crew were located. The light from the camp made it easy to find the beach.

Harriet slept most of the way. When the helicopter landed, she forced herself awake. She was really tired, but she had one more thing to do. "Ramos, take one of your men and come with us aboard the ship. The other two should remain on the beach, and not allow anyone else to come aboard until Youngsu has cleared the ship."

Coming out of the helicopter, Rose, Nadine and the First Officer Bitterman came running over. Harriet stumbled, but she managed to recover. She walked over to Nadine and took a hug. She turned to the First Officer, "We need one of the tenders to go aboard the ship."

"I want to come aboard along with you," The First Officer said.

"You are to stay with the passengers and crew until the ship is clean," Ramos said in a hard voice coming up behind her. "Where is the tender?"

The First Officer realized he was talking to a law officer backed down and pointed up the beach. "I believe it is over there."

Harriet gave Rose a quick hug. Then carrying her heavy purse, she walked that direction followed by the others coming aboard.

"You may need someone to drive the boat for you. It can be a bit tricky coming up to the ship," The First Officer yelled after her.

Harriet ignored him. She was too tired to comment. They found the tender. Harriet went to the front of the boat as the others shoved the tender off the beach. Once it was in the water the others quickly climbed aboard.

Harriet started the engines and backed the tender out through the surf taking some water inside as she did. When she was through, she turned the tender around, using the reverse throttle in one hand, and the forward throttle in the other.

The tender turned and headed for the ship. She could barely see it in the starlit sky. She didn't realize she had swum so far. No wonder she was tired. She worked the tender up next to the lower hatch, and yelled, "Throw over the bumpers."

Youngsu and Mc Craw found what looked like bumpers. They threw them over the gunwale of the tender.

"Be ready to take the lines aboard the ship!" She yelled.

She brought the tender in closer letting the bumpers feel the ship, "Now!"

Youngsu and Mc Craw both jumped for the ship taking the bow and stern lines with them. They wrapped the lines around the cleats and stood by. Harriet turned the engine off and climbed up into the ship carrying her snorkel gear. She inspected the lines on the cleats and redid both of them. Ramos and the other detective jumped up on the ship.

Harriet stopped them at the hatch, turned to Detective Ramos, "I am going to turn all the lights on. After I do, I want to take you to one of the sabotage's cabin. He is still on shore, but his cabin should be neutralized. He has bomb making supplies inside."

She turned to Youngsu and Mc Craw, "You two come with me. I will show you where the scanner is located." She walked inside the ship and placed her snorkel gear back into the locker. The red battery lights were working allowing them to see their way. She headed for the Bridge.

"I'm sure glad you know your way around," Mc Craw said. Once on the Bridge, he watched her flipping switches, "Where did you learn how to do that?"

Harriet smiled as she threw the switches. The diesel engines came alive. The lights filled the ship. "The scanner is in my cabin," she said leading them off the Bridge.

The ship was suddenly awake. Lights filled the night sky. The people on the beach could now see the lit ship.

Coming into her cabin, she walked to the couch, and produced the scanner.

"Okay guys, we have work to do," Harriet said. "Scan from one end to the other near or below the water line. Also remove all the spyware including the antenna. The Navy is coming aboard shortly, and they will be doing their own scanning. I do not want them finding our spyware."

She pointed to the two suitcases by the door, "Take those back to Rose's cabin, and replace the partition. I want to keep our spyware."

They both nodded.

"All spyware goes back into Rose's cabin?" Youngsu asked.

"Yes, as quickly as possible," Harriet said. "It is almost 2300 hours. That frigate is due then, and the Navy Seals are still coming here as soon as they drop off their prisoners."

Youngsu nodded and headed for the door followed by Mc Craw. They had a lot of work to do before the frigate arrived.

Harriet closed her door. She walked fast back to the lower hatch. She saw Ramos impatiently waiting for her. "Sorry it took so long, but I wanted Youngsu on his way with the scanner first. Now, we need to check all of the compartments where electrical appliances may be running meaning the kitchen and engine room. The crew left in a hurry. On the way I will show you the saboteurs' cabin, and where I found one of the bombs."

She led them down below deck. All of the hallways were brightly lit. They checked the kitchen and crews' quarters. They found several things on and turned them off. The engine room was working perfectly. Finally, she took them to saboteurs' cabin. They saw bomb making material stuffed beneath their bunks and in the overhead lockers.

"There are usually two men to a cabin," Harriet said. "That means we have two saboteurs". Turning, she said, "Now let me take you to the First Mate's Cabin." She led them quickly up the ladders, and into the officer's quarters. Going into the

Gonzales's cabin, she said, "I found a ten-pound bomb in this cabinet over his bunk. I don't know why it was there, or who it was intended for, but he had to know it was here."

"Is there anything else?" Ramos asked.

"No, I am completely exhausted. I need to rest before I collapse. You may remain aboard the ship, and continue checking for things to turn off, or you may go back to shore, but I am off to my bed."

Ramos could see she was not doing well, "We will remain until the passengers come aboard."

"You could check the computer for the names of the two men who occupied the saboteur's cabin. There's a computer on the Bridge."

"Then we will start there," Ramos said. "You go off to bed."

On the Beach

Morales (Gonzales) was being driven back to the beach when his phone vibrated. It was his First Officer Bitterman on the phone.

Phone Conversation:

"Sir, Miss Cummings has returned and has boarded the boat."

"What about Paniagua?"

"I believe he has been apprehended."

"Are there any military there yet?"

Christopher Charles

"Only a Detective Ramos, but I believe the military are due here at 2300 hours."

"I should be there before then," Morales said.

Then in the distance he heard helicopters approaching, "Sir, I believe we are about to have more company. I need to go."

Bitterman closed his phone and watched the two helicopters land on the beach.

The Navy Seals jumped out of the doors and took up positions around the helicopters as Lieutenant Roberson stepped out.

First Officer Bitterman approached, "It is nice to see the Navy Seals are here."

Lieutenant Roberson, all military type man with good biceps, turned to him, "Where is Miss Brown and the detectives?"

"The detectives are aboard with a Miss Cummings, and her people sweeping the ship for bombs, I believe. I don't know any Miss Brown."

Lieutenant Roberson did not correct him.

On the Road

Morales was approaching the location where they had hidden the trucks and limousine. He left the trucks and his men at the hacienda in case Paniagua should return. He was in the limousine with his driver. Besides, he did not want a confrontation with the US Navy.

He speed-dialed General Lopez:

Phone Conversation:

"Colonel Morales here sir with some good news. It seems Senor Paniagua has been apprehended, and the cruise ship is anchored off the beach where the passengers are located."

"That is good news," General Lopez said. "I am very curious how that came about."

"I will know more shortly, sir. I am returning to the beach. The US Navy is already there."

"We do not want a confrontation," General Lopez said.

"It will just be me and my driver, sir. I left the men at the Paniagua's hacienda, but I may run into a problem with their military."

"You are on Columbian soil. They have no jurisdiction here."

"They are very upset, sir."

"They have their ship, and the passengers and crew are unharmed. That is a huge relief. I will see what the Assistant Director intends to do."

"Yes sir, I would appreciate it."

Morales flipped his phone closed, opened it again, and called Esteban Morales, his father:

Phone Conversation:

"Esteban here?"

"Sir, I am on my way back to the beach. We missed Paniagua at his hacienda, but he was captured by the Americans. The ship and the all the passengers and crew are safe."

"That wasn't the object of the plan, son."

"I know, but at least no one was hurt."

"Now we cannot get to Paniagua," Esteban said.

"He lost his cartel, sir. That should help us financially."

"Where is Sergeant Fuentes?"

"He's at the hacienda with the prisoners and Paniagua's family."

"Good, you go make peace with the Americans," Esteban said, and hung up the phone.

Raul knew what was going to happen next, but there was nothing he could do to stop it. His mind visualizing Paniagua's family and men being lined up and shot by Sergeant Fuentes' men. His father looking to avenge the murder of his brother, Chief Don Morales of the Los Angeles Police Department. He could still see the innocent eyes of the sixteen-year old girl looking at him, pleading.

He shook it off as the limousine pulled off into the brush to secure it. He stepped out and made his way through the jungle back to the beach. His driver followed him after he camouflaged the limousine.

When he reached the beach, he saw the cruise ship anchored 2,000 meters out with its lights glowing in the darkness. He also saw the Navy Frigate had also anchored close to it. On the beach, it was overflowing with Navy Seals and personnel from the ship.

First Officer Bitterman saw him, and immediately announced his presence to a lieutenant standing on the beach. Seeing no reason to hide, he walked calmly towards the man.

Reaching him, he extended his hand, "I am Colonel Morales of the Columbian National Police."

Taking his hand, the lieutenant said, "I am Lieutenant Roberson of the US Navy, you are to proceed to the Naval Frigate immediately." He turned and motioned for two seamen standing by a rubber raft with an outboard motor on the back of it, "Take this man aboard the frigate."

"Yes sir."

Turning back, Lieutenant Roberson said, "You are to follow these men. They will take you aboard."

Morales nodded. He did not like leaving Columbian soil, but then the water around Columbia was still in their jurisdiction. He followed the men.

11 The Debriefing

Frigate's Captain's Office

Captain Decker, a big man with a hard bearing sat across from Captain Morgan. There were two other officers in the room with them. He reached out, turned the recording device on, and opened the phone connection to the Assistant Director Clark.

"Now we will begin," Captain Decker said. "State your name please."

"Captain Morgan of the Norsewegian Cruise Lines."

"You will tell the truth and nothing, but the truth so help-you God?"

"Yes sir," Captain Morgan said.

"How did you come about being stranded out in the middle of the ocean?"

"Where would like me to start?"

"From the beginning," Captain Decker said.

"I was approached by one of Senor Paniagua's agents. I was retired because of some circumstances that were not my fault. I needed work. I was taken aboard his boat with the promise of a possible position. There, he informed me there would be an opening soon with the Norsewegian Cruise Lines. He wanted me to take the position.

I thought that was it. I knew they would not be hiring me because of my previous incident. I did some smuggling, but two weeks later I receive this call from the Cruise Lines. Seems their previous Captain had been killed. They were anxious to replacement him. I accepted the position, and the next day an agent of Senor Paniagua told me I was to by-pass the Panama Canal and take the cruise ship down the Columbian west coast. I was to call them when I was in Columbian waters.

I immediately smelled something was not right here, but they showed me a picture of my daughter and grandson. He said they would be killed if I didn't take the ship south."

"How does Senor Gonzales fit into this?" He knew the name had been changed, but Caption Morgan did not know."

"He seemed to be aware of their plan and told me to comply. We knew it was going to be a boarding or they were going to blow up the ship. We worked out a plan to drop the passengers and crew off on a secluded beach. He left me a raft at the lower hatch to escape the ship."

"Then how did Miss Harriet Brown manage to bring the ship back here?"

"Paniagua's boat came up beside the ship after the passengers and crew were dropped off on the beach. I stopped the ship thinking it was Paniagua boarding the ship. I was afraid of what he might do when he saw the passengers and crew were gone. Then when Miss Harriet Brown appeared on the Bridge, you cannot believe the relief I felt."

"Then you do not know how she came upon Paniagua's boat?"

"No, she would not tell me. We were not on the best of terms."

"Why was that?"

"I tried to have her kidnapped earlier by a friend of mine to remove her from the ship after I learned she was a detective with the authority to take over my ship. You can see where this could be a problem."

"What were the results?"

"She escaped and managed to board the ship. She sent her two-inch high heel into my foot in response."

Captain Decker smiled, "What happened after she arrived?"

"I got to thinking what was going to happen to the ship. At first, I thought he was going to board the ship, but when she showed up with his boat, that was no longer an option. That left blowing up the ship with a missile or detonating bombs already aboard the ship. In either case I needed off.

I locked the wheel and went down to the lower hatch where Paniagua's boat was tied. I took the life raft aboard the boat and left."

"You know you left Miss Brown stranded with no hope of rescue if the ship exploded?"

"That was her luck. She did severe damage to my foot and nailed the two feet of my friend trying to hold her. He was not trying to do her harm, only detain her awhile."

"So, you left her out of revenge?" Captain Decker asked.

"Let's just say I knew she knew how to run the ship, and she would keep it going south to avoid being blown up. She could have always run it up on the beach, but then it would have blown."

"Then how come the ship didn't explode, and you were found out in the middle of the ocean?"

"That's the weirdest part," Captain Morgan said. "I had been going for some time. I figured on going south as far as I could go before I ran out of fuel, but a swell hit the boat hard. It knocked a cabinet door open in front of my feet. Looking down, I saw a ten-pound bomb with a pulsating blue light. I turned my head. There on the deck behind me were four more blinking blue lights. She had moved the bombs to my boat. I don't know how she did it. That woman must have used witchcraft.

I was scared, I tell you. They were going to blow any second. I slowed to ten knots, took hold of the life raft, and jumped overboard. Now you tell me who was doing who in. That she-devil tried to kill me."

Captain Decker turned to the speaker in the room, "Is there anything you would like to ask, sir?"

"He is to be held over for attempted murder," Assistant Director Clark said. "Bring in Chief Detective Ramos."

"We have Colonel Morales on board, sir."

"Let's talk to Detective Ramos first."

"Yes sir." Captain Decker said. He nodded to the Lieutenant beside him, "Take him back to the brig, and bring in Chief Detective Ramos."

"Yes sir." The lieutenant took Captain Morgan by the arm and moved him towards the hatch.

"You don't have to push sonny," Captain Morgan yelled. "I can still walk."

They both left the cabin.

"I would like to bring in Miss Brown, sir. She will probably have the most accurate course of events."

"Allow her to sleep a while," Clark said. "She has been through more than one person should be."

"Yes sir, we are bringing in Detective Ramos."

A moment later Ramos entered the captain's office as Captain Decker stood.

He shook hands, "Detective Ramos, sir."

They both sat down.

"I need for you to give us an overall flow of events, Detective, since you were privy to most of them."

"I will do the best I can, sir."

"Can you start with the murders in Los Angeles?"

"Yes, it was my case. Looking back, we probably should have prevented the cruise from leaving port. I also have to say that Mr. O Brian did not take the situation seriously. He hired Miss Brown's Detective Agency to protect the ship, but he took away all of their means of doing so. They were not allowed to bring their weapons or their spyware aboard. I do not know what he expected them to do. He did give them authority to take over the ship in an emergency. Then he made the two suspects Mr. Gonzales and the Captain aware of their presence, which almost caused her to be stranded in Acapulco, Mexico, when Captain Morgan had her kidnapped."

"How did she escape?"

"They were not aware of the other members of her team. She was rescued after she freed herself by stomping into the feet of her kidnapper with the heels of her shoes."

"Okay, go on,"

"She knew something was going to happen from the conversations she had with the First Mate Gonzales. She confided in me. I took a leave from the Los Angeles Police Department. I brought three other detectives with me to

Panama City, where we rented a helicopter. I tried to bring Clark, I mean Assistant Director Clark into it, but he was hampered by evidence. We had nothing hard only hearsay. He could not get anyone to move this direction. Even after we learned the ship would miss the Panama Canal, and head south along the Columbian Coast."

"When did you know who was behind the murders, and the attempted kidnapping of the ship?"

"We had no idea. I don't think Miss Brown had any idea until Captain Morgan told her when she had arrived on his boat. We knew Captain Morgan and First Mate Gonzales were part of it. Miss Brown and Gonzales were very close for a while. I think she saved his life at least two times maybe three. He owed her, but he returned the favor by drugging her with the Scopolamine drug and left her stranded at the Si Como No Resort in Costa Rica."

"Isn't that where Senor Paniagua had his headquarters?"

"That's how she knew where he was," Ramos said. "When Captain Morgan told her she had his boat, it was an easy deduction. I think she ran into some of his henchmen while she was stumbling her way out of there."

"How did she come by his boat?"

"I didn't ask her. I know she chased the ship for something like twenty plus hours before she caught it. She turned the ship and brought it back to the shore where passengers and crew were by herself and anchored it."

"How did she do that?"

"She catches onto things very quickly. Someone must have shown her how to anchor the boat. Did you know she swam to shore after she anchored it?"

"That's more than a mile swim," Captain Decker said. "That would take an experience swimmer."

"I agree with you, but I don't think she ever learned to swim before this trip."

"What happened at the Si Como No Resort?"

"She had been there before, and they recognized her. This allowed her to approach them close enough for her team to take them out. I heard she burst into the board room and shot Paniagua and another man pulling a gun. We arrived after all the action. We were in time to make the arrest, and that was about it."

"Okay, I may want to talk to you again," Captain Decker said.

"There are two more saboteurs coming aboard we need to apprehend. I have theirs names. I plan on taking them into custody when they pass through security."

"Very well, make the arrest, but we will take them into custody after the arrest."

"Thank you, sir, I think if they see military personnel waiting for them, they may try to run or involve other people."

"I agree, they are all yours."

"Thank you," Ramos said, and shook the Captain's hand as he stood.

"Have them send in Senor Gonzales next."

"Yes sir," Ramos said leaving.

Captain Decker turned to the speaker, "Sorry sir, did you want to ask him any questions?"

"No, we will talk later," Clark said. "I am anxious to hear from our Senor Gonzales."

He finished his sentence, when Morales (Gonzales) entered the office. Morales shook the Captain's hand, "I am Colonel Raul Jimenez Morales of the Colombian National Police."

The Captain nodded for him to sit, "I am Captain Decker. We are debriefing those involved in the ransom incident. This conversation will be recorded to be used in a court of law if necessary."

"I understand the necessity," Gonzales said.

"First, how did a Colonel of the Colombian National Police become involved in Paniagua plot to blackmail the Norsewegian Cruise Lines and the US Government?"

"We knew of his intentions for some time," Morales said. "We discovered he was going to blackmail the US Government because they had stolen over 800 million from him. He wanted it back."

"That was drug money." Assistant Director Clark said over the speaker.

"Oh, we do have someone else listening?" Morales asked.

"Yes, I am Assistant Director Clark, and I am very aware of the supposed 800 million he claims we owe him."

"Then you also know you kept the product that precipitated the whole chain of events. I think that was thirty tons of cocaine."

"That was to prevent the drugs from reaching our streets."

"No, it was more to shut down Senor Paniagua's operation. He lost his cocaine, and you took his money. He simply wanted it back."

"Are you defending him?"

"No, I am only stating his position, so you will understand his motives better."

"Did you have the Captain and First Mate killed?" Clark asked.

"That was pure Paniagua, but I took advantage of the situation, and volunteered to replace him. I also brought aboard twenty of my police officers in case he tried to board the ship."

"There was a ten-pound bomb in your cabin. Would you like to explain that?" Captain Decker asked.

"Easy enough, one of the crew found the bomb under the deck plates below the forward cabins. He gave it to me, and I placed it in my cabin. At that point I knew Paniagua planned on blowing up the ship. I began training the passengers and crew until they could evacuate the ship safely.

I knew the plan was to deliver the ransom note when the ship was heading south along the coast of Columbia. I set up a location, a hundred miles from Paniagua's Hacienda. I placed trucks and weapons there, and had informed the small village, we would be coming.

I evacuated the ship at that point and marched through the jungle to reach my vehicles. We drove the hundred miles to the hacienda, but Paniagua was gone. We were hoping to catch him before he exploded the bombs in the ship. You can verify all of this with General Lopez of the Columbian National Police. He was in on the plan all the way."

"Did you inform Captain Morgan of your plan?"

"Captain Morgan is not very reliable. No, I did not reveal all of the plan."

"Why did you treat Miss Brown so horribly?" Clark asked.

Gonzales smiled, "I tried to save her life."

"What, by stranding her at the same resort that Paniagua occupied?"

"He was there?" Raul asked in a surprised voice.

"He was, and she stole his boat to catch the ship," Clark said. "Of course, she did not know it was his boat then."

Detective Harriet Brown

"She is a very remarkable woman," Morales said. "You must know I love her. I would do nothing to hurt her. You and I both know it was her father who took his 800 million dollars.

Do you have any idea what he would have done to her if he had his hands on her? I simply could not allow that to happen. Now you tell me I did exactly that." He held back his emotions, and said, "Give me a minute." Then shaking his head, he said quietly, "That's how she knew where he was?"

"Yes, it was actually Captain Morgan who told her whose boat she stole. I think she was coming after you. She did not like being drugged with the Scopolamine drug."

"I accidently overdosed her, but I saw to it she had a place to recover, and I gave her a thousand dollars to catch a plane out of Puntarenas back to Los Angeles."

"It appears she did not like that option," Clark said.

"Detective Ramos said he didn't believe Miss Brown knew how to swim before this trip," Captain Decker said, "Did you have something to do with that?"

"Yes, I taught her to swim. She almost drowned in the process, but she learned very fast."

"Did you know she swam a good 2,000 meters to shore after she anchored the cruise ship. Again, another remarkable feat being she was only a passenger, and not allowed on the Bridge."

"A 2,000-meter swim would have been hard even for me. That might explain how she learned to ride a horse so quickly," Morales said, allowing his mind to drift. He knew she had never swum before. The sudden ability to ride a horse at a full gallop, a wild one at that now seems more plausible. Shaking his head, he looked up, "She was on the Bridge on two separate occasions for a few minutes. She must have been told how to anchor the ship then."

Christopher Charles

"I was told she saved your life on two occasions. Would you go into more detail?" Captain Decker asked.

He cleared his throat and went into when the wild horse bucked him over the cliff.

When he finished, Captain Decker asked, "How was she able to ride the wild horse?"

"I believe she grabbed his ears and held on until he calmed down."

Captain Decker smiled, "I will have to keep that method in mind."

"What was the other incident?"

Raul went into the snorkeling incident off the coast by the mouth of the Tarcoles River where she swam into the shark's eye.

When he finished, Captain Decker said, "A remarkable woman. Do you have any questions, sir?"

"Yes, what are your plans now," Clark asked.

"I would like to take the ship through the canal, and into the port at Cartagena, Columbia. I plan on departing the ship and rejoining my family there. First Officer Bitterman is more than qualified to continue the cruise to Miami. Actually, I have very little experience in handling a ship of this size."

"I think we can accommodate that for you," Clark said, thinking he will no longer be influencing Harriet.

"Thank you, sir," Morales said standing. "I would like to board the ship now if that is okay."

"As soon as it is cleared," Captain Decker said. "We are running another scan to be sure there are no more bombs aboard. We will be keeping the military personnel aboard the ship. They can take the lodgings your police officers used. In case there is another incident."

"That would acceptable, sir," Morales said, leaving the Captain's Office.

With the ship's antenna working again, people on the beach were calling home letting family members know what had happened to them.

On the Beach

Lieutenant Roberson received a call from the frigate stating the crew and passengers could come aboard. He approached the First Officer, "We can start the reloading of the crew and passengers. You will use the tenders for loading. The crew will go first. Leave enough crew to take the lifeboats and rafts."

"Yes sir, I will see the Chief, and get it started," The First Officer said. "I must say I am relieved to be finally leaving this place."

Aboard the Cruise Ship

Harriet heard a knock at her door. She was still in her bathing suit and clothes. She had been so tired, she fell on the bed, and went to sleep. She looked at the clock. It was five in the morning. She heard commotion outside indicating people were aboard. There was another knock. She rolled out of bed and walked to the door.

A lieutenant dressed in his white uniform, stood in front of her. "I am to accompany you to the frigate for a debriefing, madam."

Harriet looked at herself, "Give me a few minutes." She closed the door in his face and went into the bathroom. She took a quick shower to remove the salt crusting to her bathing suit and skin. Feeling better, she worked on her hair until all of the salt was out of it. Drying quickly, she put on a cute dress, and shoes. Next, she worked on her hair. Forty-five minutes later she was presentable.

Before she opened the door, she placed her forty-five revolver back inside the wall radiator. She was ready for the world, opened the door, and smiled, "Lead on, Lieutenant."

He pushed himself off the wall and led her down the stairs to the lower deck hatch. The crew was coming aboard the ship. She saw Detective Ramos, and one of his men standing back from the hatch. The security people placed everyone through the X-ray machine and checked their shoes. Security was being exceptionally tight.

When one of the male crew members walked through, the security officer nodded to Ramos. Once inside the hatch, Detective Ramos arrested him by placing him up against the bulkhead and cuffing his wrist.

When another crewman came through the security system, he was delayed a moment until Detective Ramos could return.

The man became uneasy. He looked around nervously. Finally, the security officer had to arrest him, and placed him up against the bulkhead until Ramos could arrive with the cuffs.

Harriet observed all of this waiting for the tender to empty out. When everyone was through the security, Harriet boarded the tender. Behind her came Ramos, another detective, and the two prisoners. The two crew members retrieved the lines. The pilot took the tender away from the ship.

"We're innocent!" Yelled one of the prisoners. "We didn't do anything!"

"You placed bombs in the ship, and probably killed the First Mate and the Captain," Ramos said shoving the prisoner into a chair.

One of the prisoners jumped to his feet. He leaped for the side of the tender. Unable to use his hands, his head struck the gunwale as he tumbled overboard and into the ocean.

The second man tried the same, but he was restrained by Ramos and the other detective. The tender did a large circle and came back to the spot where the prisoner had fallen in, but there was no trace of him.

After looking fifteen minutes, Ramos said, "Let's go, he probably drowned."

Later, he was found face down floating by the lower hatch.

The tender came alongside the frigate and tied up.

Harriet boarded after the prisoner was taken aboard and placed in the brig. She was directed to the Captain's office. Walking in, she was met by Captain Decker.

He stood, took her limp hand, "Welcome aboard Miss Brown, I am Captain Decker, please be seated."

"Thank you," Harriet said as she seated herself.

"This debriefing will be recorded, and may be used in court," Captain Decker said.

"Then I will have to be careful what I say."

"We just want to know what happened."

"One of the ones responsible for setting the bombs, and possibly killing the previous Captain and his First Mate jumped overboard and drowned."

"You said there were two?"

"Yes, the other one is being placed in your brig; I believe by Detective Ramos."

"Let's start at the beginning," Captain Decker said.

"Assistant Director Clark wanted to be in on the debriefing, sir," Harriet said.

"I am here," the speaker on the desk said.

"Hello Clark, thank you for sending the Navy to rescue us."

"I think most of that was already done before they arrived," Clark said.

"It was still nice to see them," Harriet said. "Now, where would you like me to start?"

"What was your contract with the Norsewegian Cruise Lines?" Clark asked.

"I am not at liberty to divulge all of it because we may be going to court. My crew of five was hired to come aboard the ship to satisfy their insurance company. We were told not to bring weapons or our spyware. Our payment would be a free cruise through the Panama Canal. Mr. O' Brian gave me a letter stating I could take control of the ship in an emergency."

"That doesn't seem like much of payment for services rendered."

"If nothing happened, it was a free vacation," Harriet said. "I had a separate contract if something did happen."

"Can you divulge the contents of that contract?"

"No, but let me also say here, Mr. O' Brian further handicapped us by informing the First Mate Gonzales, or is it Morales now, of who we really were. This led to Nadine and myself almost being kidnapped, and me being given the Scopolamine drug."

"To reaffirm, was the attempted kidnapping Senor Morales or Captain Morgan's idea, or both?" Captain Decker asked

"Morales learned of our presence from O' Brian, and he told Captain Morgan who initiated the kidnapping attempt."

"We were told you saved Senor Morales' life at least two times, can you elaborate on that?"

"I cannot see where that is important, sir. The man needed help and I helped him," Harriet said. Her voice indicated she was angry with him.

"We'll come back to that," Captain Decker said. "We understand you were very close to him, is that correct?"

"We needed to learn when the ship was going to be attacked," Harriet said. "The only one who knew that was the Captain and the then Raul Gonzales."

"Where did you learn how to run a cruise ship?" Captain Decker asked.

"I had the opportunity to be on the Bridge a couple of times. Knowing I may need to take control at some point, I thought it might be prudent to learn all I could. I tried to have Raul take me on a tour of the ship, but we ended up in the casino instead."

"I am surprised Captain Morgan allowed you on the Bridge." Captain Decker said.

"Oh, he was very angry I had been on the Bridge after he learned I could take it over in an emergency. Also, he was angry over an episode we had on the dance floor after I had escaped from the kidnappers. He was mishandling me. I gave him a spike heel in his right foot. He is not a nice man."

"It takes an experience officer to anchor a ship of this size."

"It is not so hard if you remember to place the chains five times the depth. Then it is a matter of moving the ship forward or backwards."

"Hympt," Captain Decker said, "I can see it was no problem."

"Why did you anchor the ship so far from the shore?" Clark asked.

"It was dark. I could not tell the distance. I could only really see the bottom of the ocean with the sonar. When I reached a hundred feet, I dropped the anchor. I was thinking three or four hundred meters at most. It was very hard to swim the 2,000 meters."

"Where did you learn to swim?" Captain Decker asked, wanting to back up Morales' statement.

"Raul Gonzales taught me to swim when he took me snorkeling. I almost drowned when he shoved me overboard the first time."

"You only swam two times before you swam to the beach?"

"I said it was a long swim. I was completely exhausted. There was also a current that kept taking me north. I had to consistently adjust for it. That's probably what made it so difficult. I have no idea how far I swam. I was also very relieved when Detective Ramos' helicopter landed. I had no idea how I was going to handle Gonzales. Fortunately, he was already gone."

"Tell us about the drugging," Clark said. He was still very angry over this.

"Raul took me snorkeling a second time on the coast just outside the Tarcoles River in Costa Rica. A shark attacked us, so we cut our snorkeling short, and decided to have lunch at the Si Como No Resort. You should also know we were aware something was about to happen in a day or so. I called Detective Ramos and made him aware. He was at Panama City with three other detectives."

"Did you save Senor Morales' life in the shark attack?" Clark asked getting back to the subject.

"I don't think that I saved his life," Harriet said. "I saw the shark, and he didn't. I swam hard and struck the white shark in the eye. He responded by striking out with his tail. He struck Raul in the side and chest knocking him unconscious.

It was probably my fault for punching the shark's eye. I got him breathing again. We left the area quickly."

"The shark would probably have taken a chunk out of him if you hadn't attacked it." Clark said.

"I don't know that for sure, sir. I just made it angry."

"Let's go back to the resort," Captain Decker said.

"We came back into the river and docked at the Si Como No Resort. I made the mistake of leaving the table to go to the bathroom. When I came back, something did not feel right. It could have been Raul acting weird, or just a sense I had just made a mistake. Anyway, I tasted the lemonade. It was the worst lemonade I had ever tasted. My salad had a white substance on it I did not recognized. My senses were on overload. I didn't eat it, and sort of moved it aside.

Then he offered me a section of his fish he was eating. Figuring he would not drug his own food I took a bite. Well, he did drug it. Before I knew it, I was drinking the lemonade and eating the salad before he had it taken away. I don't remember anything after that. I woke up nine hours later sometime after 11PM. I found the contents of my purse on the bed, and a thousand dollars beside it."

"Did you know Senor Paniagua was there?" Captain Decker asked.

"Not at the time, or I should say I did not know he was the target. His name was mentioned, but I did not connect anything. I was stopped by two large men in black suits. They directed me towards the front of the hotel. They were carrying guns under their coat. I was not looking very good. I could barely walk. My head was hurting as I stumbled towards the front desk. I was working through the effects of the drug."

"How did you happen unto Paniagua's boat?"

Christopher Charles

"When I reached the docks, I found same man Raul had paid to watch our boat. He was sympathetic to my situation. I told him I needed the fastest boat available and gave him the thousand dollars. He directed me to a large red and white boat.

He untied it and threw the lines in as I started it up and left the dock. I was a little out of it. Otherwise I probably would not have stolen the boat. It was fast. I knew the ship was going to sail down the west coast. I just punched the throttle all the way forward and hoped I could catch it. I only caught it because it stopped to drop off the passengers and crew."

"That's still a lot of ocean," Captain Decker said.

"Yes sir, but the boat had radar giving me a twenty-mile radius. I figured if I stayed within fifteen miles off the coast, I would see it on the screen. There were several smaller images, but I knew the ship would make a larger one."

"Okay, let's go to when you boarded the ship," Captain Decker said.

"First you should know I was shocked to see the ship was empty. I had no idea what to expect. I knew someone was on the Bridge. He had slowed the boat, so I could board. I also saw a large raft in the middle of the lower hatch."

"Captain Morgan said he stopped for your boat because he thought it was Paniagua coming to board the ship." Clark said.

"That's what he said. I didn't know up until then who was trying to do us harm, or whose boat I had. It all came together rather quickly. I also realized Paniagua probably had someone plant bombs aboard. You have to know I told Gonzales everything after he administered the drug. I went back to Rose's cabin and found everything had been removed. I went to Youngsu's cabin and found his bag beneath his bed. I had forgotten about it. Inside was his scanner that detected low emitting frequencies. I took it and began searching the ship.

Detective Harriet Brown

I found two four-pound bombs in the engine room below floorplates taped to pipes. After I removed them, I had to find a place to put them. I figured if I threw them overboard, they might trigger the others on board. I decided to place them on the boat, send it adrift, and let Paniagua blow up his own boat. I found three more forward. Two were in a crew's cabin below the water line. You have one of crewman in custody now. The fifth bomb was a good ten pounds. I found it in a cabinet above Gonzales' bed. You will have to ask him why it was in his cabin. It would have blown a large hole in the side of the ship, but it would not have sunk it."

"When did Captain Morgan leave the ship in Paniagua's boat?" Captain Decker asked.

He left when I was still below deck looking for more bombs. I heard the boat pull away. I ran back up to the Bridge to warn him, but he had smashed the radio. He had also taken the life raft, not a nice man. Though, I have to say in his defense, he was being pressured by Paniagua. He had his daughter and grandson. He even sent Captain Morgan a picture over the internet."

"Then how did you find where he had left the passengers and crew?" Clark asked.

"The ship had a course direction screen. It would show you where you are on the course, and it would show you where you have been. I simply turned the ship and returned on the previous course following the line on the screen. The throttles can go backwards and forwards. A reverse on one throttle, and a forward on the other throttle turns the ship very fast."

"Let's move to the raid on the Si Como No Resort," Clark said.

"As I said Ramos was already at the beach when I swam ashore. Gonzales had left to find Paniagua. He went the wrong direction." She said with a smile. "Mc Craw, Youngsu, and myself climbed into the helicopter with the detectives and headed out. When we landed, I only took Mc Craw and Youngsu with me into the resort.

They saw us land, but we were no threat. I calmly walked up the steps to the entrance only to be stopped by two very large men in black coats. We did not look dangerous. We had no weapons showing. They allowed me to be close enough for Mc Craw and Youngsu to take them out.

I moved into the hotel and walked to the front counter. The clerk immediately recognized me when I fainted in front of his counter. He ran around to help about the time Youngsu, and Mc Craw entered. He was quickly subdued, and his phone lines were all disconnected.

We went in further, crossed the pool when we spotted two more men in black. Being the decoy, I walked towards them. One of them recognized me from the night before and allowed me closer. I dropped a few tears telling him I was sorry for the night before, but Senor Paniagua wanted to see me. I didn't want to lose my job.

Trying to help, he knocked on the door to inquire. The door opened. I ran inside pulling my gun from my purse. Mc Craw and Youngsu coming up behind me took out the two men, while I lined up on Paniagua. He threatened to blow up the ship and kill all of the passengers and crew. So, I shot the large switch from his hand taking two of his fingers with it. The switch flew to the corner of the room.

A man beside Paniagua threw himself over the switch as another man at the table drew his gun. I shot the man in the shoulder sending the gun, and him backwards to the floor. The man with the switch squeezed it shut coming up from the floor. I could not bring my gun back fast enough. Paniagua's boat blew up.

Mc craw came through the door shooting his pistols in the air and shouting. It quickly quelled any further resistance. Detective Ramos arrived, and the Navy Seals landed on the beach. It was all over very quickly. I was exhausted, but I called Rose to see if the ship blew up. It didn't, but I still wanted Youngsu to check it again with his scanner to be sure. We flew back to the ship and boarded it. Youngsu searched the ship, and Detective Ramos found out who the saboteurs on the ship were. I went to bed."

Captain Decker took a deep breath and asked, "Where did you get your guns?"

"Mc Craw picked up the pistols from the men in the black suits."

"I don't have any further questions," Captain Decker said, "Sir?"

"I think that is enough for the debriefing," Clark said. "You can stop the recording."

Captain Decker turned the recorder off, "The debriefing is over for the moment. I would like to talk with our prisoner next."

"Yes, that would be advisable. Harriet, Senor Gonzales is going through the canal, and leaving the ship at Cartagena, Columbia. He says he has family there. Would you like to listen to his debriefing?"

"Can one believe anything he has to say?"

"Why don't you listen, and decide for yourself," Clark said.

"Okay, turn it on, I will try to keep an open mind."

Captain Decker took the disc back to the beginning of Gonzales debriefing, and started it up.

Harriet listen until it was finished, then she stood, "I need to go back to the ship now. Thank you, Clark." She turned and walked out of the office.

"That is a remarkable-women," Captain Decker said.

"You have no idea," Clark said.

Christopher Charles

"Okay, are you ready for the prisoner?"

"Let's move along."

The lieutenant reentered, "We have the prisoner outside, sir."

"Good, send him in." Captain Decker said.

A moment later, a crewman was pushed into the room, and forced to sit in the chair opposite the Captain. The Petty Officers who brought him in remained standing on each side of him carrying revolvers.

Captain Decker looked at the crewman. He was a wiry small man able to crawl into small places. He kept his head down waiting for his punishment.

"Before we start, you should know everything you say will be recorded, and could be used in a court of law. Do you understand what I just said?"

The man nodded his head.

"I will need an affirmative or negative from you," Captain Decker said.

"Yes sir."

"Then we will continue. You were found with bomb making materials in your cabin, and a bomb taped to the bulkhead below your bed in an attempt to sabotage an American cruise ship that could have killed thousands of Americans not to mention the loss of property. That automatically puts you into the category of a terrorist. That means Gitmo or as you might know it as Guantanamo Bay, Cuba. There's no lawyer or justice system to protect you there, or I could turn you over the Colombian National Police, who are very anxious to see you, or I can have you lay over for testifying against Senor Paniagua and place you on American soil with the protection of our legal system. What is it going to be?"

"I will take the last offer," The Crew Man said.

Detective Harriet Brown

"Then state your name:"

"Arturo Molina."

"How long have you worked for the Norsewegian Cruise Lines?"

"One year."

"What was the name of you bunkmate?"

"He was my brother, Jose Molina."

"How was he employed?"

"We came aboard together, sir."

"How did you get the bomb making material aboard the ship?"

"We brought in the bomb parts a little at a time. Some of it came aboard with the other supplies."

"How long in the planning has this been going on?"

"Paniagua's people killed my father and threatened to kill my mother unless we did as they said. That was a month ago. They lived in a small hacienda outside of Cartagena. We could not even go home to his funeral."

"We have Paniagua in custody. He and his men are being transported to Gitmo as we speak. Are you willing to testify Paniagua instructed you to place the bombs aboard the ship?"

"Is there any way to protect my mother?"

"I will see what we can do."

"I don't care what happens to me, but I want to see Senor Paniagua dead!"

"Then I can rely on your testimony?"

"Yes sir."

"Now many bombs were placed on the ship?"

"Four were placed in the ship, and I gave a ten-pound bomb to the First Mate Gonzales. He was to place it anywhere he thought best."

"He was part of Paniagua's people?"

"You did not know that? I saw him leaving here. He was there to make sure we placed the bombs."

"How did you know he was part of Paniagua's people?"

"He took over the First Mate's position, didn't he?"

"He said the position became open, and he took advantage of it."

"I don't know, sir," Molina said. "I only know he was aware we were placing the bombs. I even gave him one. I believed he would have told Paniagua if we had refused."

"Were there any others involved with Paniagua on the ship or part of the Norsewegian Cruise Lines?"

"There may have been, but I don't know of anyone else."

"Okay, Senor Molina, I will see what we can do to protect your mother," Captain Decker said. He turned to the speaker, "Do you want to ask any questions, sir?"

"Yes, who killed Captain Waverly and First Mate Williamson?"

"My brother, and I didn't. We only placed the bombs!"

"Did you place the bomb in Captain Waverly's car?"

"You said I would not get Gitmo if I cooperated."

"That is correct," Clark said. "We have the bomb makings we took from your cabin. It should not be hard to match it with the car bomb. We want the truth, now!"

"The First Mate caught me placing the bomb in the engine room. My brother had to shoot him. It was either that or Paniagua would shoot our mother."

"And Captain Waverly?"

"I placed the bomb as ordered while he was in Mr. O' Brian's office."

"Who ordered it?"

"Who do you think? He had a gun to my mother's head, and my father lay on the floor dead."

"How did you communicate with him?"

"He phoned me and sent me the video."

"To repeat, who ordered the killings?" Clark yelled.

"Paniagua! Paniagua," Molina shouted.

"Your mother was rescued, and is now on the cruise ship," Captain Decker said.

"Thank you, sir," Molina said.

Captain Decker turned to the lieutenant, "Return him to the brig."

The lieutenant tapped Molina on the shoulder and led him from the Captain's Office.

Detective Ramos, no longer needed, returned with his men, taking the helicopter back to Panama City. They would take a flight back to Los Angeles from there. The helicopter was costing him 350 dollars an hour. He really could not delay longer. Harriet was sleeping. She was exhausted. He did not want to wake her. He would see her at home. He did not trust Gonzales or was it Morales now. He knew he was getting off the ship in Cartagena. Then he would be out of her life. He kept that thought as he boarded the helicopter.

12 Panama Canal

Harriet returned to the ship. The crew was still coming aboard. The sun appeared over the horizon. It would be another two hours before all of the passengers, and lifeboats were aboard. The rafts were deflated and brought aboard as well. They left the supplies on the beach for the small village to use as they pleased. This was the food, tents, cooking gear, etc. It was a bonanza for the village.

Harriet was still tired. She took advantage of the delay to take a nap. She thought about taking a jacuzzi, but then she would have to redo her hair, and makeup.

Laying on her pillow, she heard Nadine open the door and look in on her. She faked she was sleeping. She was not up to answering anymore questions, especially about Raul. She heard the recording. He said he loved her but was that all an act to please the Captain. How did she feel about him? He could have left her a note instructing her what he wanted her to do. No, that was no good. She heard, go back to Los Angeles. If she did, Paniagua would have blown up the ship. Maybe that was his intention all along.

No, he really did want Paniagua, but what about the bombs? He was handed one. That's why the lifeboat drills. The ship was expendable, the passengers and crew were not. That also meant the two saboteurs knew him. He was going to Paniagua hacienda to stop him from blowing up the ship, or to murder him? Why did she think that?

Finally, unable to sleep, she rolled out of bed, and walked out into the living room. They were bringing the passengers aboard now, but it was still slow going through security.

She saw Nadine standing on the balcony, and shouted, "I am going to see who is in charge of the ship now."

"You will probably see Gonzales, opps, I mean Morales. I saw him boarding earlier."

"We probably need to clear the air," Harriet said. "Who is running the ship?"

Coming inside, Nadine said, "The military is aboard. Maybe one of them."

"I'm going to check it out," Harriet said leaving the cabin. She knew Rose and the guys were already aboard. They had everything secured. She walked down the steps, and up another series of steps the sailors like to call a ladder. She entered the Bridge, and saw the military trying to replace the broken radio.

The First Officer was there checking the instruments. He looked up when she entered. "Are you coming for another lesson Miss Cummings, or is it Miss Brown now?"

"I don't think I need more lessons, sir, but I thought you might want my help."

"No, we will not be needing it," The First Officers Bitterman said. "Colonel Morales will not be the Captain since he is disembarking at Cartagena, and Captain Morgan is being retained aboard the Navy Frigate."

"Then that will make you Captain of the ship," Harriet said. She knew she could push the issue since she still technically had control of the ship.

"Yes, you do understand, now you will please leave my Bridge. I do not want to see you up here again." He looked at her hard, "Do we understand each other?"

"Perfectly sir," Harriet said. "It appears you are not very appreciative of having a ship to be a Captain of." She turned and left the Bridge. At the hatch she stopped, and asked, "When are we getting underway, Captain?"

"Within the hour, and my name is Captain Bitterman."

"Thank you, Captain Bitterman." She turned and descended the stairs. She walked back to the fantail and looked out at the beach. The tender was still picking up the passengers. A few crew members were still on shore. The village people were tearing down the tents, and claiming the items left behind.

She heard footsteps behind her. She knew who it was. Raul came up beside her, "I'm going to miss this place."

"You have a strange kind of humor, sir," Harriet said not looking at him standing beside her.

"You know I was only trying to protect you at the resort." Morales said.

"It appeared more like you squeezed all the information you could out of me, and then threw me away. Do you have any idea how it feels to wake up in a strange place having no idea how you got there, and you do not know anyone around you? We have not even discussed the pounding headache, and the death warmed over feeling."

"I'm sorry, but things were about to start happening, and you were a prime target."

"You did not know that until I spilled my guts to you."

"O' Brian told me who you were."

"You could have told me who you were, especially before you drugged me. I can be cooperative."

"It was poor judgement on my part," Raul said. "But looking back, if I had not, we would not be standing here."

"I understand you knew there were bombs aboard. You were even given one."

"Yes, I took all the passengers, and crew off the ship. If I had taken the bombs off, Paniagua would have known, and not carried through with his blackmail threat on a ship I controlled. He would have picked another ship and blown it up. It was necessary for him to believe he was being successful. He had computer linkages to the bombs. He would have known if they were removed from the ship but placing them on his boat was brilliant. I never thought of doing that."

She was hearing him. It all sounded very reasonable, but she felt there was something he was not telling her. Also, she wanted him to clear himself. She was willing to believe anything that sounded reasonable. "So, who were those people in Guatemala, fake grandparents?"

"No, they were my grandparents on my mother's side, whose name is Gonzales."

"You could have left me there. It would have been kinder."

"Yes, the thought crossed my mind, but then my grandparents would have been involved, and the timing would have been off. Besides you might have stolen the black stallion and rode back to ship."

"You regret teaching me to ride him?"

"No, that was one of the good things I did, but by far the best one was teaching you how to swim. How did you manage a two-thousand-meter swim?"

Christopher Charles

"It was very scary looking down into the blackness. My arms got so tired I could only move my legs. The snorkel helped a lot. I didn't have to turn my head to breathe. I more or less floated and kicked my legs slightly. The fins propelled me forward with little effort. I did not believe I would make it for a while."

"I would still like to be your friend," Raul said.

"I heard you were leaving the ship when we reached Cartagena tomorrow."

"Yes, I have been demoted from First Mate to passenger. It seems they found out I didn't have experience in sailing a ship this size. The First Officer has taken my place."

"It seems this ship loses its officers often," Harriet said. "Maybe you should stay on. You might be Captain again by the time we reach Miami."

"No, being Captain of a cruise ship is not my idea of a career. Being a police officer is much more exciting. Look what we accomplished this time."

"Thank you for including me, but I did not see anything exciting."

"You brought the man responsible for killing your father to justice, and the way I hear it you shot his fingers off. You had the opportunity to kill him, but you didn't, that shows mercy."

"It shows I am not a killer," Harriet said. "I did not cross the line."

"Sometimes it is best to remove the vermin. Now your country will spend millions to kill him, and you could have done it with one shot."

"That's rather harsh."

"That's reality, but sometimes we need to work things out. Ring out all the emotions before we can go on. You know he would not have hesitated a second in killing you."

"I still could not just kill him when there was another option."

"Yes, that's what makes you who you are."

"Okay, a truce until we reach Cartagena tomorrow."

"I accept," Raul said.

They heard the ship's horn blow indicating the ship was getting underway.

"How about something to eat in the ballroom," Raul asked. "It will not be the Captain's table, but we can possibly obtain a table next to the dance floor."

"It is a little early, but I am starved," Harriet said, "I have not eaten since I don't remember."

"Then it is the ballroom." Raul said taking her arm. "Remember, I do not pull any rank now."

Harriet smiled, "Neither do I."

The ship had taken on the Navy Seals, and the Navy Frigate was following them through Panama Canal. The bomb scare seemed to have passed. The Frigate carried the prisoners, Captain Morgan, and the saboteur, Arturo Molina.

All of the lifeboats and tenders were in place. First Mate's red speed boat was loaded aboard the ship. It now belonged to the First Officer.

The First Officer, now Captain Bitterman, set the ship in motion. He signed off on the course set to the Panama Canal. He left the Second Officer in charge and proceeded down to the ballroom for a decent meal. He had not eaten since they were placed on the beach. He was hungry. He squared his shoulder and walked down the steps. He had visions of being promoted to Captain of the ship when they reached Miami. Someone has to be Captain for the return trip.

Christopher Charles

He walked into the ballroom and found the captain's table. He was the only one sitting at it. He did not realize he should have invited some of the guests to the table. He ordered a thick steak and a bottle of champagne.

The steward came quickly with the champagne, "The chef is still putting things together, sir. It will be a while."

He looked over at the table across from his to see Morales and Harriet, each were eating his large steak. He called the steward over again, "How did they come about their steak?"

"It was the only two he had on hand, sir. It is a mess in the kitchen. The freezer was off, and everything is unfrozen. The chef is trying to rescue everything. He is under a lot of pressure. He will have your steak as soon as possible."

"The Captain's table takes priority. He should know that."

"Yes sir, I will inform him. Who should I say is the Captain?"

"I am Captain Bitterman, I will be eating here now."

"Yes sir, I will tell the chef immediately."

The band came in. They began setting up. It was early, but Chief Myers had instructed them to play. He wanted things back to normal quickly to calm the passengers. Though most of them were in their cabins sleeping.

The passengers and crew had become aware of what happened to the ship, and the part Harriet had played in it. They were being especially nice to her trying to thank her. They had actually closed the kitchen down for two hours, but they also needed to please the new Captain.

The steward brought out his vegetables, "The chef is still trying to locate your steak, sir. Is there something else you would like?"

"What do you have?"

"We found the lobsters, sir. We can boil them right up."

"Okay, lobsters then," Captain Bitterman said in an irritated voice.

"Yes sir! Right away sir," the steward said, and hurried off to the kitchen.

The band began to play a soft melody as Harriet and Raul Morales were finishing eating.

Harriet looked over at Raul, "Are you related to a Los Angeles Chief of Police? His name was Don Morales."

"I do not have any immediate relatives in the United States that I know of, why?"

"He killed my father, and tried to kill me on several occasions," Harriet said.

"There are a lot of Morales in the world."

"Yes, some are not so nice."

To change the subject, Raul asked, "Are you up for some dancing?"

"I am still very tired, maybe one Waltz."

Raul raised his hand, and mouthed, "Waltz," to the band leader.

He nodded, turned to his people, "Waltz."

Harriet wiped her hands and walked out on the floor. Immediately the music when into a Waltz. Taking Raul's hand, she moved about the floor. It was like old times feeling her feet flow over the floor. She felt the magic again allowing the music to take her as Raul led her around the floor.

When the Waltz was finished, she almost collapsed, and knew she was still very tired, or maybe it was more. She looked up at Raul, "I think I need a few hours of more sleep."

"Then why don't I meet you when we enter the canal. That will not be until two or three this afternoon."

"Let's make it three."

"At the fantail at three," Raul said, as he helped her back to the table. She picked up her purse. Raul led her out of the ballroom. He watched her go up the stairs, turned, and proceeded to his stateroom thinking maybe he was forgiven. He received a vibration on his phone, opened it to reveal his father, Esteban Morales, on the line:

Phone conversation:

"Yes sir, we are proceeding towards the canal now."

"Bring her home with you. I would like to meet her." Esteban said.

"Who, sir.

"Why, Miss Harriet Brown, she is becoming very popular here. We are having a celebration party for the capture of Senor Paniagua."

"Yes sir, but she may not come without her team. She is feeling a little insecure at the moment."

"Bring them! General Lopez will be here. He is very anxious to meet all of them."

"The ship should dock in the morning around eight. We could be ready to go by nine."

"Do you want the limo to pick you up?"

"And my car."

"Okay, I'll have both there by nine."

"They will have to be back aboard the ship by 6PM, unless they give them another day because of attempted kidnapping."

"Let me know. I also have another surprise for you."

"Are you going to tell me what it is?"

"Then it would not be a surprise."

"You should know I will not be going on with the ship."

"That is probably good thinking, even though General Lopez said he would protect you."

"He does not have that much influence in the United States. I will call you when we leave the ship."

"Good, talk to you then."

Raul pushed the phone into his pocket. Walking back to his cabin, he asked himself. "Do I really love her? How does one know? She makes him feel good. He likes to be around her. His heart pounds when he dances with her. Does that classify as love? How is he going to convince her of these feelings after he deserted her at the resort?

Then how does she feel about him. He was doing very well up until the desertion. Now he is at the bottom looking up. Maybe meeting his family will help. She liked his grandparents. He will push for her to come to his home.

Harriet entered the cabin to find Nadine in the jacuzzi. "That's looks heavenly. You want some company?"

"Come on in, the waters great," Nadine said. "I see you met our Colonel again."

"Yes, he was his charming self," Harriet said dropping her clothes to the floor. She climbed in allowing her body to sink into the whirling water. It felt good.

"You going to meet him again?" Nadine asked

"We are meeting at the fantail at 3PM to watch the canal entrance together," Harriet said. "Right now, I need to sleep, but this feels so good."

"There is something about him," Nadine said. "I don't know what it is yet. Maybe it's the name, Morales."

"Have Rose check to see if there is any connection. Paniagua was connected to Chief Morales maybe he is connected to Raul Morales."

"Are you hoping there is not a connection?"

"I don't know how I feel at the moment other than I am very tired." She felt herself starting to fall asleep in the warm water, "This is enough for me."

She stood and worked herself out of the water. "If I stay longer in there, I will probably drown." She wiped herself dry, slipped into something light, and headed for her bedroom. She stopped a second, "You can have Rose, and the boys up here when they wake up to see the canal, if they want. That's about 3PM."

"I'll tell Rose."

Harriet stumbled to her bed and fell in a heap. She was exhausted. She didn't know Nadine came in and pulled the blankets over her.

Nadine smiled, and said to herself, "She has had to learn so much in such a short time. Now she is faced with love coming from the wrong source. Why doesn't she fall in love with Detective Ramos? He obviously loves her, or he would not have flown down here to rescue her. She does not see her shinning white knight only the villain."

Nadine woke her at two thirty to allow her to dress herself before the boys arrived, and her appointment with Raul at three.

Harriet looked up to see Nadine. What time is it?"

"Time for you to be out of bed, if you plan on meeting the man who is pulling your heart strings at three."

She stumbled out of bed, began dressing herself, "He is not pulling my heart strings. I control my emotions."

"Do you want to sleep longer?"

"No!"

"I say no more."

Harriet managed her clothes before the boys came knocking on the door. Behind them came Rose. She carried her spyware suitcase. Harriet closed her bedroom door to finish the process of putting on her makeup and doing her hair.

Mc Craw came in, looked around. The air conditioning had been on, it felt good compared to his room below deck. He looked at the jacuzzi, and noticed it still had water in it. "I think I will be taking advantage of the warm water." He slipped his pants off leaving his trunks on. Slipping over the side, he was in the water with the jets hitting his back.

Youngsu watched him a moment, "I forgot swimsuit, back in a minute." He slipped out the door.

Harriet walked out of the bedroom, refreshed, and looking very nice. She smiled big, "You all have a nice time." She walked swiftly towards the door.

"You going to see that bastard again," Mc Craw yelled from the jacuzzi.

"Maybe," Harriet yelled back as she closed the door.

"That man is bad!" Mc craw said. "Why can't she fall for someone decent?"

Harriet was down the hall descending the stairs. She knew how they felt. Why was she setting herself up again? Maybe it was the fact he had a bad side that appealed to her. It was like watching fire consume a building. You know it is being destroyed but it is fascinating to watch. She walked back to the fantail. He was there waiting for her.

He smiled and held out his arms.

She allowed him to hug and kiss her on the cheek. She was not quite ready to allow him to kiss her on the mouth yet. She turned to the rail, and watched the ship enter the locks that would take them to the lake.

When the ship entered a lock, it would fill with water raising the ship in the process. The higher lock would open allowing the ship to move forward at a higher level. They had very similar locks on the Great Lakes to move from one lake to another.

They watched the process for an hour. He had his arm around her, held her close, "My parents want to meet you when we arrive in Cartagena. You are sort of a hero. I would like you to meet General Lopez, my boss. He especially wants to meet you."

"I will think about it," Harriet said. "I want to do something with my team in Cartagena. They have not been treated well on this cruise. I have a lot of making up to do."

"Bring them along. My father insisted upon it."

"I will see what they say," Harriet said. "Let's go find something to eat now. I am suddenly feeling very hungry." She did not want to commit this early. She will allow him to dangle awhile. She had control of her emotions. Nadine did not have to worry.

"How about we try the Blue-Sky Bar?" Raul asked. "They have good steaks there."

That sounded safe, "Okay, but I may go for something other than steak."

"They have an Italian dish there you might like."

"You are sounding better, lead on."

Harriet's Cabin

Rose was into her computer trying to get into Columbian's births and deaths section. She finally found the Morales'. She saw Esteban Morales name. He had one son, Raul. Checking further, she found Esteban had two brothers a Don Morales, and a Jose Morales. They had moved to Los Angeles with their mother thirty-five years ago. That was the connection. She also knew Paniagua had Chief Don Morales killed in prison. She wanted to tell Harriet, but she decided to allow her to have a good time first.

Blue Sky Bar

Harriet took a seat behind a booth in the bar. A band was playing soft music allowing people to talk. Raul took the seat across from her. The waiter came over and handed them a menu.

Raul looked up at him, "We will both have your Italian Special"

"Yes sir, and to drink?"

"Champagne of course," Raul said. "This is a special occasion."

The waiter looked at Harriet. She nodded, "That will be fine."

Moments later two glasses were poured with champagne, and the waiter left.

Raul lifted his glass, "To love and all of its mysteries."

Harriet tipped her glass to strike his, "To love that is very scary."

They both took a sip of the Champaign.

Christopher Charles

Harriet accidently took a larger sip, and felt the fizz go up her nose.

The next thing she knew, she was on the dance floor dancing close to him. She liked it. She allowed him to hold her close.

She felt the pressure building. She did not want him this close, but she could not resist. She felt relieved when the music stopped, and they came back to the table. Their food was already there.

She continued to eat very slow hoping to delay more dancing. The waiter came over and removed the plates.

He started to ask her to dance when she said, "Is there desert?"

"I thought I would take you out to watch the sun set over the lake. It is very special."

"So, it is desert or the sunset?"

"I will bring you back for the desert, and you can have both."

"Okay, let's go," Harriet said.

They walked back to the fantail. Below them they could hear the music playing in the ballroom. It was soft. The water was perfectly still. The sun was setting in the west sending its rays north and south.

She looked up at him as he kissed her on the lips. She suddenly released her restraints kissing him back passionately. Finally, minutes later she pulled herself back from him, "We are probably going too fast."

"I do not have much time to convince you to marry me."

"I don't know that much about you," Harriet said.

"You are going to meet my family tomorrow. Ask them any questions you like. I am sure they are going to fall in love with you too."

Harriet swallowed hard. Recovering she asked, "Are you asking me to marry you?"

"Yes, if you will have me."

"I love you very much, but I am not thinking straight at the moment. You turn my emotion all kinds of ways. Let me meet your family, and I will let you know then."

"I know this is a big step, but we are connected. I can feel it. We belong together."

"I don't think good around you. My emotions become all confused. You have to let me straighten them out."

"Okay, then tomorrow we go see my family. I will not press you. I want you to be sure."

"Thank you," Harriet said softly as he kissed her again. She allowed herself to kiss him emotionally. When her emotions were beyond reasoning, she somehow found the strength to pull herself free, and whispered, "No more, please no more. I cannot handle it." She broke his embrace, "I will see you tomorrow at the lower hatch at 9AM. I am going to keep you at your word, to bring my team."

"Yes, as long as you are coming," Raul said. He watched her running back inside the ship. He felt the emotions stirring in himself. He really wanted her, but he would have to wait. Calming himself, he continued to stare out into the setting sun.

Harriet's Cabin

Frightened, she almost ran back to her cabin. He had this strange effect on her. Maybe she was still responding from the Scopolamine drug. She could feel her tears wanting to surface. Reaching the door, she stopped, took a few deep breaths, gaining control of herself. Then opening the door, she entered.

Rose was at the table looking at her computer. Mc Craw stood on the balcony with Youngsu looking at the sunset.

Nadine saw the distressed look on Harriet's face, "What happened?"

Harriet ran to her, placed her head on her shoulder, and whispered, "He wants to marry me, and I'm scared."

Nadine patted her on the back, "It's okay, dear, we'll talk about it later."

Harriet regained her composer as Rose looked up. Harriet quickly wiped the tears away, then she said, "We have all been invited to Raul's family home for lunch tomorrow. We are leaving here at 9 AM tomorrow."

"Maybe you should look at this," Rose said as the boys came back inside. "Your Raul Morales is related to our late Chief Morales. He is his uncle. It seems going after Paniagua was more than drugs. It may have been revenge."

"He said he did not have any relatives he knew about in the United States."

"I am sure he would know if he had an uncle who moved there forty years ago. His father's brother after all." Rose said.

Harriet began clearing her head. The emotions of the moment before were being controlled. She looked at her team, "He asked me to marry him, and it seems I know very little about him."

"You want me to take spyware," Youngsu asked.

"Could you set it up without being noticed?" Harriet asked.

"I have ship's transmitter antenna," Youngsu said "I have all spyware that was on the ship."

"It's going to be tight security," Harriet said. "If he learns we spied on him, I may lose him."

"You need to learn more about him," Rose said. "Under normal circumstances this would not be very nice, but he has already lied to you about his family connections, and his involvement in this case."

Nadine continued, "Normally I would say this is not a good idea if you are thinking of marrying him, but you need something more than emotions to make this decision. If you find out his family is bad, it will be very difficult to back out of a marriage. They kill people down here on a regular basis."

"You need to know what you are getting into before you marry this guy," Mc Craw said. "Let's do the spyware."

"Okay, but it will have to be done with extreme precision," Harriet said, thinking to herself. If their spyware comes up with nothing, then her answer will be "Yes." She needed some way to make a decision that was not emotional.

13 Raul's Hacienda

The next morning Harriet was up early. She was wearing slacks with ten spy bugs in her left pocket. She wore a loose blouse to allow the moist air to move through it. She was combing her hair when Nadine came in with her cup of coffee, "Let me teach you to say something nice in Spanish. Now repeat after me: Gracias por su hospitalidad y por tratarme tan bien"

Harriet repeated it, "What did I say?"

"Thank you for your hospitality and treating me so nice."

Harriet repeated it several more times until she had it down.

"You need to say it with feeling to make it genuine."

Harriet tried it again, "How was that?"

"Better but say it like you play the piano."

Harriet took Nadine's hand, looked up at her with her big blue eyes, "Gracias por su hospitalidad y por tratarme tan bien."

"You have it." Nadine said, "Let's not overdo it."

Taking her purse, she headed for the door.

They met the boys coming up the stairs. Youngsu wore an open long sleeve shirt to cover the transmitter strapped to his arms. He also carried a few bugs in his left pants pocket. They were not carrying anymore spyware. They were only interested in transmitting.

When they reached the lower hatch, Raul was waiting for them. The limousine and Raul's SLK 230 Mercedes were beside the ship waiting on the dock.

He gave her a hug. The two of them left the ship with the others following behind. Limousine driver handed Raul his keys and opened the door for Harriet. The other driver opened the door for the limousine allowing Nadine and company to enter. He stepped into the shotgun seat. The limousine driver took his seat. In moments the two vehicles were heading towards the city.

Raul had lowered the top allowing the warm breeze to strike their faces. Harriet had placed her rolled hair band on to hold her blond hair. She smiled allowing the breeze to strike her face. Not going fast, the limousine moved easily behind them.

They moved on through the city and up on a road following the coast. Harriet had memorized the streets going through the city. Some of the streets she could not see, but she memorized the buildings next to them.

Raul noticed she turned her head at times. He knew she was memorizing the streets again. He was not going to trap her at his house.

The coast road was two lanes. It had narrow curves that at times only allowed one car to pass through. He was not driving fast, but the narrow road made it seem that way. There were fences along the coast side in sections especially where the curves were sharp, and the side of the road dropped off several hundred feet. She was glad they were driving on the inside of the road. She would have to close her eyes on the way back.

Harriet was not talking because the wind made her shout to be heard.

Raul noticed she was uncomfortable, and yelled, "I can raise the top."

Harriet shook her head, "Let's just enjoy the wind."

An hour later they approached a long drive going off the road, that led up the hill, and into the jungle. Suddenly the jungle was gone leaving a manicured lawn, and a paved driveway that led up to a very large house that overlooked the ocean.

There was a gate with two guards and a guard house. It was part of a high electric fence that ran around the house. The gate opened. The guard phoned the house making the residence aware of their arrival.

Raul drove through and up the driveway. He drove around the large circular portion and pulled his small sports car up to the steps. The limousine parked behind him.

Harriet stepped out of the car. She removed her hair band, ran her fingers through her hair, trying to remove the knots, that may have accumulated.

Mrs. Morales, a short woman with large hips, but dressed very nice in a long Spanish dress, walked down the marble steps from the house with a big smile on her face. She took her son in her arms, hugged him tight. She knew he had placed his life-in danger again. She was thankful he was alive.

Harriet and the others waited with the limousine.

She looked up, "Who are these friends of yours?"

Raul went through the introduction, and finally with some emphasis said, "And this is Harriet Brown."

"The one the papers are making all the fuss about?"

"Most of it is true," Raul said. "They can only stay for a short time. They must be back aboard the ship by six."

"Then we will do the best we can to entertain them in the time we have," Mrs. Morales said shaking Harriet's limp hand.

"You don't have to make any fuss over us," Harriet said. "Raul was anxious for us to meet you and invited us up here for a few hours." Harriet looked around as she received her hand back, "You have a very beautiful house, Mrs. Morales. I can see why Raul is so fond of it."

Mrs. Morales turned to Raul, "Why don't you go see your father about lunch as I show your guests the house."

Raul started to give Harriet a hug, thought better of it, turned, "I'll be back in a few minutes."

"Let me take you inside first before we show you the grounds," Mrs. Morales said as she led them back up the marble steps.

A butler opened the door on cue, and the group entered the house. She took them into a great hall that was being decorated, "We are having a welcome home surprise party for Raul tonight. It is unfortunate you cannot stay. I am sure he would have liked it"

"Yes, it would have been fun," Harriet said. She noticed a Steinway Piano, "Do you play the piano," Mrs. Morales?"

"I do on occasions. I studied piano in college. Perhaps if you stay tonight, I will play for you."

"I would love to hear you play," Harriet said.

She led them into a board room that was occupied with a large ten by four oak table with six chairs around it. The room was part library.

Harriet noticed Youngsu placed two bugs under the table, one at each end as Harriet kept Mrs. Morales occupied. "Where did you import the wood?" Harriet asked. "It seems to have come from China."

"A very good guess," Mrs. Morales said as she led them from the room. She took them out onto a back patio that overlooked the ocean far below. Harriet knew the highway was right below them five hundred feet. It was a perfect view of the ocean to pick up a South-Eastern satellite.

Youngsu had already placed his first transmitter on the lower rail. He did it so fast and nonchalant, that she did not notice, and she knew he was going to do it.

Mrs. Morales took them back inside feeling very satisfied she was impressing her guests with her fine house. She took them one step further showing them her husband's study. A place she is never allowed in. Nervous, she did not keep them long. "This is my husband's favorite place in the house." It had a beautiful desk with inlaid wood and rose wood cabinets.

Before they left Harriet managed one bug, and Youngsu managed another under the desk lip.

Feeling she had overstepped the line, Mrs. Morales quickly eased them back out, and took them to the front yard.

Down the hill a hundred yards Harriet saw a large barn, "Do you keep horses here?"

"Yes, we keep about ten horses. Raul likes to ride. He has been riding since he was a child. He is very good on a horse."

"Yes, I am sure he is. Maybe we could see his horses before we leave."

"If time permits," Mrs. Morales said.

Raul, going down the stairs that went to the recreation room in the basement of the house, was thinking how he was going to tell his father he wanted to marry Harriet. He found his father with a close friend, Senor Emilo Federico playing pool.

Seeing him, his father, a six-foot-five black hair man with a small stomach showing, put down his pool stick, grabbed his son, and squeezed him, "It's nice to see you home, son." Turning him around, he said, "You are just in time. I was talking to Emilo here about uniting our families. It's time son. You have proven yourself to be a man and earned a title. We both need grandchildren."

"Yes sir, but why so soon?" He was thinking fast. He wanted to get married, but to Harriet not Emilo Federico's daughter. "Can we talk about this later, sir?" Raul asked becoming embarrassed.

"Sure, sure," Esteban Morales said allowing his enthusiasm to die.

"I have brought guests back with me from the ship, remember," Raul said. "They're upstairs. I would like you to meet them."

"Is one of them Miss Brown?" Esteban asked.

"Yes, she is here with her team," Raul said.

"Is she the one who rescued the ship?" Senor Emilo Federico asked.

"Yes, the same," Raul said.

"Then I want to meet her," Senor Federico said.

They came up the stairs as Mrs. Morales and company were walking back to the house with Harriet.

"I think we promised them a lunch, Raul," Esteban said. "Why don't you go see where they are in preparing it?"

"Yes sir, but maybe I should introduce them first?"

"That won't be necessary," Esteban said pushing Raul towards the kitchen.

Watching him leave, Senor Federico asked, "Do you think he has feelings for this Miss Brown?"

"He may have, but he is marrying your daughter, Gabriela Guevana Federico. That will not change," Esteban said as they walked out on the steps.

Watching the group approach with his wife leading, he said, "She was at my wife's family a few days ago. She learned to ride a horse almost like magic. She saved Raul's life. It's probably why he is affected by her."

"Maybe she had prior lessons," Senor Federico said.

"No, she had never been on a horse, yet she rode that wild stallion of theirs like she had been riding for years."

"You say she rescued him?"

"That stallion bucked him off a cliff. She rode back to the barn and retrieved a rope on the same black stallion. My mother-in-law said she came in riding full out, reared him to a stop, and jumped off. When she came back out of the barn, she leaped up on his back, reared up to turn him around, and kicked off for the jungle like a pro."

"She saved his life," Emilo said. "I think that was important."

"Yes, it is the way she did it that's amazing, and makes one wonder who she really is."

Mrs. Morales had reached the porch steps. She began the climb up to her husband. Harriet and the others followed her.

Senor Morales walked down to meet Harriet, "I suppose you are Miss Brown?"

"Yes, it is my pleasure to meet you, sir." Harriet said. She offered him her limp hand.

Accepting it, he said, "Welcome to our home." He turned to Emilo, "And this is Senor Emilo Federico, he is anxious to meet you."

She turned, extended her hand, "It is my pleasure, sir."

"We've all heard so many extraordinary things about you," Senor Federico said.

"Most of what you heard I believe is exaggerated, sir," Harriet said.

"Maybe, but will you allow us to make this judgement call," Senor Morales said.

Harriet smiled, "I will only try to correct the exaggerated portions, if that is okay, sir."

"Fair enough," Esteban said. He took her arm leading her back inside, saying, "I think I promised you a lunch."

His wife was left for Senor Federico to escort inside.

He led her to another outside patio where a table had been set up with a large awning covering it. A pig had been cooking in a large covered pit. It had since been taken out and carved. People were moving about putting things on the table.

Raul was already there talking to the waiters. When he saw them entering, he moved towards Harriet, but he was blocked by his father, who seated her at the head of the table. He took the seat on one side of her. Senor Federico took the seat on the other side, leaving Raul with his mother at the other end. The rest of the crew took the other open chairs around the table.

Harriet knew she would be grilled. She did not want to disappoint Raul, but she did not want things to be exaggerated.

Mc Craw helped Nadine, and Youngsu helped Rose to their chairs.

Food began to arrive along with beverages. The waiter going around to each of them giving them some choices, roast pig thick, or thin. Champagne or water. Salads were served around.

"We heard you saved our Raul's life when that black demon bucked him over the cliff," Esteban said.

"I just threw him a rope. The horse did all the work and pulled him up."

He looked back at Raul, "Would you like to fill in the details?"

"I don't know much because I was hanging over a cliff, but she had that black stallion pulling me up with a rope she retrieved from the barn a quarter of a mile away."

"You mean the same stallion that bucked you off the cliff was now saving your life?" Emilo asked. "How was that possible?"

"She tamed the animal," Raul said.

"Would you mind telling us how she did that?" Esteban asked.

"She grabbed his ears, and held on tight until he calmed down," Raul said.

Esteban turned back to Harriet, "How long did you hold his ears?"

"Until he stopped bucking, sir." Harriet said with a smile. "I think he was afraid I would grab them again because he behaved very good after that."

"I think we have another way of training our horses, Raul," Esteban said, and smiled. "I would never have thought of that."

"She also saved my life when we went snorkeling a couple of days ago. A white shark attacked me while we were diving, she swam into it, and struck it in the eye. It swung its tail hard, hitting me in the chest, and side, knocking me out cold. She pulled my head back and got me breathing again."

"She hit it in the eye with her fist?" Esteban asked.

"She said she held her arms straight out and swam straight into his eye. It was only her second-time swimming, sir."

"She just learned to swim?" Emilo asked.

"I took her out a few days earlier, and almost drowned her before I realized she did not know how to swim."

"So, you taught her swim?" Emilo asked.

"Yes sir, she learns very fast. I had her diving, and swimming before we left the area."

Emilo turned to Harriet, "You have only been swimming two times in your life?"

"Actually, I have been swimming three times, sir. The last time was two days ago or was it one day. I have not had much sleep over the past week, sir."

"She swam 2,000 meters after she anchored the cruise ship, sir," Raul said.

"That's well over a mile I believe," Emilo said. "I don't know many who could swim that far."

"It was very scary, sir," Harriet said. "I really could not see where I was going."

"Did she swim at night?" Esteban asked.

"Yes sir," Raul said, "She was the only one on the ship. All of the rafts and boats were on shore. She had no choice."

"Let's hear about the ship," Esteban said, turning back to Harriet. "I heard you sailed it by yourself."

"Yes sir, Captain Morgan smashed the radio, and left on Paniagua's boat taking the only remaining life-raft with him."

"Wait a minute here, you just said Paniagua's boat."

Yes sir, I used it to reach the ship?" Harriet said.

"Where did you get his boat?" Esteban asked raising his voice.

"I rather not say," Harriet said.

"Were you connected to Senor Paniagua?"

"No, I only met the man once, and shot his fingers off when I did," Harriet said. "He was going to blow up the boat."

"You mean ship?" Emilo asked.

"No, I mean his boat. It had Captain Morgan on it." Harriet said calmly.

"I think we need to back up here," Esteban said. "Let's start when you acquire Paniagua's boat."

"I still rather not go into it, sir." Harriet said.

He looked at Raul indicating he was to tell him.

"I drugged her and left her at the Si Como No Resort in Puntarenas, Costa Rica. When she came out of the drug, she was angry and took the fastest boat on the dock. It happened to be Senor Paniagua's boat. She chased the ship some sixteen plus hours before she caught up with it to find it empty except for Captain Morgan. He deserted her leaving her with a ship full of bombs ready to go off. He didn't know Miss Brown had moved all of the bombs to Paniagua's boat."

"Paniagua was at the Si Como No Resort?"

"Yes sir," Raul said. "I must have been within a hundred feet of him and didn't know it."

"Evidently Miss Brown knew," Esteban said in a low irritated voice.

"No, I only learned it was his boat when Captain Morgan told me before he took it. That was why he stopped the ship for me to board. He thought it was Senor Paniagua boarding."

"Then Captain Morgan was in on it." Esteban said.

"They had his daughter and grandson," Raul said. "He did what they told him."

"How did you learn how to run the ship?" Emilo asked. "That is no easy task especially anchoring a ship of that size."

"The officers on the Bridge allowed me to watch. They told me how the screens worked. I was there when they anchored offshore once. It was all very interesting. I never thought I would need the information."

"She must have done something very seriously wrong for her to be left at Si Como No Resort by my Raul," Mrs. Morales said.

"No," Raul said, "I was only trying to take her away from Senor Paniagua. Her father was Mr. George Brown, the one who took Senor Paniagua's 800 million. I also did not want any interference, when I removed the passengers and crew from the ship and went for Senor Paniagua's Hacienda. She had control of the ship when there was an emergency.

I deeply regret drugging her. I know now I should have taken her into my confidence and told her what I intended to do. Though, we would have missed Senor Paniagua then, and the ship would be at the bottom of the ocean."

They did not ask her how she found the bombs on the ship. Maybe they knew Raul had knowledge of the bombs. He certainly was aware of the saboteurs.

The food arrived. The conversation turned to small talk. When they were finished, "Morales pulled out a cigar, "Do you smoke, Miss Brown?"

"I have never learned the art, sir," Harriet said.

"Would you like to learn?"

"If you will show me."

"My pleasure," Esteban said. He took out a new cigar. He removed the wrapper and handed it to her.

She looked at the end of the cigar, "I've seen men cut the end of these. Is that important?"

"We usually bite the end of it off."

Harriet put the cigar into her mouth, and tried to bite it off, but it would not come. She took it back out, "I think I need sharper teeth, sir."

"Here, allow me the honor." He took the cigar back, and quickly snapped the end of it off. Handing it back, he said, "I think that will do it." He took out his lighter, flipped it on, as Harriet placed the cigar in her mouth again.

Lighting her cigar, he said, "Suck in the smoke slightly to get the end of the cigar burning."

She managed. The end of the cigar came to life. She smiled, "Thank you for teaching me how to smoke a cigar."

"My pleasure," Esteban said leaning back in his chair taking a big puff from his cigar.

Harriet imitated him and blew out a large puff of smoke. She almost gagged, but she held it in.

Mc Craw did not like her smoking, "I think we need to be getting back to the ship. We have a long drive."

"By all means," Esteban said. "I will have the limousine drive you back to your ship."

"Maybe we could encourage Harriet to stay for the celebration tonight, since it was her exploits we are celebrating," Emilo said. "General Lopez will be here. I am sure he will want to meet her."

Harriet's phone beeped indicating she had a text message. She flipped it open.

It Read:

"The ship will lay over until twelve noon tomorrow to repair the radio."

Looking up, she said, "The ship is not leaving until twelve tomorrow. They need to fix the radio."

"Then you can stay for the celebration," Emilo said.

"I think we should be leaving, Rose said. "I need to check on some things, and I wanted to check out the city before we leave tomorrow."

"Yes," Mc Craw said watching Harriet take another puff from her cigar. "We should all be getting back."

Everyone stood as they began walking out. Rose and Nadine began making their goodbyes, shaking hands with everyone.

Raul walked over to Harriet, "My father would like you to stay too. I think it is important. You wanted to get to know them."

"Yes, I know how important it is, but will you take me back to the ship when I want to go?"

"Better yet, I will give you the keys to my car," Raul said handing her the keys. "That way you may go back anytime you choose."

Taking the keys, Harriet smiled, "Then I will stay for the celebration tonight." Running, she caught up with Nadine and Rose, "I'll be staying, but give me a call if you hear anything important. I have Raul's keys I can leave anytime."

Mc Craw noticed she was not coming, "You should come back with us. I don't trust these people."

"I need to get to know them," Harriet said. "They may become my family."

He gave her a hug whispering, "I know what you have to do, but it doesn't mean I have to like it, and stop smoking that damn cigar. It don't look good on you."

"Thank you for your advice," Harriet said as she closed the door to the limousine. She watched it drive away. They had their work to do, and she had hers. They were both in their best positions. She turned back to Raul waiting for her, "I am all yours."

"The party is going to be a big affair I am told. We need to find you something to wear. I will call a friend of mine and see if she might have something for you."

"You should have told me I would have brought something from the ship."

"Give me a minute," Raul said pressing his speed dial. A voice came on the line:

Phone:

"Gabriela, a friend of mine from the United States needs a dress for tonight's celebration. I was wondering if you might have something."

Pause:

"You have, good!" he turned back to Harriet, "What size shoe?"

"Six or six and a half depending on the shoe."

Raul repeated it over the phone and closed it. He turned back to Harriet, "She has the same size. She will be here in an hour. She will bring everything."

"Who is Gabriela?"

"We grew up together. We are very old friends. She is Emilo's daughter."

"Does she know how you feel towards me?"

"No one knows yet," Raul said. "I didn't want to tell them until you said yes. Now what would you like to do for an hour?"

"Let's go look at your horses."

Inside the house Esteban and Emilo walked back to the basement to finish their game of pool.

"He got her to stay," Emilo said. "He does have some influence over her."

"Yes, it appears that way, but I will handle it." Esteban said.

Harriet and Raul walked down to the lower barn. All of the horses had been brought into the barn. They were being fed as they walked by. They approached a large brown horse as Raul said, "We just acquired this horse last month. He goes by the name of 'James.' He is supposed to be very fast. Maybe if you are still here tomorrow you could ride him."

"I think I am into gentle these days. Does your father ride much?"

"He is a gentleman's horseman meaning he likes to have fast horses, but he does not like to ride them."

"You like to ride."

"Yes, when I have the time. I haven't had much of that lately."

"Maybe we had better head back to the house," Harriet said. "The object of my visit was to meet your family."

"Yes, Gabriela should be coming anytime."

Twenty minutes later they were at the house. A black limousine had arrived. "That is her car," Raul said.

"Hmm, she likes limousines too."

"She doesn't know how to drive."

Christopher Charles

They entered the house and found Gabriela in Mrs. Morales' room. Entering, Raul introduced them, "I am going to leave you in Gabriela's capable Hands."

Gabriela, twenty-three, was a shy pretty girl. Her build was similar to Harriet's, but her dark eyes and hair enhanced her delicate features. "I am supposed to make you look nice for the celebration," she said.

"I appreciate your help," Harriet replied. "I decided to stay suddenly and did not plan on staying for your celebration. Therefore, I didn't bring any clothes."

"I brought lots of clothes. You may choose anything that fits."

Harriet looked at several dresses. She found a sheer one that fitted her well. It did not expose too much, but enough to be interesting. She found shoes to match.

She managed to place a bug on the bed frame as Gabriela was putting her own dress on. She had two left and slipped them into her pocket. She fixed her hair and makeup, she was ready.

Gabriela continued to dress herself. "How long have you known Raul?"

"I just met him on this cruise. We really have not had much time together. He wanted me to meet his family, so I came along today."

"It is more than that," Gabriela said "General Lopez is coming, and the President may also show. They want to make a big fuss over you for capturing Senor Paniagua."

"How long have you known Raul?"

"Forever," Gabriela said. "Our parents are very close. We grew up together. I am supposed to marry him they tell me to unify our families."

"Do you love him?"

"Of course, but like a brother. He would do anything for me, and I would do anything for him."

"Is there someone else you really love enough to marry?"

"I have had my chances, but they have all been denied by my family. I think I am destined to become his wife."

"How would you feel if he married someone else who he really loves?"

"He would have to get married in secret, and never come back here. His family would divorce him."

"But how would you feel?"

"I wouldn't want to never see him again, but I hope he can marry someone he really loves, and I can marry someone I really love."

"Then you do have someone you want to marry?"

"He's already asked me to marry him, but my father would have him shot if he knew."

"Surely not that drastic," Harriet said.

"You don't know this family, do you? They are trying to build an empire. They want to unite our families into one. Marriage is the simplest way of doing this. They will remove anything that stands in their way."

"What would you say if I told you Raul wants to marry me?"

"I would say you will probably be dead tomorrow, if they found out," Gabriela said. "I pray he runs away with you and changes his name. At least then he would be happy, and I would be happy for him."

"I have not said yes, but we are very close."

"You should leave immediately," Gabriela said. "Your life is in danger."

"I plan on leaving after the celebration tonight."

'You don't understand, Gabriela said in a whisper, "The celebration is announcing Raul and my engagement to be married. They find out you and Raul are in love, they will react, and do you harm."

"Are they really that violent?" Harriet whispered.

"He has been in love before, and they have all disappeared."

"Does he know this has happened?"

"No, there is always some excuse made up."

"He must have tried to reach them."

"Of course, but they simply have disappeared."

"How does General Lopez know this family?" Harriet asked.

"General Lopez and Senor Morales are old friends from school. Raul is destined to replace him."

There was a knock at the door. Mrs. Morales entered the room, "If you are ready Miss Brown, my husband would like to entertain you in a game of pool in the basement." She looked at Gabriela, "We still have to do your hair my dear. Tonight, is very important."

"Where is the basement?" Harriet asked.

"You will find it. Walk toward the back of the house. You will see a stair leading down."

Harriet felt uneasy remembering the warning she was just given. The basement would be a good place to do her in. She walked towards the back of the house. She saw the stairs and started down quietly. She could hear them talking in Spanish. Now she wished she had picked up that language.

She made it all the way to the bottom before they recognized she was there. Turning, Esteban said, "Would you like to join us in a game of pool?"

"It would be my pleasure if you show me how to play," Harriet replied.

"It is a very easy game, you merely hit the white ball. It in turn hits your ball that is supposed to go into one of the pockets." He proceeded to show her how to hold the stick. "It's an even push into the white ball and not a jerking motion to send the white ball the correct direction. We will play a practice game to show you."

Harriet watched them play a short game. She noticed how they held the cue stick using the table at times or their fingers. They even had a stick called a cradle to hit balls in the center of the table. She would be using this a great deal to prevent her from having to bend over very far, which she thought was the object in the gentlemen's minds.

They set the balls up and broke them. Harriet noticed they hit the set balls off center to force them to break better and send some of them into the pockets.

She used the table for close shots, but anything that required her to lean over, she used the cradle. By her second game she was beating the both of them. She had placed a bug under the table.

Esteban was showing his temper. He struck the balls harder, causing them to bounce the wrong direction, or strike the pocket and bounce out. "I hear you, and my son have been spending a great deal time together."

"I think he was doing his job trying to find out what I knew," Harriet said.

"You were swimming together before the shark stuck," Esteban said.

"Yes, and he proceeded to drug me with the Scopolamine drug when we returned to the resort. He came very close to killing me, but his objective was to find out what I knew. When he learned all he could, he dumped me, and left me to wake up in a strange room."

"You were angry?" Emilo asked.

"I worked it out over sixteen hours chasing the ship."

"Then why did you agree to come to his home?" Emilo asked.

"I don't hold grudges. He explained his reasons."

"How close are you to my son?"

"I think you will have to ask him for that information. I consider him a very good friend."

"Hmmm," Esteban said as he nailed a ball in the pocket very hard. "We are announcing his engagement tonight to Miss Gabriela Guevana Federico. Does that bother you?"

"Are you trying to create a situation here, sir?" Harriet asked. "I respect whoever Raul wishes to marry. Do you have any intentions towards me?"

"You do catch on rather quickly," Esteban said. "You may stay and enjoy yourself, or you may leave whenever you please. We wish you no harm."

"Thank you, sir. Now if you will excuse me, I think I will see how Raul is doing."

The large ballroom was decorated, and the band was setting up. Food was dispersed throughout. She saw Raul talking with a servant. He saw her approaching, smiled, and walked towards her.

He started to kiss her when she pushed him back, "We cannot to do that. You are getting engaged tonight."

"Yes, I just found that out."

"I just left your father. He was questioning me about my feelings for you. He tried to box me in. He's one dangerous man."

"Yes, we may have a problem."

"We will have to behave ourselves until you are sure what you want to do."

"Will you marry me?"

"If I say yes, I will probably be killed according to Gabriela. Are you sure you want to go against your family, and never see them again?"

"I'll work it out. Will you promise you will stay long enough for me to do that?"

"I will give you the night," Harriet said. "It will be your decision."

"I will work it out." Raul said.

The guests were arriving filling the room.

Large round tables lined the walls leaving the center for dancing. The band was to one side of the dance floor next to the piano across from the head table. Harriet was seated at the head table along with the Morales' and the Federico's. General Lopez sat beside Harriet, and Mrs. Morales sat across from her. Raul and Gabriela sat beside each other next to Mrs. Morales.

Champagne was distributed freely around the tables. Harriet directed her attention to General Lopez, a big man with a large head and big shoulders.

"I hear you have captured Senor Paniagua in Costa Rica," He said.

"Yes, it was a lucky guess, sir. I had been there before. His guards recognized me. This allowed me to approach them, and my team to neutralize them."

"Very good strategy." General Lopez said. He did not question how she came by being there earlier. Senor Morales had already told him.

The band began playing a Waltz. Raul started to stand, when General Lopez asked, "Would you do the honor for a very old man to have a dance?"

"I have been waiting for you to ask me," Harriet said standing.

General Lopez helped her with her chair and took her to the dance floor. He was a very good dancer. Harriet stayed with him moving through the turns easily.

She also placed a bug on the inside of his front coat pocket.

He tried several turns. She stayed with him allowing the music to take her.

"You dance beautifully, my dear. Did you take lessons?"

"I just follow the music sir, and of course your lead."

They moved smoothly over the floor. Raul watched with envy, but he held his tongue.

When they returned to the table, General Lopez helped her with her chair, smiled, "That was the most pleasant Waltz I have ever danced."

"She's a natural tease," Mrs. Morales said in Spanish. "She even smokes cigars."

Harriet looked at her and smiled.

Esteban Morales leaned over to his wife, "Why don't you play the piano, my dear. I always loved to hear you play."

"What would you like to hear?" Mrs. Morales asked.

"Do one of your favorites."

She stood, walked over to the piano, and pulled out several sheets of music. When she found the one she liked, she placed it on the piano. She cleared her throat. Everyone suddenly was very quiet.

Esteban leaned over to the General, "You are going to like this. She is very good."

"I am sure she is," General Lopez said.

Mrs. Morales motioned for one of the servants to come over to turn the pages. When she was ready, she began playing the music. It was classical Bach. She made several mistakes, and she missed the rhythm in places, but overall, she was able to complete the piece.

When she was done, she bowed as everyone politely clapped. She returned to her seat with a big grin on her face, and leaned towards Harriet, "My son says you play the piano. Would you like to play for us?"

"I do not want to compete with you, madam," Harriet said. "You played so beautifully."

"We won't hold you to my standards, dear, but I would be pleased if you would play for us."

General Lopez stood, and helped her with her chair, allowing Harriet to stand.

She looked quickly at Raul's smile. She felt better. He had evidently told her she could play. Reaching the piano, she sat down slowly, and closed her eyes. She allowed her emotions to flow.

Mrs. Morales leaned over to her husband, "What is she waiting for?"

Harriet could feel the emotion of the hate coming from Raul's family, and the love pouring out from Raul. She decided to move into the love emotion first.

Keeping the emotion, she allowed her fingers to move across the piano keys.

Christopher Charles

They started slow, and in the high notes simulating innocent love. As her emotions grew the notes became louder and down an octave. Then passion taking over the music flowed from her soul filling the room with her love. The notes coming fast as her love emotion intensifies.

Then suddenly the notes drop to a very harsh tempo. She was banging the keys as the evil forces were trying to break up this perfect emotional love. The soft love notes trying to find an opening through the harsh tones coming out. Finally, the love notes become louder as they slowly move the harsh notes aside. Coming out full bloom, the love triumphs the harsh notes, and carries the day. She brings the story to a conclusion and moved into the high notes once more.

Finished, she stood, and bowed. No one clapped or dared to say a word. Harriet walked back to her chair as General Lopes pulled her chair out for her.

"That was the most emotional piece of music I have ever heard. We are all stunned a bit. You must forgive us."

"Sorry, I only play what I feel." Harriet said.

Estaban saw the tears in Raul's eyes, and immediately took him by the shirt, "We need to talk now! To my study."

Raul rose from his chair and followed his father.

Mrs. Morales said, "That was far from anything classical, wasn't it, General Lopez?" She said in Spanish knowing Harriet did not speak a word of Spanish.

"You just heard something very beautiful, Mrs. Morales. You should enjoy the moment. I don't think you will hear anything like it again." General Lopez said in Spanish.

Harriet saw Raul leaving with his father, and knew he was going to make his case now. She was trembling and felt very cold.

General Lopez, realizing the situation, said, "I am sure everything will work out to the best, dear. You must have more faith."

She smiled up at him, "I just did something very foolish. I walked right into their trap."

"You are what you are, and they are what they are. You must always keep that in mind. You expressed how you feel. Now allow them to react and express how they feel. It will all work out. You will see." He was well aware she was in love with Raul, and that he loved her. After she played everyone was aware. She will be lucky to survive the night.

Esteban Morales Study

Esteban sat in his chair and pointed to the chair in front of him for Raul. When he was seated, Raul said in Spanish, "I love Harriet, and I want to marry her, sir."

Esteban looked at his son a moment. Finally, he said in Spanish and in an even tone, "You are going to marry Gabriela Federico, or I will have your girlfriend killed. Is that understood?"

Raul looked at him a moment. He could tell his father was serious.

"You need to grow up young man. Playtime is over. You will marry Gabriela and complete your destiny. Love is for fools and the weak."

"Sir, I am going to marry Miss Brown."

"Then she is a dead woman," Esteban said.

"You wouldn't kill her?"

"I've done it before, and I will do it again," Esteban said firmly.

Christopher Charles

Raul suddenly remembered his other two love affairs. They were both suddenly missing. He always thought they had moved on and found someone else. He looked up at his father, "You actually had them killed?"

"We are serious here. How do you think you advance in rank so fast?"

"I thought it was because General Lopez was your friend."

"No, it was more, there were vacancies that needed to be filled. How did you think you were able to become the First Mate on the cruise ship?"

"The First Mate was killed along with Captain Waverly leaving the position open."

"Senor Paniagua only wanted Captain Waverly killed to replace him, with Captain Morgan. We had the Molina brothers kill the First Mate. They only wanted Senor Paniagua killed, and we promised to do that for them, and of course a little money helped."

"That's why Molina gave me the ten-pound bomb. He knew I was part of the plan to kill Senor Paniagua."

"Now you are catching on."

Raul's mind flashed to Paniagua's family. He could still see the pleading eyes of the Paniagua's sixteen-year old daughter. Looking his at his father, he asked, "The Paniagua's family at the hacienda?"

Esteban smiled, "Sergeant Fuentes took care of the problem."

"They were only children."

"Children grow up, we were not leaving any loose ends."

Raul could not say anymore. He heard his father talking, but he could not respond.

"Have no doubt, I will have her killed. You will become engaged to Gabriela tonight, and you will marry her in two

Godfrey stood when she entered and found her a chair in front of his desk. He had a concerned look on his face.

"Is it that bad," Harriet asked. "I thought they approved the contract."

"We are not dealing with the cruise lines anymore. They have turned everything over to their insurance carrier. Legally they were insured. It is up to them to settle the contract. You may still get your two million, but I would not hold my breath. They will be dragging this out as long as possible."

"I was expecting something like that," Harriet said. "I assume we still have our cruise tickets?"

"Yes, the cruise lines left that in place."

She walked into his office a very rich young lady, now she walked away probably very poor.

To Be Continued to Book Three, Kidnapped: